Permanent Removal

Alan S Cowell

First published by Jacana Media (Pty) Ltd in 2016

10 Orange Street
Sunnyside
Auckland Park 2092
South Africa
+2711 628 3200
www.jacana.co.za

© Alan S Cowell, 2016

All rights reserved.

ISBN 978-1-4314-2343-9

Cover design by publicide
Set in Warnock Pro 11/14.5pt
Job no. 002640
Printed and bound by Creda Communications

Also available as an e-book:
d-PDF ISBN 978-1-4314-2344-6
ePUB ISBN 978-1-4314-2345-3
mobi file ISBN 978-1-4314-2346-0

See a complete list of Jacana titles at www.jacana.co.za

So you thought the bad old ways had died with the birth of the new, that the whispers and lies of the past had been forgotten in the freshly minted land of Mandela. You'd be dead wrong. Alan Cowell's high-speed thriller rips a wormhole in the rainbow nation and throws us back to a time when right and wrong were fixed in blood and love came off second best. In a broodingly atmospheric story that piles on the suspense, Cowell lays bare the fragile human hearts that beat uncertainly in the aftershock of apartheid. There are no heroes here except dead ones. And even they're not perfect.
– **Charlotte Bauer**, writer

A political thriller by a legendary New York Times *correspondent who knows South Africa, its history, its secrets and its intrigue so well.*
– **Robin Wright**, author and former Africa correspondent

When old friends reluctantly revisit their role in The Struggle *against apartheid, they find they have secrets to hide, betrayals to forget and new loves to pursue.* Permanent Removal *is a tautly told tale of inner torment – contemporary, courageous, compelling.*
– **John Borrell**, author of *The White Lake*, and former *Time* magazine bureau chief in Africa

With a journalist's eye for detail, and a consummate knowledge of time, place and circumstance won the hard way, Alan Cowell weaves a spell-binding tale of a society steeped in blood and deception, and still far from truth or reconciliation. Permanent Removal *should be required reading for every South African, and for everyone who wants to know, or thinks they know, about the struggle to end apartheid, and its legacy.*
– **Allen Pizzey**, CBS News

Cowell has done it again, proving himself master of all genres. Paris Correspondent *was the funniest of novels on modern journalism. Now,* Permanent Removal *raises the bar for political thrillers. It's taut, romantic and, at the end, a shock. You'll love it.*
– **Charles Glass**, author of, among others, *Americans in Paris, Deserters* and *Syria Burning*

A refreshing new work by an author who delves into the brutal past and the trembling present in an approach which is both stimulating and provocative, and certain to cause controversy. Disturbing, unusually structured and enthralling.
– **Wilf Nussey**, author and retired foreign correspondent

Prologue

When she left The Place, she felt free. The tin roofs and dirt roads receded in the rear-view mirrors. Passion and its artful satisfaction replaced the preoccupation with "the issues". She drove with ever-greater urgency, crossing town, watching the landscape change before her eyes. So what if They followed her?

At the beginning, the cars were rusted, cast-offs. The roadsides choked under a litter of greying, abandoned garbage bags and rags of newspaper caught on rusting wire. You could smell the sweat, the poverty. People walked miles looking for work, money, relatives, carrying their shoes over their shoulders to save on wear and tear. Then, the mess gave way to silvery high-rises, glass-flanked behemoths clustered on the golden reef, the gateway to the other side: the quiet lawns under the sprinklers' rainbow, the discreet remote-controlled gates, the late-model German cars hissing on highways of smooth asphalt, bearing their cargoes of golf-sleek men and bejewelled women.

Once or twice, her sense of mission rebelled and she swung the blue Kombi around in a perilous 180 to return to The Place, where people lived on the edge. Most times, anticipation lured her on – love in a place of tennis courts, private pools, discretion. If there was a salve to her conscience it was, simply, that these crazy moments were the exception to prove the rule. A necessary aberration, a cleansing. Hungers sated, she would return gladly to The Struggle.

Part One

They will use the flashing patrol light to force the sky-blue Honda to pull over – an old trick, but effective. They will manacle their captives and switch licence plates. They will drive the four men back towards the dunes. In the first instance, there will be knives and bludgeons. Then petrol to incinerate the bodies and the Honda. Dirty work, no doubt, but someone had to do it.

Part One

One

THE LETTER ARRIVED IN THE FINAL delivery before I closed the house and set the alarm sensors for a long absence. I resisted an irrational temptation to call a last goodbye to someone who had been there only in my imagination.

The cab – not, please note, an official vehicle placed at my exclusive disposal – was waiting across the frosted lawn. The driver yawned, reaching for a Styrofoam cup of something warm and steamy. The music on the car radio sounded vaguely oriental, but this was an era before the quarter-tones of the mosque and the muezzin's call became, for us, the symphony of menace. Down the street, between petrified trees and iced-over SUVs, newspapers were being delivered to other people: my subscriptions to the *Times* and *Post* and *Journal* had been suspended indefinitely – an act of giddy liberation. Untethered from my daily rites, I felt remarkably, peacefully, alone.

I went through the final fussy mental checklist of a protracted itinerary – passport, cash, medications, credit cards, traveller's cheques, money belt, shortwave radio, maps, workout kit, letters of introduction, contact book, backup USB, PDA, Swiss army knife (not in the carry-on, of course – even in those days!), batteries and cables and connections for the technology that burdens the modern wanderer. Past travellers took with them great steamer trunks and cases of victuals – limes, porter, salted hams, firearms in anticipation variously of scurvy or pirates or hostile receptions.

These days, you prepare as if you are some kind of techno-turtle, carrying your cyber-shell on your back: bound to the world wherever you are, wired or wireless, made whole by e-mail and internet access.

I looked back at the white colonial home, memorising the empty porch and shuttered windows that mocked any dreams of a family seat, a cradle of generations. Then I fell into traveller mode, staring without seeing past the cab's stained, Perspex division into the gloaming.

My mind was already far ahead, across miles of ocean and desert and bush that I would traverse at a sanitised altitude of seven or eight miles, untouched by storm or pestilence. Or so I thought. But your ghosts always find ways to haunt you. When they are awoken, it is well to be prepared.

I have sometimes asked myself how events might have unfolded if the letter had arrived in time for me to absorb its contents, in time to weigh its implications so much earlier. Or if I had never seen it at all. But "what ifs" has never been my style. What happened, *the past*, may be written about – as in this attempt – but not rewritten. Not if we are honest. Not if we seek to avoid making the same mistakes over and again.

An early transatlantic connection deposited me in London with just enough time to switch terminals for the overnight flight to Cape Town. In my previous existence, Embassy Suburbans – with tinted windows, driven by armed, over-fed minders wearing fishing vests and cargo pants – ferried me across bumpy tarmac; the kind of ostentatious discretion that people associate with American policy in the half-light between diplomacy and mischief. At dingy airport lounges in Cairo or Tashkent at some unwelcome hour, with large insects buzzing in pools of flickering neon and soldiers in ill-fitting uniforms cradling worn Kalashnikovs, second-tier officers ensured that I traversed their ambassador's territory without embarrassment or offense. Envoys handed over sealed cables: eyes only, and so forth. Not anymore.

Thomas J Kinzer, Ambassador Extraordinary and Plenipotentiary, abbreviated sometimes with faux bonhomie to "TJ", had become Tom Kinzer. Lecture-circuit guru, TV soundbite dispenser, conference invitee and attendee, panel moderator, occasional op-ed contributor.

When journalists asked – with decreasing frequency – I told them I embraced this early change of life, this transfer from public to private sector, from the closed world of diplomacy to the open exchange of ideas. But there were times – in the right company, at the appropriate hour and with the requisite lubrication of Jack Daniels, when I would vouchsafe a degree of bitterness at having played the diplomatic game so dutifully and with such consummate duplicity. Only to be knifed by my own side. A high-flying career sustained by the rapier thrust of ambiguity had been lost to the political sabre-slash.

The metaphors of treachery are always those of the blade.

Somehow, in the very early retirement deal, along with the annuity and healthcare provision, I wanted my morality back. But how could a scarred diplomatic warrior insist on the return of openness, honesty? Would a courtesan demand the restoration of maidenhood?

Materially there was no real hardship. I could hardly complain of mistreatment when my garage housed a late-model Jaguar (despite the attentions of my ex-wife's lawyers in Washington and Paris) and my calendar was generously booked with paying engagements. But, left to dangle in the wind, your name not mentioned inside the Beltway without the appended question "wasn't he the one?", financial reward is not everything you consider to be your due.

On that journey from a northern winter to a southern summer, I had particular cause to attend the conference to which I had been invited, far beyond the stated agenda.

True, I felt stimulated by the challenge of steering debates with some of the host nation's great thinkers, by the flattery of sharing a podium with the likes of Suzman and Gordimer. Folders of pre-conference material told me the theme was "Truth and Reconciliation – Prerequisites of Justice?" The list of speakers was impressive, a galaxy of moral celebrity – Tutu and Mandela, Boraine and Bizos. The kind of people for whom the subject under discussion was the indigestible, daily reality, lodged in the national throat, not some nebulous college-campus theory.

But voyagers harbour subliminal motives. Nostalgia moulds journeys as surely as flight schedules. I had travelled this way before, much earlier in my life. I found myself asking: would the mountains be lower now, the passions less intense, its objects less gilded?

As the flight attendant leaned over to lower the window blind, I caught sight of myself, slightly stubbled, but still presentable – dark around the chin and with the beginnings of greyness at the temples – peering back at my own reflection with an expression somewhere between bemusement and apprehension: was I, Thomas Kinzer, arch-cynic, one-time manipulator of governments and dark events, looking for some magical return to innocence?

I have never been prone to airborne excess. Yet on this journey, feeling unready for sleep, I took a little more wine than usual with dinner, and, surprising myself, requested a Scotch on the rocks instead of decaf. I tried reading some of the standard authorities – Gobodo-Madikizela, Krog, Joubert – but could not concentrate. I swung the small, personal in-flight screen into place and flicked through a digital sheaf of movies, not altogether gripped by any.

On the real-time navigation display, the airplane resembled a child's cut-out toy, already south of the blue Mediterranean and the empty reaches of ochre desert, starting its long haul towards the tip of sub-Saharan Africa, coloured green – fecund, mysterious. I had once found the place names exotic. Kano, Accra, Nairobi. A line across the map was marked "Equator".

Far below, I imagined pin-pricks of light signalling the course of sightless, powerful rivers: fishermen's pirogues, hewn from single tree-trunks, drawn up on the muddy banks of dark villages. The inner eye, as Wordsworth put it, resurrected long-ago visits to towns built as administrative centres by the European colonial powers decaying inexorably, their night spots seething, their medical dispensaries empty.

Memories from an earlier, unchronicled life bubbled from forgotten depths: security guards with night sticks snoozing fitfully outside aid workers' guarded villas, patrolling the razor-wire barricades of traders' padlocked storehouses; a web of single-track roads through tunnels of impenetrable bushland, ribbons of rusty sand, impassable in the rains.

Far below, there would be ramshackle churches (usually less ramshackle for the wealthier Catholic dioceses) and village huts shaped like round, chocolate cakes topped by straw, the perimeters swept clean by women fearful of snakes, perching like birds on small, three-legged stools; a baby, usually, strapped to the back, another clamouring for the breast and another in gestation, hostage to the dreaded virus that would leave her children orphaned before they followed their widowed mother into an early grave.

Then you could imagine how it would all change when pre-teen gunmen and soldiers with amulets rampaged through these places, exhilarated by sudden screams, mortal panic. Kigali, Geneina, Gulu, Bukavu, Sharpeville, Kolwezi. Names on a different map, unrelated to aerial navigation. A drumbeat of horror.

I thought I should make a note of these ideas in order to provoke debate at the conference by asking – mischievously, maliciously – whether it was only in wealthy lands like the one I was visiting that "Justice" and "Reconciliation" had meaning. Whether, elsewhere, such themes represented an impossible luxury, subjugated to the grim dictates of daily survival against hunger, sickness, poverty, oppression. As it turned out, I would need much more powerful navigational tools than an airline's digital gazetteer.

I finally opened the letter at that late hour when the picked-over meals have been cleaned away and the seats have been tilted back and the overhead cabin lights are dimmed; when the insomniacs commune with laptops and the cabin attendants pray for a quiet night.

The stamps were bright, gaudy, showing birds and fish identified in minute script as lilac-breasted rollers and coral rock-cod. The envelope, made of cheap paper, was smudged with much handling, as if too many people had wished to touch it, to speed it on its way.

The postmark was from a remote station in a province of South Africa. I did not really need to open it to guess who had sent it, and, by association, what it might say. Even if I had not broken its seal of sticky tape and failing gum, I doubt that I would have been able to – or wished to – side-step the events that came to inspire some of the more sensational accounts that I want to correct with this narrative, this testimony. One headline still rankles: "An American's Shame in the New South Africa."

There were two documents, one handwritten in blue ballpoint on a single piece of lined paper that might have been torn from a school notebook.

"Our Dear Tom," it began. My eyes prickled. I blinked to focus.

"We send you our warm greetings. We wonder if you will remember us, the Widows. We wonder if you remember that you said you would help us find why our great Husbands died. We remember you said you would find the person who betrayed them. We remember you said one day you would return and Justice would be done. So now the new clues are here so you can help with all the powers of your Great Country."

It was signed: "The Widows of the Cooktown Four."

Enclosed with the letter, a newspaper clipping offered what seemed to be a transcript or excerpted record of some kind of hearing or interrogation. One passage had been singled out with hieroglyphics of emphatic underscoring and exclamation marks in the same blue ballpoint ink as had been used in the letter.

Question: What happened then, Mr Theron?
Answer: Information was received that Nyati and a number of black activists would be there to meet the white liberals. The activists were identified by means of informers. One informer, really. It was important for us to know where and when the meeting was taking place because that would tell us whether the conditions were right to undertake the operation. And I reported that evening we would make an attempt or investigate the possibility of undertaking the operation.

Question: What were your orders?
Answer: We were ordered to ensure the permanent removal of Nyati from society. To take him out, eliminate him.

Two

ONCE THE LETTER WAS OPENED, so was Pandora's Box. Sleep became almost impossible, a restless semi-consciousness, veering between blank wakefulness and not-quite-slumber. A flickering peep-show from my past – names, faces, tennis parties, gunfire; still, cold bodies; live, warm bodies; funerals – left me grasping for the present before I slid into soft-focus replay of younger days.

South Africa had been the arena of my first diplomatic assignment. Not, as later, a nation feted by the world as a joyous experiment in rainbow harmony, (offset, of course, by the monsters of AIDS and criminal violence) but in more sombre days, when the sinews of oppression were taut and seemingly permanent. I had been sent to a country in the final, violent paroxysm of a bloody conflict, one defined in absolutes: black, white; Afrikaner, African; minority, majority; tyranny, freedom; capital, Kapital.

I had been sent there to represent a superpower that hedged its bets, insisting – how conveniently we forget this now! – that the oppressors could be persuaded to set the terms of their own demise, while the oppressed waited patiently for redemption.

Above all, I had been sent there in my youthful prime, prey to every intoxication of thought and flesh in a land that offered both in industrial proportions. It had been my testing period, before the required adherence to official policy built its carapace over raw instincts of spontaneity, hardened the rushing arteries of indiscretion.

I had been duped by the elation of the victims, suffering their only ticket to freedom, who foreswore their own present to deny their enemies a future. I had been entrapped by the passions of revolutionary times in the pell-mell rush towards a new order in which the sins of the past would be automatically expunged.

In short, I had believed freedom was indivisible. My commitment to the God of policy had wavered. I had loved and left and been left. I had arrived an innocent, an ingénu. I departed with scar tissue still raw.

The sun came up somewhere over the Kalahari Desert, and the sky brightened rapidly towards Cape Town. When I raised the window blind, the light was so piercing that I almost winced.

They came at me in a pincer movement as I stood impatiently at the immigration desk, annoyed after my long flight that it was taking so long to process my entry form and temporary visa.

There had been a delay when the immigration officer in her crisp, white uniform ran my passport through the computerised scanner. Furtively she moved a hand below the counter, presumably to raise some kind of discreet alarm to which the two men responded.

One of them was smooth skinned and slightly plump, the other stringy and lean, a hint of roughness around his knuckles. Initially, I hoped that they might be part of the reception committee, bearing an invitation to a quiet lounge with freshly brewed coffee and chilled fruit juice while my suitcases were picked off the conveyor belt and the formalities were taken care of, as so often in my diplomatic days.

"If you could just step this way, sir," the white officer said. "Nieuwoudt. Airport security."

"It will not take a moment, a minor matter," his colleague said. "A slight discrepancy. No cause for alarm. My name is Faku."

With some reluctance, I followed them, confused and ill-tempered. They had taken possession of my passport, my carefully filled-out immigration form, my currency declaration – in other words, they had taken control of me.

I walked between them, unblocking the muttering line that had formed behind me of passengers awaiting their moment at the immigration desk before the raised rubber stamp of official welcome formally descended on their passports with the quiet, satisfying thump of validation.

I carried my shoulder bag with its laptop and documents. The plainclothes men led me back from the row of immigration desks, away from the gateway to the baggage collection point. Strangers followed my movements with undisguised and faintly hostile curiosity.

What was I? Some kind of illegal immigrant, arms dealer?

"Discrepancy? I don't think I quite follow."

"Step in here for a moment, *meneer*," the stringy officer said. His use of an Afrikaans courtesy sounded like a sneer.

"You will soon be on your way," Faku said, adding as what he seemed to think was a joke: "One way or the other."

The room had no windows. Two chairs on one side of a Formica-veneered table faced a single chair on the other. A grid of neon lighting in the ceiling bounced back off a linoleum floor marked with burn marks from some phase of pre-history when people smoked indoors.

"Please sit down."

"What is all this? I really don't understand. I'm here for a conference. Officially invited by the sponsors, including your President."

"There is no need for temper, Mr Kinzer," Nieuwoudt said. "Just a few simple questions."

"What kind of questions, for God's sake. It's been a long day and night of flying from Washington."

"Washington." Faku repeated. He had flipped out a folding notebook held by a strand of elastic. Now he wrote in it. I could see my name and passport number and a date. There was a file number that looked vaguely familiar. And the word "Washington." He noticed that I was reading his notes upside down. He flipped the notebook lid closed and smiled at me.

"But your flight came in from the UK." Nieuwoudt shoved my immigration form across the desk to me. In the section marked "Origin of flight" I had written: "London."

"I made a connection in London."

"Aha."

Faku wrote again. But I could not see what he wrote.

"From Washington? You made a connection in London from Washington?"

9

"There is no direct flight. For God's sake. Is this some kind of third degree?"

"An interesting choice of words," Faku said. "Why would you accuse us of torture? Is it something you are familiar with?"

I drew in a deep breath and gathered my thoughts. I was a former American ambassador. My name and rank were still on file in Washington. I did not need to answer their questions. It was a matter of time before I demanded that they allow me a call to the local consulate to avoid an international incident.

"I want to cut the chase," Nieuwoudt said, sounding reasonable.

"Cut to the chase."

"As I said, I want to cut the chase. Your passport is an ordinary American passport. Is that true?"

"Of course."

"But in our database you are listed as a diplomat. So why would a diplomat travel on a non-diplomatic passport?"

"Your database is out of date. Obviously."

"Or your mission is not as stated." Faku looked up from his writing and stared at me.

"What on earth are you suggesting? I am here as an official guest at a conference. Look!"

I fumbled in my shoulder bag to retrieve my credentials and handed them my dossier of invitation letters, accommodation advice, travel advisories. In the past I would have stonewalled, demanded an apology, stood on the dignity of my nation and my calling to public service. Now I simply wanted an end to this farce, this shake-down or whatever it was, and be on my way. Of course, it is never wise to offer officialdom an iota more information than is being requested. Instantly, I regretted my excessive helpfulness.

Nieuwoudt flicked through the folder. The widows' letter fell from its pages and Faku swept down on it, scanned it quickly, then paused to read it more carefully, before handing it to Nieuwoudt.

"Thank you, Captain," Nieuwoudt said.

"That is no problem, Sergeant," Faku said. "It seems as if our friend, Mr Kinzer, has more than just a conference on his mind. We had better take a photocopy."

They did not seek my permission.

Alone in the room with me, Faku leaned back in his chair. Below his dark suit jacket, his shirt buttons strained over his stomach. He made no attempt to conceal the hand-gun in a leather shoulder-holster.

"You see, Mr Kinzer, when people come to our country and they have certain missions that are not on the official agenda, it is our job to make sure our country is safe."

"If your database told you I was here as a diplomat many years ago, then it must have told you I harbour no ill will against it."

"Our database tells us many things, Mr Kinzer. Many things indeed and about many people." His belly trembled to the rhythm of a throaty chuckle.

Nieuwoudt returned to the room. He handed a photocopy to Faku, who folded it into squares and sandwiched into his notebook. He rose from the table, shuffled my papers into their dossier and took a last glance at them.

"Nice hotel, eh, Sergeant, where they have put him up. We should be allowed to stay in such places!"

"VIP, Captain." Nieuwoudt said, allowing himself a thin smile.

"You see, Mr Kinzer, many things have changed since you were here. For the better. Correct, Sergeant?"

"Correct, Sir. Many things are different. So it is better, Mr Kinzer, to let the dogs lie asleep."

He took a rubber date stamp and ink pad from a desk in the corner of the room, stamped my passport and, in a handwritten annotation, added the words: "14 days. Single entry. Conference purposes only."

Faku handed me my documents and opened a side door I had not noticed, leading directly into the arrivals hall with its crowded carousels.

"Welcome," he said.

I collected my baggage and looked back over my shoulder. The door to the small, airless interview room had closed seamlessly. There was nothing to suggest that the room existed, that anything had happened at all. Uncertain as to what this encounter might mean – other than some kind of bizarre case of mistaken identity by two over-zealous officers – I made my way without incident or further scrutiny through customs and into the shimmer of a Cape Town morning.

Outside the airport, beyond the glass doors, there seemed to be some kind of demonstration, led by a young woman with a bullhorn, chanting against official corruption. Riot police in blue uniforms, holding German shepherd dogs, leashed and snarling, had the protesters pinned behind barricades. There were crudely painted posters: "No to Arms Deals!" "No to Kickbacks!"

The young woman with the bullhorn seemed barely out of her teens but confidently led the chanting, as if she were some kind of African Joan of Arc, cloaked in righteous rage.

For a moment, I stood poised, drawn towards the protest, towards this strange echo of my earlier times here, yet aching for rest.

"Conference purposes only."

Faku had materialised again at my shoulder. "Official delegates, that way," he said, pointing to a cordoned area inside the terminal building, designated by a large banner proclaiming: "Truth and Reconciliation. Pre-registration." As I turned away from the protest, I saw a rock arc into the police lines. Immediately afterwards a teargas canister drew a counter-trajectory in white smoke.

The conference organisers had sent an entire team to extract me from the melee – a driver, a greeter and a sort of factotum equipped with a clipboard on which were clamped my speaking schedule and a brief professional biography to be approved for the conference website. No reference was made to the rumpus outside the airport. Or to my brief encounter with Faku and Nieuwoudt.

My resume left an unexplained gap between the entries for Princeton and Harvard Law School and those for my more senior diplomatic assignments, omitting my earlier experience in South Africa. The title "Ambassador" was used liberally, with no explanation for the brevity of my final posting in Paris before the brusque order to return to Washington, to hand the ambassadorial keys to a motor trader from California who had made significant campaign contributions – an exchange surely more familiar to him than to me.

My "personal interests" were listed as: reading, travel, music. Familiar camouflage, obscuring anything even remotely personal.

The reception committee was composed of women in their middle years. Something about their single-mindedness, their solidity reminded of the widows who had composed the letter, the tricoteuses of the revolution, moulded by the resolve and stoicism that marked their generation, never knowing whether a child or husband or brother or sister would survive the day without a fatality, a burning, an arrest, a disappearance. A beating from one side or the other. Now, they wielded their clipboards and schedules like rewards of victory – emblems of safety and certainty in a halfway peace.

They would drive me, they said, to my hotel. I would rest. Lunch was free time. The first appointment: a formal reception early that same evening, at another hotel. Sessions would start the following day: 8:30 am sharp. A local SIM card was included with my conference documents – a pay-as-you-go, with complementary start-up credit. Mini-bus transport would be arranged. Secretarial facilities available if needed. The conference language would be English, with ad hoc translation into isiXhosa, isiZulu, Sesotho and Afrikaans.

The women talked, laughed. I laughed. I had forgotten how easy – and important – it is to laugh; how much laughter functions as a prophylaxis against the sense of doom that can all too easily overcome the uninitiated.

In a blur, through the windows of the mini van, I was vaguely aware of squatter camps spreading over the sandy, windswept Cape Flats. Slender columns of black smoke rose above the shanties as they had in the old, revolutionary days. My escorts chose not to allude to them or explain them. The bridges over the busy, chaotic four-lane highway were covered in steel mesh to prevent the launch of projectiles or bodies.

The landmarks were comfortingly familiar – the twin cooling towers of the old power station at Langa and, of course, Table Mountain – a somewhat more photogenic marker. With laden mini-bus taxis challenging our every manoeuvre and dark-windowed BMWs offering no quarter in the fast lane, we swept along the curve of freeway past the Groote Schuur Hospital, alongside the grounds of the university and the Rhodes Memorial (Rhodes Mem, in the shorthand of college students). Buck and zebra grazed on the mountain's lower slopes.

From a rise near a Holiday Inn, the Mother City offered herself for inspection. The bare lands of District Six, slowly reviving after the uprooting of its mixed-race population back in the apartheid '60s; the port where container ships docked and the Yacht Club offered berths to more elegant vessels. Below the wall of Table Mountain, three cylindrical apartment buildings delivered a remarkable architectural affront to one of nature's great vistas. I remembered they had been nicknamed the Tampon Towers to acknowledge both their bizarre design and their singular inappropriateness to their setting. Past Signal Hill, out to sea, Robben Island slumbered on the glittery ocean.

"Our President was there. On Robben Island. You see," the factotum who had introduced herself as Sheryl Makwazi said. "He was imprisoned there. Even him. For 27 years he was in jail. Eighteen on that island. Hard labour. Breaking stones. Comrade Mandela. Madiba."

The mini van transported us to one of the newer hotels along the Victoria and Alfred Waterfront, a development had not existed in my earlier days as a junior attaché. I was slightly disappointed to see that the area had become one giant strip mall with boutiques and fancy eateries, bookstores, cafes, parking lots, apartment houses, yacht marinas. In my memory, it was still a longshoreman's working place with godowns and quays, and a single restaurant, the Harbour Café, serving Greek salad with bricks of feta and raw onion, and a chunky, white, saltwater fish called kingklip.

Finally, after many thanks and assurances that another mini van, with the redoubtable Sheryl riding shotgun, would collect me at 6:30 pm sharp for the opening reception, I was released to my hotel room and my memories.

Fighting sleep, I placed a call back to Washington. It would be early there, 24 hours in local time since I had left an eternity ago. I wanted to catch her before she went off to her job in one of those interdepartmental outfits that pokes its nose into other people's business.

I knew she rose early in the day and I had a question to ask her concerning her time as my first boss in the embassy here in South Africa. I caught her as she was about to leave her brownstone. She listened; I thought I heard her sigh.

"I'll get back to you," she said. No suggestion in the way she spoke of surprise or pleasure to hear from me.

I unpacked on auto-pilot, hanging a light-weight suit in a closet, placing shirts and underclothes in drawers, plugging in adaptors to hook up my laptop and cell-phone charger. Spilling out of the suit-bag's compartments came a belted safari jacket and bathing shorts, T-shirts, chinos, walking boots, a travellers' fly-fishing rod, digital camera, sun hat, sneakers, flip-flops, condoms (packed more in hope than expectation: as I had often told junior diplomats in my earlier life, spontaneity should never be left to chance.)

I stripped and showered; inserted the local SIM card into my cell phone. My room looked back, towards Table Mountain. I watched as the cable cars crept up and down its splintered buttresses, crossing half-way between the base station and the summit where clouds formed and reformed: the tablecloth, the locals called it.

The letter I had opened on the plane referred to the killing of Solomon Nyati, a small-town schoolteacher who had risen to great prominence as an opponent of apartheid, a harbinger of what his land might one day become. A prophet in his own land.

His death had been one of the most chronicled of political assassinations. Three of his comrades perished with him, their names woven into the national liturgy: Zinto, Ngalo, Mboniswa, Nyati – The Cooktown Four. I had met them all, drawn to their struggle. A white security police officer, Kobus Theron, had openly admitted that he led the death squad that killed them. In his quest for amnesty, he had appeared at the hearings known as the Truth and Reconciliation Commission – a model of justice and catharsis that would be pored over at our conference.

Lily Nyati and the other widows believed the truth had not been told. They wanted to know why, how, with whom he had operated. They wanted to know what Theron had omitted.

They had given me an impossible task. And two men with police warrant cards and free run of a major international airport had made my mission even more daunting. But the widows had ambushed me, left me no choice. That much was obvious, no matter the restrictions inscribed in my passport.

I re-read the letter, parsed it a dozen times, examining its omissions as much as what it said. The widows had not sought the identity of their husbands' murderer – or murderers – but the reason for the killings. Perhaps I was reading too much into it, but they seemed also to be inquiring about a person in a different role – not victim or perpetrator, but a Judas figure, "the person who betrayed them". Clearly, at whatever inquiry had inspired the newspaper clipping enclosed with the letter, evidence had been produced that, on the fateful day of the killings, an informer, or informers, had tipped off the assassins.

Of course, they were right to clamour for justice, even if mistaken about my ability to enlist the policymakers in Washington in their crusade. Yet the balance of forces had shifted. No longer the emissary of a higher power, I would have to fight alone.

My cell phone rang out and the screen showed a number in Washington, although I did not recall giving my local whereabouts to anyone back home.

"Sleeping dogs, Tom." It was my former ambassador returning my call. "Leave it alone. Please. For all our sakes." Her choice of metaphor sounded oddly familiar. I wondered who she had been talking to since I called.

The sun was long past its zenith, the afternoon fading. A call from the hotel front desk, jangling in the quiet whisper of the air-conditioning, told me that people were waiting to take me across town to the opening reception of the conference.

As I clambered into the mini-bus, my minders handed me a photocopied addendum to the agenda:

"Opening address to be delivered by Cde Lily Nyati."

Three

She had changed in the obvious ways of grief. There was a harder look to her eyes. Over the years, Lily Nyati had become something of a well-known person — not quite a celebrity, for that would imply some cynical manipulation of her plight — but an emblem, an icon nonetheless: the widow of the fallen warrior, swathed in his mantle, bearing his cross, his sword.

She had created a charitable foundation to promote reconciliation. She had been at the forefront of the racial debate. She had tried, without success, to prevent her hometown, her shrine, from falling into anarchy. In a way she stood in the tradition of Winnie Mandela — a woman defined initially by an absent husband but growing on her own terms in the vacuum created by his departure.

Her sole mission was to remind those who might forget that her land could not yet move on until it confronted its recent history with greater disclosure and penance. She reminded her compatriots that the mystery of her own bereavement had not been resolved. When she saw me, the fusion of loss and rage burned in her eyes, far more than any indication of pleasure at our reunion.

After the pleasantries — "how well you look" and "you have not changed one bit" — she drew me to a quiet corner of the lawn, away from the pre-conference, cocktail-and-canapé reception that seemed designed to reward less enthusiastic attendees. I was faintly aware of lush scents and bright colours at the fringe of vision — bougainvillea, frangipani. An empty space had opened between us and the delegates clustered around buffet tables alongside the pool.

"We were desperate," she was saying. "We did not know where to look. The letter was our last hope."

"I am sorry it took so long to reach me."

"But you can still help."

"I can try."

"You must try."

I found myself saying: "I will try," but I was not sure she heard me. She had taken my hand when we met and still held it, squeezing it tightly.

"People think I am a little ... obsessed," she was saying, speaking quickly as if there was not much time. I found myself looking over her shoulder, lest Nieuwoudt or Faku lurked behind the flame trees. "But it is because they do not want to face what I face."

"I thought it had all been resolved. Well. At least the details are known. From the transcript you sent."

"That, yes. But you see, you will know this. In your country these matters are taken to their conclusion. Watergate. Impeachment. Monica Lewinsky! But here, we go only so far" – she bracketed her fingers between her thumb and index finger – "and then look the other way. We say: let us stop now. The pain is too great."

"But they know who carried out the killing."

"Of course. But they are free, those ones. They killed the Pebco Three and the Cradock Four and the Motherwell Four and the Cooktown Four, and they are free. They have stood in the open and said what they did. But that is not all of it."

"Lily, what else can there be?'

She pulled me closer. Her hand held mine tightly.

"They were betrayed."

"By?"

"That is what you must find out, Tom. Please. I am sorry."

She released my hand and stepped back.

"Sometimes the past will not let me go. And when I saw your name on the speakers' list, I started hoping again. I am sorry."

"I will try."

"Is that diplomat language?" she said. She smiled, almost coquettish. "Because we have seen a lot of diplomats coming through here and making promises."

"I am no longer a diplomat."

"But you are an ambassador?"

"A title. No more. A retirement benefit. Like a gold watch."

She laughed. "So you do not need to be diplomatic. You can discover things."

"I would not know where to start."

"You must start where Nyati was the night he died. You must start with the people who met him. The last people who saw him."

"I will try my best."

"No, you can do more. Nyati thought you were his friend. He thought you made America his friend. He thought when you came to see him, it was not just you but all the Americans coming to see him. The American people. You brought the American people to support The Struggle, to encourage him, to show us we were not alone. So you must help him now. Will you?"

"You know I will do everything I can."

She smiled, as if a victory had been won, but then grew sombre.

"But you must be careful," she said. "Perhaps we should not ask you. When you first came to us, we thought you were – what do you call it – a spook, a spy. CIA. Dirty tricks. But now the shoe is on the other foot. Our enemies are still out there, Tom. They will try to stop you. They will play the dirty tricks. Like before. Maybe worse."

Across the lawn, a small, busy man detached himself from the cocktail crowd and bustled his way towards us, clad head to toe in purple. Despite advancing years, he was still the figure he had been when I first saw him in the 1980s preaching in his church in Soweto – chirpy, demanding, burning with a self-confidence that denied every attempt to crush him. Like the rest of us, he wore a laminated tag, proclaiming his name and profession: Desmond Tutu. Archbishop Emeritus.

A young woman – mid-to-late teens, early 20s, I could not guess more closely – took Lily Nyati's hand. She was slender, bony even, with close-cropped hair and angular features that, combined with her spectacles, gave her the same frail and owlish look as I recalled from her father. She wore a short, dark skirt and a T-shirt, the uniform of youth. She stood slightly akimbo, as if cloaking her vulnerability to the shocks of a world that had convinced her to expect only the worst.

"My daughter, Solomon's daughter," Lily Nyati said. "Celiwe Nyati, daughter of The Struggle."

I thought I recognised her from the airport demonstration and I noticed that her eyes showed the bloodshot tinge of contact with teargas. But this did not seem the place to inquire.

Instead, I smiled, foolishly happy to meet a new generation of the family. When I last saw her, she had been a bundle in a blanket tied to her mother's back.

"I knew your father," I said.

"I am happy for you. I wish I had that privilege."

"Lily, my dear, they are waiting for your speech," Tutu broke in, blessedly covering my embarrassment.

"Archbishop, do you know Thomas Kinzer, the ambassador from America. Ex?"

"Ah, my good friends, the Americans. Perhaps not so diplomatic. But welcome. Welcome in our rainbow nation."

He forced one of his distinctive, staccato laughs and led Lily Nyati and her daughter away across the lawn, an intense, enclosed trio in clashing colours.

Over her shoulder Lily called out to me: "Do not forget, Tom. Do not forget your promise. We trusted you then. We trust you now."

Her daughter looked back at me as if to suggest quite the opposite.

"Promises? That sounds very mysterious. Have you known Lily long?"

"Some time. Thomas Kinzer."

I extended my hand as I glanced at the intruder's laminated identity tag: Zoë Joubert, Centre for Governance (NGO). (Mine said: Thomas Kinzer (Ambassador). I recognised her name as the author of one of the ground-breaking papers on the psychology of those who had carried out some of history's worst and most intimate cruelties, from Josef Mengele in Nazi Germany to Eugene de Kock in her own country. For someone steeped in the darkness of human evil, she seemed determinedly bright.

"I read your paper, on perpetrators. Rather compelling."

"Ah! A diplomat indeed."

"Retired," I said. "A retired diplomat."

"But I didn't know diplomats made promises. Well, not ones that they could keep, in any case!" Despite her smiling, I thought I detected an edge to her voice.

Zoë Joubert stood straight-spined as if she had been taught at an early age to draw herself up, in the manner of an equestrian or ballerina. Her appearance, I admit, confused me. I had always associated the NGO set with the sandals-and-sarong tradition of aid workers at far-flung "projects" involving village handpumps and seed beds.

But she defied the caricatures. She had that poise that comes from a certain type of education, the kind that teaches the social arts, the ability to communicate through deft questions and fluid conversation, to deflect the impudent from prying too closely before they are invited to do so. Her hair was professionally tended, waves of chestnut and dark honey drawn back from her high forehead, accentuating the aquiline cast of her features. Her tan suggested a liking for the outdoors more than stuffy libraries or closed, nocturnal communing with computerised databases. There was something of the beach about her: I found myself wondering whether her skin would taste of sea salt.

To this day, I cannot adequately explain her sudden, immediate impact. Even now, when so many other impressions and events have been laid over the palimpsest of what you might loosely call our relationship, I recall a swirl of emotion unsullied by the equally stark memories of what subsequently transpired.

Her eyes crinkled over half-moon spectacles, producing the slightly intimidating prospect of a well-respected academic about to test a student's thoroughness in preparing a paper. At least, she had not fled. The thought left me absurdly pleased.

"You seem very young for a pensioner," she said in what I took to be some kind of teasing inquiry.

"Well. It's a long story. I could tell you over dinner," I heard myself blurting out. "I'm sorry. That must have seemed rather forward."

For a moment she seemed as nonplussed as I felt. Conference

small talk was not, I guess, supposed to include such brash overtures.

"No, no. Please. Let's have dinner. A good venue for a long story."

Perhaps she figured that someone who owed a promise to Lily Nyati could not be all bad. And perhaps, too, she simply wanted to know more about what the promise entailed.

We turned back towards the crowd where a mistress of ceremonies tapped the microphone. The amplifiers emitted a loud whistle then subsided. Lily Nyati was waiting in line with the others – Alex Boraine and Antjie Krog, Nyameka Goniwe and Desmond Tutu.

From the hotel's French windows, another group of people had issued forth across the lawn, a cluster of thick-set security men surrounding the all-too-familiar Father of the Nation. It was the first time I had seen him other than in television news footage. He looked slightly smaller and more shrunken than expected. During my first stay in his country, when he was serving time in Pollsmoor Prison after his long spell on Robben Island, his name had been a mantra, an incantation. The distillate of hope and defiance, uttered by the masses to taunt the white authorities like a matador waving a red cape at a fuming bull.

"Mandela," I said, immediately regretting such a gauche statement of the obvious.

"Madiba," she said fondly, using his blue-blooded clan name, as if to re-affirm the implicit assurance that, in Mandela's new order, there would be no levy of pain – no guilt tax – for his former jailers.

"Have you known Mrs Nyati long?" I whispered as the audience fell silent.

"A long time. From before. We met in The Struggle." She leaned towards me, laying a hand on my arm to signal that we should be silent in such august company.

"And her husband?"

"He was murdered just after I met him. I only wish I had more time to spend with him."

Four

"Mr President," Lily began. "Comrades, Excellencies, friends. Thank you all for coming to the Mother City, Cape Town. Thank you for your interest in our new struggle. In the past, as you know, we fought for our freedom and our democracy. That was our first struggle. Against apartheid.'

She pronounced the word with a half-smile and what sounded to me like a mocking snarl, stressing the final syllable as if squeezing the vowels in her throat, strangling her one-time oppressors with their own language. The sound, the word itself, left some of her audience uneasy, as if it were a breach of decorum to mention the unpunished crime in the era of reconciliation.

Beyond the podium and the pool area, the hotel's December rituals were unfolding regardless of our earnest, self-absorbed gathering – the pampering of foreign guests, the subtle suggestions that nothing, really, had changed to upset the natural order. Bearing aperitifs and bowls of nuts and potato chips on silver salvers, waiters in white tunics and purple sashes slid between tables of guests from "overseas".

Some of the men wore what might have been a uniform, gold-buttoned navy blue blazers and pale slacks – habitués of the great hotel's luxury, migrating like birds to the warm southern summer. The women favoured floral frocks in pastel shades, offset with pearls, the tribal dress of their annual invasion.

Nothing in their manner betrayed a sense that Lily's words carried beyond the magic circle of delegates held nervously in her thrall, certainly not to those clinging to a different spell altogether, cast in a time before people like Lily Nyati gave speeches on the sacred lawns of the Mount Nelson Hotel, named for a different Nelson altogether than the one who stood before us on the low podium.

"Now we have a second struggle, not with the oppression of the old system, but with the legacy of the old system."

Listening to her, I imagined her as a schoolteacher, like her husband, chalking the letters onto a board: Oppression, Legacy – underscore O, underscore L. "For decades, for all our lives for most of us, we lived under the tyranny of the system called apartheid" – the word again, the capital A, the tremor of resurgent memory. Underscored.

"We lived with the Pass Laws and the Group Areas Act, the so-called homelands." Underscore P, L and G, A, A and H. "We lived with the torture chambers and the *sjambok*. We lived in a police state where our only crime was the colour of our skin. Every day we were wounded a little bit more. We were wounded by our failure to throw off oppression. Our own children called us cowards. We bled from the cruelties of the system and our own impotence to end it. Today, that system is no more."

She paused to drink from a water glass. Among the crowd of delegates and participants – black, white, foreign, local, drawn from the current and former regimes – murmurs of assent fell into a darker silence of memory, foreboding.

On the hotel terrace, happy hour ticked away. Second rounds were called for. Whiskery cheeks flushed; pearls nestling in modest décolleté glowing with the beginnings of demure perspiration. Condensation frosting tall glasses.

"Waiter, over here waiter, if you please. Same again. Chop chop, old chap!"

Lily Nyati punched a clenched fist into the air.

"The system is no more so we say: Viva to that!" she proclaimed. One or two people curled their fingers in agreement. Others exchanged bemused looks: where was all this leading?

"But we cannot say we are healed. Can we? Yes, we have our freedom, but our hearts are still wounded. Our souls bleed. And why? Yes, we have had commissions and inquiries, the Truth and

Reconciliation Commission. The TRC." – the chalkboard again – "But look at our beautiful country today. Look at the perpetrators, the collaborators, those who lived so happily with apartheid in their suburbs while we were slaves in townships. Surely, we say, surely they must burn now with remorse and pain. But how many of them really know what they did? How many think: oh, well, we got away with it? We did not have to pay and we are still here in our big houses with our maids and gardeners, our cars and our jobs? And for us, the victims, what do we have? Do our husbands open the door to greet us and say they are home? No. Because they are dead. Do our children rise from the grave to embrace us? While the perpetrators walk free we are left with our pain. We are not healed."

She cast her eyes over a skittish, close-knit band of diplomats from European countries and the United States.

"Comrades, we are here, I hope, to think of two kinds of solutions. One is practical. I know that many among you from our overseas friends become nervous when we say: look at the Swiss. They paid for what they did in the Holocaust. In billions from banks. They did not want to. They were forced to. By their victims and the sons and daughters of their victims. So who will pay for apartheid? Will the big companies who made their profits pay those profits back? Ford, Toyota, Barclays, Standard Bank, BMW, Pick n'Pay? Anglo American? De Beers? What about the governments who supported them with their policies? What about the people, the Americans, who used constructive engagement to protect the regime? What about those, the British and their Mrs Thatcher, who called Comrade President Nelson Mandela a terrorist? Will they pay?"

She paused again and lowered her written notes, laughing quietly, looking about her on the podium. There was a strand of bitterness when she resumed.

"No. Even my own government will not ask its friends for that. Instead it will buy some more weapons from them. *Amandla!*"

The sour irony of the battle cry drew a ripple of approval from the more militant souls.

"But I am not here to talk about money, or even corruption. I am here to talk about how we as individuals come to terms with our wounds, how we bathe them and make them heal, as we would our children when they have hurt themselves at play. And when we do that, what is really making the healing? Love. Love heals. When we pray, we beg the Lord: only say the word and I shall be healed. And that is the crux of matters here and now in our beautiful country. Where is the love? We do not love those who hurt us. They do not love those they hurt. But without love, our land will go forward like a sick man pretending he is well, like patients with HIV saying they merely have a common cold, until they fall suddenly and die. Look at us, the widows of Cooktown – Zinto, Ngalo, Mboniswa, Nyati. We know the names of the men who killed our husbands. We have seen them at the so-called Truth and Reconciliation Commission. We have heard them tell us in the most terrible detail how they did it. So brazen! Standing there and saying: yes we did this and this like so. We shot this one and burned that one and stabbed that one. We removed them! Removed! Eliminated. And yet they are free! Free as you and I who fought and suffered for our cause, free to walk on our beaches and mountains."

A handful of reporters scribbled notes. The strobe beat of the photographers' flashlights ticked up a little.

The Western diplomats were glancing at their watches, praying for the witching hour when the embassy drivers arrived to whisk them away to the next fusion of warm wine and bland small talk. I recognised their plumage of summer suits and hounds' tooth twinsets, as much as their instinct to avoid embarrassment at all costs.

Elsewhere within the audience, from the less constrained activists from the NGOs, a low rumble of endorsement and recognition built like approaching artillery fire.

Lily Nyati gestured for silence, scanning the crowd. Her eyes found mine. A single tear trickled down her cheek. She was looking straight at me. So was Zoë Joubert.

"Now we face a great challenge. And it is this, for all of us. From Cradock and Port Elizabeth and Cooktown and Motherwell. We must see the perpetrators brought to justice. We must see them show true and deep remorse. We must hear them say: your husband was a human being. It was wrong what I did and I am deeply sorry to the core of my being. And for our part, the victims, the survivors, we are told by all the experts that we must see them as humans, not monsters. And the experts in the universities and the think tanks say we cannot do that until they show remorse. We must reach the point where we can forgive because until we truly forgive we cannot be free of the hatred that burns within us. These killings of our loved ones, these burnings, these disappearances, they live with us. They poison us. They tie us to the perpetrators and we cannot be free. But how can we know these theories are true if the perpetrators do not come to us? If they do not confess to us? If they do not put the theories into practice?"

"Comrades. Excellencies. Above all, we must know why. We will not know how to live our lives without these dark shadows until we know the reasons, the causes, the orders, the treachery. It is not enough to say: I did this and this and he was dead. We must have the whole picture and we must know for once and for all that the guilty ones have paid."

She turned now to confront the phalanx of political bigwigs sitting behind her.

"It is now the time to ask the biggest question that we have all avoided: should we, the victims, forgive at all? Is there a place in our rainbow nation for any of those in their boardrooms and offices and Casspirs and torture chambers who oppressed us? How can we forgive the spies and traitors who still walk among us? Comrade President, how can you ask us to forgive them when they walk on our graves?"

She sat down abruptly, suddenly small, hidden below a maroon beret, swathed in a brown chequered blanket.

The waiters tending the buffet tables had stopped their work to listen, silent, immobile, ignoring commands to top up jugs of Pimm's No. 1 Cup, or to refresh gin and tonics. The diplomats had ceased shuffling as if entranced – deer in the headlights. The reporters looked on expectantly, aware that something shocking had happened even if it did not fit the usual categories of news. Slowly Mandela began the applause and Tutu helped the exhausted Lily Nyati rise in acknowledgement of her accolade.

At her side, her daughter raised her mother's fist. She lifted her own in the salute that people of Celiwe's age would hardly remember in its original context.

"*Amandla*," the daughter cried, her voice strong where her mother's had been failing, her eyes bright and fierce where her mother's had clouded with tears and exhaustion. "*Amandla!*"

"*Awethu*," some in the audience roared back. Power! It shall be ours!

The slogan, so familiar during my first stay in their country, revived the memories: dust and stamping feet, choking teargas, plumes of fire, rattles of gunshots, hurled rocks, Molotov cocktails.

Lily Nyati gazed at her daughter with apprehension, fear perhaps. She had called for apartheid's final reckoning and her own child had taken up the challenge.

"*Amandla*," her daughter cried.

"*Awethu*," the crowd roared back.

Then, the voices slid into the harmonies of *Nkosi Sikelel' iAfrika* – God Bless Africa – the national anthem once the marching song of the revolution.

Beside me, Zoë Joubert joined the singing. A sweet, firm voice that I would normally have associated with a convent upbringing or a church service; a white woman in elegant clothes singing in fluent African languages in the cadences that bound her to the struggle.

Across the lawns, on the hotel terrace, the foreign guests who came for the African summer to escape their own winter paused in their cocktail hour, as if somewhat puzzled by the native customs, or wondering if this was some form of cultural manifestation – like tribal dancing and the playing of marimba music – to be expected in these odd, new times.

The official delegation swept away, carrying Lily Nyati and her daughter with it. She looked back at me as if to say: now do you understand? I was left alone with Zoë Joubert, nervous in a way I could not recall since my first romantic expeditions in high school. She moved away slightly, as if Lily's words had put our earlier banter into a different light.

"Some speech," I said.

"Some woman. She behaved as if she knew you very well."

"Back then. A little."

"And Solomon?"

"Oh yes. Solomon, too. Solomon was something else."

"You got around." She said. "Funny we didn't meet."

"Different circles, I guess."

In my previous life, I had learned to arrange my facial features into a mask – polite, non-committal, more interested in developing my interlocutor's narrative than in offering any clue to my own. A trick of the trade in a world where even the most modest snippet of information had a value to be counted, stored, extracted without reciprocal disclosure.

Talking now to Zoë Joubert, I felt the same expression settling into place as I tried to bring some order to the unfamiliar feelings inspired by meeting her.

I wanted her to trust me. When I looked at her, heard her voice with its merest hint of a lilting, local accent, overlaid with some mid-Atlantic tones that I could not place, I wanted to radiate reassurance. I wanted to stem the dark undertow that propelled her questions as she sought to place my walk-on part in the drama of her country. I wanted many things that I had lived without for a long time.

I wanted to smile and I wanted her to smile back at me. I wanted to push aside the shadow of the mission set for me by Lily Nyati. As any beat cop knows, the greatest suspicion in homicide cases falls on the last person to have seen the deceased alive. And, in the Nyati case, that person was standing right in front of me, raising troublesome questions: who was the "we" she spoke about, was that the same as "meeting group" in the excerpt of testimony the widows had enclosed with their letter?

Yet. Yet, if I had met Nyati, Zoë Joubert seemed to have been thinking, what was the reason for that encounter? What was my secret, hidden agenda?

I found myself smiling in anticipation of our dinner date. Or was date too strong a word? The temperature seemed to have climbed towards evening. As Zoë Joubert crossed the lawns of the Mount Nelson

Hotel, chatting and shaking hands with fellow conferees, I noticed that she had removed her jacket – a tailored affair in beige linen over a sleeveless, silk top in a shade of dark burgundy. There seemed to be some kind of marking on her upper left arm, an unusual blemish in what I was already telling myself was a vision of perfection.

Five

WE ATE GENEROUSLY, HUNGRILY AT one of the smart bistros on the Waterfront with pink tablecloths and matching napkins and an array of silverware. I was slightly surprised that she accepted my pre-emptive offer to pay the bill; something about her sense of independence had steeled me for a battle over sharing the tab, but she seemed happy enough with my old-fashioned fiscal chivalry, as if it were only right and proper that a stranger should pay tribute in this time-honoured fashion without taking her acceptance as an invitation to courtship. She had changed her outfit since the afternoon and now wore a light, cotton blouse with sleeves that covered her arms.

She drew a lot of attention from other men; moonstruck husbands peering past their wives, young bucks with the brazen eyes of frequent triumph. I steered the conversation away from Lily Nyati and onto relatively neutral ground – the status of her rainbow nation, the politics of the conference and – heretical though it seemed – the post-Mandela era. I ran through my diplomatic CV in a self-deprecating way with no hint of bitterness, glossing over its final chapter: the decision to quit had been mine; enough was enough. How long could one continue to be an ambassador – however extraordinary or plenipotentiary – in an era when jet planes and e-mail had made plumed hats and crafted dispatches something of an irrelevance?

Get a life, they said.

So I had.

"And you?"

"Nothing nearly so exciting. Groves of academe. Civil society. The two seem natural allies. Wine?"

"Thanks. And before that?"

"Oh, well. Little rich girl, I guess."

"Nothing wrong with being rich. Not in America, at least."

"Well there certainly was in South Africa. At least in the old days."

"And now?"

"And now, well, there's a handful of people called formerly disadvantaged who are getting advantaged pretty quickly. And plenty of people who were advantaged then and seem to be getting even more advantaged now! Then there are the ones who will never even know what advantage means and they are the majority."

I let her guide me in the ordering. She checked with the table staff on the freshness of the Knysna oysters and said two orders of three would suffice, given their generous proportions. Perhaps a salad for the table? She suggested the fish – sole off the bone would be good with a bottle of dry white wine. She pointed to it on the menu and I had difficulty with the pronunciation: Buitenverwachting Buiten Blanc. She laughed at my linguistic clumsiness, but not in an offensive sort of way. She corrected me and explained that it was the name of the estate that produced it, quite close by.

"It means 'beyond expectation,'" she explained. "In the old days, you couldn't get to university without a good grade in Afrikaans. Now we have 11 official languages!"

The oysters, big and luscious, arrived with a garnish of condiments and brown bread, heavy with the taste of ocean.

"I can manage English and French. And a smattering of roadblock Arabic," I offered.

"Roadblock?"

"You know the kind of thing. Don't shoot. Which way to the airport please?"

"You never learned any of our languages while you were here?"

I caught a hint of reproach and shook my head ruefully.

"Not even roadblock, I guess," I said.

"Well it's never too late," she said. I must have looked alarmed because she smiled and said: "Don't worry. I'm not starting you on a course of isiXhosa or isiZulu. You won't be staying that long, in any event."

"I don't know," I said. "I'm a quick learner. It depends on the teacher."

She turned to ask a passing waiter to remove the oyster shells. I don't really recall who was the more embarrassed at my gauche gallantry, her or me.

Even if I had been the most skilled of Don Juans, the most artful of suitors, I doubt that our first-date conversation would venture much beyond sparring and formality to delineate areas that could be considered common ground, set the markers of shared belief, compatibility. The rules were unfamiliar; I felt uneasy joining a joust in which my motives might be misread: I was not even clear about them myself.

I escorted her back to the hotel in a shared cab. (The journey was brief but the risk of violent crime argued against walking the nocturnal streets.)

The elevator stopped at my floor and, bidding her goodnight, I stepped out. The doors closed behind me. I found myself suddenly annoyed at my lack of courage, my inability to divine her assumptions about me. I tried to tell myself that these were early days: I had known her for only a matter of hours – this was certainly not the time to attempt the leap from a casual encounter to liaison, amour.

You might sense an affinity, a spark. But if you do not have the self-confidence to assume that your overtures will be reciprocated, you hold back, prevaricate. Not, I hasten to add, that I had ever commanded the cynical arts of a Lothario. Indeed, I had displayed a consistent talent for allowing my heart to dictate to my head. (Some would express the metaphor in earthier terms.)

I returned to my room, befuddled with advancing jetlag, my body clock out of sync in more ways than one.

When I accepted the conference invitation, I thought I understood – and could handle – the perils of this kind of travel across the years, back to a place of so many landmarks. But I had not expected such potent spells to be cast so soon after stepping from my time capsule, to find myself in a version of the present whose markers I no longer recognised, caught up in a minuet driven by forces I could not begin to define. The term "conference purposes only" suddenly seemed to offer remarkable scope to pursue far more than dry debates and ardent polemics.

To my surprise, after some initial hesitation on both sides – call it shyness, if you will, or inexperience – Zoë Joubert seemed to share the enthusiasm.

If, at a coffee break between panel discussions, I approached her, she would break off conversation with other delegates and greet me with an ardent intensity. I am not given to tactile behaviour, but found my hands reaching out and had to restrain myself from that kind of glancing touch on the sleeve or shoulder that implies so much. When I felt her eyes on me, I would turn and a smile would light my face. For the first time in years, there was no way of computing the likely course of events.

What remained of my professional cynicism, my tradecraft, sounded warning bells that I should not mix emotional entanglement with the Nyati inquiry. But it was increasingly, overwhelmingly evident that I would go where my heart led – if only to rediscover the delirious sound of its beating.

"You are like love birds, you two," Lily Nyati said once when she joined us midway through the earnest discussions that had brought us all together. "Whenever I see one of you, I see the other."

Zoë Joubert laughed and reddened. I think I choked on my coffee. Lily Nyati smiled, but there was no humour in her eyes. She was saying to me: do not confuse your missions. Find out the truth about Solomon's last evening, but do not hurt this woman in the process.

There was another sub-plot that I hoped she would keep between the two of us: when I first met her and her husband – shortly before his death – I had been travelling with Jessica Chase, a foreign correspondent who had written the seminal newspaper profile of Solomon Nyati. The article brought his name before an international audience for the first time and had inspired me to seek her out soon after I arrived to begin my tour as a junior press attaché.

Now, his widow was warning me not to mix work with pleasure again, not at her expense.

"So, Zoë, are you finally divorced from that poet?" Lily asked in another of her interventions.

"Quite some time, now, Lily." Zoë laughed to hide a blush.

"And, Tom. You. You married in the end after you left here?"

"Married and divorced, Lily."

"A society lady?"

"Some people said so."

"Like Zoë here, then."

"Lily, really!"

"OK. Then, a mine owner's daughter. A rand lady!"

After the final conference session, I planned a run around the contour of Table Mountain and Zoë Joubert offered to guide me on the unfamiliar trails. I accepted happily.

We spoke little on the drive from the hotel, across town and along Langstraat to the twisting road leading over to Camps Bay before the turn-off to the cable car station. The following day, she told me, she planned to drive over 500 kilometres along the coast to meet her old friends – the cabal from the 80's, she exclaimed with a smile – at a resort where they often vacationed together to renew their old bonds of friendship.

And what else besides friendship, I asked myself.

She drove one of the new Beetles, a convertible. The rear seat was already stacked with cooler bags and tennis rackets and those flat boards people use to spin through the ocean surf. I could see wetsuits and duffels and wondered who, exactly, she had packed for.

My plans were vague. I had anticipated a long, uncharted absence from Washington, thinking I might, as the whim took me after the conference, ride the Blue Train to Johannesburg, or visit a game-park in Tanzania or perhaps tack my way by airline flight and train through Africa, from Harare to Nairobi and onwards. Cape to Cairo! But now all that had changed.

I had, I suppose, suppressed a lot of the questions that diplomats were supposed to associate with chance encounters. Often enough, in the days of ideological rivalry and sparring, a well-briefed foreign service officer might be lured into some *liaison dangereuse* with a glamorous stranger only to end up ensnared.

You learned to look for the coincidences that seemed improbable; the invitations to advance into realms of intimacy that came just a little too easily; the tell-tale knowledge of some personal detail that could not be squirreled from any public database.

Zoë Joubert had entered my life effortlessly, moved to the centre of my waking hours, but she had not intimated any readiness for an unseemly rush to the boudoir. We had simply seemed destined to share the same orbit from the very first encounter on the lawns of the Mount Nelson Hotel. Could that behaviour have been part of a subtle double-bluff to hoodwink a naturally cautious target with little recent experience of sexual adventure? But who would be her control? I could not imagine the local goons like Faku and Nieuwoudt reaching anywhere near her levels of sophistication and mental rigour. Ideologically she had opposed all they stood for. Maybe, then, a bigger player. But why? And why was I even thinking of myself with the old mindset of a high-profile, security-cleared public servant privy to confidential cables and closed briefings? I had no current value, or even secrets, unless you counted the undercover role Lily Nyati had assigned to me in her desperation to understand her husband's death. An affair would hardly compromise a divorced pensioner, even a relatively young one like me.

At first, we ran in an easy rhythm, but on the return leg she quickened the pace. I lengthened my stride to keep up with her. In her jogger's Lycra, her movements were as fluid as those of a leopard. I had read somewhere that the female leopard, brazenly available, courts the male with assiduous stalking. But that anthropomorphism in reverse seemed false: it was I who was doing the pursuing, and not very effectively at that.

As my speed increased, she seemed to draw on unsuspected reserves to accelerate again, a challenge to my slightly more advanced years. I was aware of the cable car ahead of us, climbing to the soaring buttress at the top of the precipice.

High above, a white, fuzzy fringe of cloud had begun to cascade over the lip of the mountain. Below, the late afternoon sun still burned fiercely on the Atlantic as it rushed to its tryst with the Indian Ocean beyond Cape Point. In the distance, stretching towards the snaggle-tooth mountain ranges of wine country, the Cape Flats unfolded in monotonous poverty: one dismal wooden shack pushing up against the next in a ceaseless, daisy-chain coupling. The great homes of Bishopscourt and Newlands and Claremont rose up like a scented palisade keeping the hordes at bay, even as it drew their eternal envy.

Again I took up the pace, not simply to keep step with her but to overtake and be the first to arrive back at the cable car station. In her jogger's vest, she made no attempt to hide the blemish on her upper arm – a mangled furrow of dark, hard tissue looked very much like the aftermath of a gunshot, possibly a crude blade. Or perhaps simply a birthmark.

We were pounding now, no longer jogging but running, no longer in rhythm but competing for a hair's breadth lead, a neck, a stride. If I had entertained thoughts of chivalry, I abandoned them. If I had thought I might let her win, I forgot the idea because it was all I could do to acquit myself with some kind of honour. Her stride seemed impossibly long, stretching and bounding on perfect legs, her arms scissoring with tight efficiency, her hair falling loose from its elasticated bands and streaming free.

She was not looking at me at all. Her eyes focused exclusively on the car park, moving towards us at a giddy pace. Walkers, strollers, joggers stood back to make way. Some cheered but most looked askance as if this were not the place for such shenanigans. Try as I might I could not claim a lead over her. Neither could I allow myself to fall back. My lungs were bursting but I could not slow down. Perspiration stained my sweat-shirt and ran between my shoulder blades. I knew my hair would be plastered black on my forehead and above my neck, exposing the retreat from youth.

We were close now; no more than 50 yards and incredibly she found the reserves to accelerate once more. I doubted I could hold this pace but pushed to break through the pain of cramps and tiredness in my calf muscles. At the final moment, just yards from the base station, she nudged ahead then slowed, allowing me an impression of victory.

We climbed into her car and drove in silence to the hotel. She parked and we crossed the lobby, astonishing some of them more sedate guests in their cocktail-hour finery with our clamminess. The hotel seemed full of men in dark suits, women in neat, black dresses clutching small evening bags. I half-recognised some of our co-conferees. A world-famous novelist, winner of many prizes and awards – a man with a straggly beard and lizard eyes – approached and began to inquire about Zoë's paper on perpetrators.

"I was intrigued…" he began.

For a moment, she seemed inclined to hesitate but I took her hand, propelling her forward towards the bank of elevators that sped up and down the atrium, leaving the writer to gaze in ill-tempered astonishment at an affront he evidently considered scandalous.

We entered a glass-sided lift. She pressed the button for her floor almost at the top of the hotel. We soared high above the lobby. Far below, the famous writer and the other delegates dwindled into miniaturised forms of themselves. I had not let go of her hand. We left the elevator together, walking quickly and urgently along the deep beige pile of the corridor carpeting, below small chandeliers, past cream-painted doors and fancy, half-moon tables laden with vases of cut flowers.

A trolley bearing fresh towels and replacement bottles of shampoo blocked the way but we danced around it in step. We reached her room and she entered the key-card. A small green light signalled us to enter. The maid had already turned down the queen-sized bed (chocolate mint on pillow!) and the big picture window with the drapes undrawn showed us the broad sweep of the mountain that had been the arena of our joust.

A girl in her early teens jumped up, laying aside a magazine. A backpack lay on the bed beside her, a tennis racket strapped to it. She was wearing a navy blue skirt and white uniform shirt. A matching blazer with a school coat of arms in gold had been tossed over an armchair near the window. I could hear water running in the bathroom.

"Hi, Ma," she said, addressing Zoë Joubert but looking quizzically at me. "All set?"

"Mills! So Dad dropped you off early?"

Six

TABLE TALK – A DIFFERENT restaurant this time with heavier, Mediterranean food and waitresses wearing white tank-tops printed with the word "Greek" in blue.

She has insisted we meet to "get things straight" while her daughter joins friends back at the hotel coffee shop for an end-of-term splurge of burgers and shakes. The noise from other tables is insistent, so we lean together, mutually unfulfilled. She is wearing a loose black outfit and her hair frames the oval of her face. There is no make-up. To ease our embarrassment, I have asked the usual questions required of conversations with parents devoted to their children.

School?

An upmarket academy for boarders. (She hangs her head in mock shame to make this elitist, counter-revolutionary confession).

Prospects?

Straight As, Harvard or Oxford.

Zoë Joubert flushes with pride but does not dwell on the logistical and custodial arrangements she has with the father, identified to me as long divorced, still "best friends."

Her tanned, brown hand slides across the white tablecloth and takes mine, loosely, more in consolation than ardour.

"I'm sorry," she says.

"There's nothing to be sorry for."

"I think I gave the wrong impression. I lead a very quiet life. This has all come as a surprise to me. Hotel rooms! Dinners à deux!' She smiles ruefully and withdraws her hand despite my slight pressure to suggest it is fine where it is. "I'm not used to it. And we are virtual strangers."

"I don't feel that way. It's been just a few days but I feel I have known you much longer. Frankly." I'm blushing as I recall these words, just as I blushed when I uttered them.

"You know," she says after an awkward silence, "in the German spa towns, people sometimes take up with other people for the length of their cures and baths and massages, and the term they use for this dalliance is the *Kurschatten* – the spa shadow. The person who is there and not there, a figment, without a counter point in reality. And, of course, when the cure is over and the mud is washed off, the shadow disappears and reality reasserts itself. But I'm not a shadow, Tom, and neither are you."

"Reality is what you make it. It can be the future. It doesn't necessarily mean disappointment. What has happened between us is not a shadow, a figment. You know that. And so do I."

"But you know nothing about me, Tom."

"Then tell me about you. About The Struggle. The old days."

"It's history now," she says.

"Isn't there a saying about ignoring history at your peril?"

She takes a sip of wine.

"How much time do you have?" she laughs then becomes serious. "Well, we all lived at a place called Old Deep. A mine settlement outside Johannesburg. I don't know if you would have known it? Cottages with narrow stoops and tin roofs? Dirt roads? Not on the usual diplomatic circuit! Where you lived was important in those days – I'm sure you remember."

"We called ourselves the Old Deep Action Committee – ODAC. Can you imagine? But we wanted to make a statement against the system. It was a bit like a commune. Crèches for the babies like little Mills. Gardening cooperatives. The alternative society." She says this with her fingers imitating quotation marks.

"I had a grant, money from home, but I didn't want to make too much of it, to make it ostentatious. No one was going to call me a trust-fund liberal. So we lived simply. A simple married life. Rod – my husband – had his notebooks and pencils. The poet of The Struggle."

"You can smile now but it was deadly serious then. There was a cost. Okay, we weren't thrown out of the windows at John Vorster Square.

But our lot paid a price – Aggett, Lubovsky. They died, dammit. Died for their country. Sorry, I didn't mean to be sharp. People forget. It wasn't all play-play. Sure we had escape routes if we'd wanted them but we didn't just want to go back to Ma and Pa and the big house and the servants. The cops gave us a hard time. Obviously not nearly as hard as for the blacks, or the freedom fighters. But they tapped the phones, poured acid on the cars, slashed the tires, strip-searched you for handing out pamphlets at the demos. Teargas in the nursery. That kind of stuff. For the bigger fish they could arrange a suicide, a fatal car accident. But who were we supposed to talk to? How were we supposed to contribute? Please stop me if I'm boring you."

"No, no. Please."

She recounted the story with unexpected passion, as if memory had rekindled the ardour of the fight.

Did I encourage her recollections as suitor or spy? Even now I'm unsure.

"We've all moved on," she was saying, "a prosperous bunch, really, with our law firms and foundations and newspaper columns and businesses. But then, it was so intense. Who did you talk to if you were separated by the system? What we wanted was a multi-racial front, a rainbow struggle. But a lot of blacks didn't trust us. Why should they?"

"So what I'm getting around to saying is that our problem suddenly seemed to be solved when we heard about Nyati. He was our Mandela. He wasn't in prison. He was free, available. He was open to multi-racial politics and his credentials were impeccable. If anyone could show us our place in The Struggle it was him. But how could we meet him?"

"We?"

"Yes. We. ODAC. The Old Deep set."

"All of you?"

"That's an odd question. Yes, all of us, I think. I don't recall. I only know we went to meet him in Port Elizabeth and he came to meet us and he never got home again. And you? How did you meet Lily? I thought from the way she looked at you during her speech that there must be something sort of special?"

Seven

I HAD MY LEGEND PREPARED, built around the grain of truth at the core of all such fictions, the grist of all good lies.

Those many years ago, to borrow from the language of the times, I was a temporary sojourner in Nyati's land, assigned by law to living in its different worlds defined by skin colour, joined only by the shared humanity that official separation was designed to deny.

On my side of town, the sidewalks were neat, the highways smooth. A network of domestic flights crisscrossed the land. (Of course, the flights – like German and Italian trains in the 1930s – ran on time.)

In the shopping malls you could find Picassos in art galleries and hypermarkets the size of aircraft hangars, bulging with produce. Restaurants flourished, along with bars, music stores, bookshops. The best jobs, the best land, the best of everything went to the whites, and when people went home, many went to homes like mine with pools and tennis courts. The cars were late model, German and Japanese. California in Africa!

But then, of course, quite literally over the hill, were the townships. Homes cramped and pokey; squatters jostling for space in shacks of cast-off zinc and plastic sheeting; the police in their blue uniform and armoured yellow Casspirs enforcing their writ with the rifle and the whip, buttressed by a huge edifice of law and edict that redefined the term Orwellian in terms of skin colour: the Group Areas Act, the Morality Act, the Pass Laws. Designed to ensure that no one passed where they were not wanted.

If you had written a fable on the lines of Tolkien, you would have come up with a simple narrative: Race Ogres, the evil ones, pitted against the sylvan oppressed; a master race forging its weapons in great furnaces, forcing its slaves into the deep, dark tunnels of the mines to excavate the raw materials of their own subjugation. Plough-shares into swords, bullets, gun-barrels. Looking back, apartheid's great reach into the very souls of the people almost seems improbable. But it happened.

"It was my first tour of duty, not long out of law school. A long way from the Upper West Side. In Pretoria. And what we were doing – the policy – was called constructive engagement. Remember? Of course. You would have been very aware. It was anathema but it was the policy. The idea was to stay close to the regime and persuade it to permit limited change. No revolution. No Red Onslaught. It was the way we looked at things at the time. East-West. The fight with Moscow."

Across the road from the restaurant, through the big plate glass window, a skinny boy in rags lolled against a streetlamp, waiting to beg small change from post-prandial diners. I caught our reflection superimposed on him. Zoë Joubert was still looking at me, chin cupped in hand. She was sitting very still, as if intent on absorbing every word. I felt as if I was on trial, singing for a free pardon as surely as the perpetrators at the TRC.

"Africa was a checker board of client states – that's how the newspapers put it – some theirs, some ours. We didn't want to lose South Africa, not after Mozambique, Angola. Not with the Cubans on the borders of Namibia. History now. Of course you remember the protests, the riots, better than I. The cops would move in and open fire. More deaths. Funerals became protests. I always found it weird that one of the very few lawful forms of assembly for blacks – apart from soccer games – was funerals. Well, maybe not so weird. So the funerals were held and the songs were sung and the comrades toyi-toyied – isn't that what they called that war dance? I felt drawn to the whole thing. It sounds pretty pompous but, for once, maybe the only time, I felt I was in at the ground floor of history. I started heading down to the Eastern Cape. We had a consulate in Port Elizabeth and that gave me cover for the trips."

"Cover?" There was a knowing edge to the question.

"Wrong word. Sorry. I was from the State Department, not the CIA. What I meant was just the routine stuff of my job. Administrative work. Liaison with the local press – the *Eastern Province Herald*, the little freelance agencies riddled with young idealists" – I avoided the words "agitators" and "leftists" that peppered the embassy dispatches – "the local black reporters from *City Press* and so forth. I'd go to the funerals and listen to the slogans and the speeches. See who was saying what. Get the mood, the flavour. Because you could tell a lot about the impetus, the anger, the resolve, just from listening to those speeches. And you could see how rattled the authorities were getting, how many troops were deployed, how many police, what kind of bullets they were firing – bird-shot, buck-shot, live rounds. Who am I to tell someone in your position what that meant? You were there. You were a player. You and all the others helped make it all possible."

"Not that you would know now, thank goodness," she said with a surprisingly warm smile, as if was slightly preposterous to think of the onetime master race being acknowledged in the new order. "We all did things then that we thought would help. Maybe they did. Maybe not."

She changed tack.

"So how did you meet Nyati?"

"A friend set up a meeting." I saw her next questions form. What friend? What motive? But she did not pursue them and I did not elaborate.

In theory, my journey to Nyati's home required ambassadorial authorisation. To outsiders, it could have been interpreted as a signal, a shift in policy, a calculation that apartheid's days were numbered so it was time to befriend its heirs. It was a decision that a junior diplomat had no authority to take. But I took it anyhow.

"So I went over to Cooktown and sat with him, listened. And that's how I met Lily and the others. Smuggled into the township on the floor of an old VW Kombi, covered in blankets, straight past the cops. I think they figured something was going down. They kept cruising past his house. Looking in. White guys with guns. But I'd given them the slip. We talked for hours. I even tried to persuade the ambassador to visit with him – strictly hush-hush, of course. But the next time I was at the house was for the funeral."

"I was there, too," she said. "I don't remember seeing you. But then, there were 35,000 of us!"

"Not an easy day to forget."

But easy to recall for those who had been there. Red revolutionary banners billowed over the heads of clerics ablaze with righteousness. The air choked with dust and sound as the police on the perimeters seized the high ground on a ridge overlooking the township, fingering their trigger guards with nervous anticipation, little suspecting that this day would initiate the reversal of all they stood for. A *Wendepunkt*.

The crowd became a tide carrying me along, embracing and enfolding me in its sound, its roar, its sharp odours of sweat and fury. The young men and pre-pubescent boys – "the comrades" – formed themselves spontaneously into warrior groups, *impis*, raising their knees, pounding their feet, swinging their arms in imitation of a guerrilla fighter firing bursts from an AK-47. I didn't know at the time, but their slogan translated as: one settler, one bullet.

"*Amandla!*"

"*Awethu!*"

"Nelson Mandela. Hai. Hai. Oliver Tambo. Hai. Hai."

And then the songs, the lilting loss-filled strains and the brutal exhortations to murder, all in one great swelling chorus.

"*Senzeni Na*" – what have we done? What had they done indeed to merit their enslavement?

And, addressed to the guerrilla fighters in their camps, "*Hamba kahle, Mkhonto, Mkhonto, Mkhonto we Sizwe*" – go well, Spear of the Nation.

I heard what I wanted to hear – the yearning, the bursting chorus of those so desperate to throw off oppressors who shared my skin colour. The thousands of voices rose like the thunder that rolled across the African veld to herald the rains, from the Great Fish River to the drylands of the Karoo. The hair rose on my neck and my sweat turned cold, and I raised my clenched fist with theirs as their anthem consumed us all – more powerful than mine because its revolution was raw in the making and mine was past.

"Nkosi Sikelel' iAfrika" – God Bless Africa.

The fire burned in me along with the multitude, branding us all with its simple morality: the regime, the government that we as American officials chose to deal with, was evil beyond redemption. The resistance, this great, cresting wave of humanity that carried me through dirt streets between the matchbox houses and the burned-out homes of quisling black policemen, was good. The cause was just. The comrades' demands represented no more than we in America took for granted – freedom, democracy, human dignity. This moment, the distillation of a great struggle, had nothing to do with the Cold War, the KGB, the Cubans, the battle for Africa. It had to do only with a future in which this lumpenproletariat that stamped its feet and bellowed its songs and slogans all around me would be given the same liberty as was my birthright.

We weren't the only ones to grasp the significance of the moment. At midnight, with the turned dirt still fresh on the graves, the Race Ogres declared a state of emergency that granted their warriors in their armoured trucks near total powers of arrest without charge or trial, indemnity from prosecution. Roadblocks sprang up. Men with guns smashed doors at 3 am. Cells filled. Blood ran in the fury to sluice away everything Nyati and his comrades stood for.

But in the process the apartheid regime severed its links to the distant world. In New York and London, be-suited bankers, tired of the hassle of anti-apartheid protesters on their doorsteps, called in the debts. American businesses pulled the plug on their subsidiaries, not out of any great ethical concern but to safeguard their reputation elsewhere. Confidence died. The economy shrank.

By killing Nyati, his murderers guaranteed their own defeat.

I visited the four bereaved women as they sat with their youngsters around them. Lily Nyati carried one small child in a blanket drawn across her back in the African way to share the warmth and synchronise the rhythms of breathing and heartbeat. It was a girl, she said, Solomon's youngest child. A girl he had named Celiwe. Before his death he told me what the name meant: the one who was asked for.

At that time, on the day of the funeral, I had no cause to doubt the assurances I gave that I would work with all my being to unmask the perpetrators; that I would never cease in my inquiries until every last stone was unturned, until every last link in the chain of command and obedience had been exposed, until every last traitor and informer had been brought to book.

At this point I should perhaps offer another confession which I did not make in my dinner conversation with Zoë Joubert: in that same spirit of devil-may-care abandon, during those wild days in the Eastern Cape, among the banned people and the revolutionaries, the nature of my relationship with the journalist Jess Chase turned intimate. Who initiated this chapter in our entanglement is irrelevant. When we finally fell into one another's arms in some remote motel outside Port Elizabeth – I had knocked on her door, not she on mine – I believe she was expecting me, finally, to make my move, for the door was not locked. I mention this to explain – or perhaps justify – the unprofessional intensity of feeling that I came to associate with this period in my life. If I am honest with myself, I should also acknowledge that, once it was all over, I spent much of my time looking in vain for someone capable of inspiring the same passions.

"In fact," I was telling Zoë Joubert, "I got caught on the TV coverage with all those red banners and clenched fists. Didn't do me much good back at the embassy. All the older guys, political officers, agency types, telling me I was out of line. What the hell. Because, of course, they soon came to see that the game was up for our policy. All because of kids throwing rocks and petrol bombs. And people like Solomon and Lily Nyati."

"And where were you when he died?"

"I was at home," I told Zoë Joubert. "Just at home."

What I did not say was this: I heard the news from a political activist in the Port Elizabeth region, a woman from the Black Sash movement. She called me in Pretoria, in the early, pre-office hours, shocked and sobbing over the phone – clearly indifferent to the consequences of betraying her feelings to those who routinely monitored her conversation.

She told me how the victims had always been careful to keep

their movements to themselves, to travel without advance warning of their plans, to vary their routes, to stop for no one save clearly identifiable, uniformed police. But, she said, none of that would make any difference if their movements had been betrayed, foretold.

The morning was bright and wintry on Africa's highveld, with a hint of frost crusting the yellow, dry-season lawn. A domestic worker had left a tray of coffee and biscuits outside the bedroom door along with the morning newspapers. Discreetly, she had placed two cups on it. I thought of returning to bed as if nothing untoward had happened until I could break the news gently. But my secret lover was already stirring, sensing from my grunted, guarded conversation that something awful had occurred. Her response surprised me.

She brushed aside my attempt to console her. She barked questions about what, exactly, I had been told: how, when, where, why – for God's sake, why (although the answer to that was clear enough in any logical sense.) She grabbed the newspapers, but the news had arrived too late for them. As a reporter, a foreign correspondent, Jessica Chase had been Solomon Nyati's closest chronicler. She had become his admirer and confidant. Some said it went further than that: she was his gatekeeper, at least, an ex-officio advisor, far beyond the realm of objective journalism. (The embassy files contained a security police report suggesting a little more, though I never gave it much credence. For all that was said, there was no bias to her dispatches, no ideological message, subliminal or stated. The bare facts, honestly recounted, spoke for themselves.)

She dressed without showering, by turn stricken, alarmed, remorseful, enraged. She left the house with a spray of gravel from the rear tire of her motorcycle as the big steel gate opened. I recalled tasting the bile of anger at the back of my throat: if Nyati and his comrades had been betrayed, then surely someone must pay.

We left the restaurant to return to the hotel. I had told the story of my life to Zoë Joubert and I had airbrushed Jess Chase out of it completely.

The coffee shop was empty so I assumed her daughter had gone ahead to their room. The moment did not seem to permit any suggestion of closer intimacy. As the elevator rose towards my floor, I tried to take her hand but she pulled back.

"I'm leaving very early tomorrow, for the coast," she said. "So I suppose this will be goodbye, Tom."

"Goodbye?"

The elevator stopped at my floor. She stepped out with some reluctance and we stood together in the corridor as it sped onwards.

"Zoë, I really want to see you again. Meeting you has been very special for me."

"For me, too. I wish it were all so simple. And there is Mills to think of. We didn't exactly fool her, you know. She's not naïve."

The child's name provoked a silence.

"Is there someone, you know, significant?"

"Only Mills. Don't be silly, Tom. And you're a former ambassador. You're supposed to be a bit more diplomatic."

"Well, as diplomats used to say, given goodwill on both sides … Surely there's some way we can meet again. We have got to know each other pretty well and I have lots of free time. Sorry. I didn't mean it that way. I meant I would dearly love to spend more time with you. Coffee. Lunch. No demands. I would love to drive that way again, anyhow."

"Tom. It's a free country these days. I can't stop you driving wherever you like. But I can't make promises I can't keep. Give me a couple of days to get settled and maybe it will seem different. I'll call you. We'll see."

Part Two

With the blue light flashing, Theron overtook the Honda as it slowed to a halt. The backup, driven by De Kock, boxed it from behind. In no time at all the steel handcuffs were on the captives' wrists, the prisoners split up between the cars. De Kock disguised the Honda's licence plates with a false set from Headquarters. The detainees realised that no matter how they wriggled to get their hands on the interior door handles to throw themselves clear, the child-proof locks – of all things – prevented their escape.

Eight

IN LIMBO, AWAITING ZOË JOUBERT'S signal.

The familiar reflex: when in doubt, work. In this case on the task set by Lily Nyati; however inadequate my qualifications to meet her expectations, however great the distractions of waiting.

I make to-do lists, wrack my brains to recall names of people who might help, cross off tasks when modest accomplishments are achieved – an appointment fixed, a purchase made.

I download sheaves of transcript; procure A-4 legal pads and a stout, black, leather-bound notebook of high quality vellum. It will become the incomplete journal on which I have based this attempt at a narrative.

I pore over the record of the Truth and Reconciliation Commission, particularly the sections concerning the murder of the Cooktown Four and the remarkable, public confession of Kobus Theron, the white security policeman who admitted to leading the death squad that killed Nyati and his comrades after their meeting with the Old Deep set. Oddly, for all my attempts to pinpoint Zoë Joubert's activities during that era, using a variety of search engines, I turn up no matches and it strikes me as odd that she has left no trace, no footprint, in the testimony of the commission – the Domesday Book of The Struggle. Has something been redacted? And if so, how would I know?

When you root around in history, you can never tell what will emerge from the careful constructs of official narratives, the undergrowth of obfuscation. You are a clumsy hunter stumbling over rocks and tangled, hidden roots, stirring unsuspected life forms, alerting the prey to menace. I was venturing into the events that formed a new nation's self-image, its pride, its sense of exceptionalism. And I had travelled far beyond those bureaucratic frontiers laid down in my passport by Faku and Nieuwoudt. That was fine as long as my inquiries went no further than the laptop in my hotel room.

Ultimately it was obvious that my investigation could not simply be conducted in some forensic bubble of web searches and paperwork. I would have to talk to the people who might know something and might be able to help.

Inevitably, that would mean blowing whatever scant cover my presence at the now-concluded conference might have offered. There was little choice if I was to fulfil my mission. Zoë Joubert still had not announced her intentions. Time was ticking on in other ways, too: my visa limit had been set at 14 days – a highly unusual restriction for reasons I did not understand. Once those days were up, I would become an illegal immigrant to be removed, expelled, declared *persona non grata*.

But the last thing I wanted to do was to report in to some dingy bureaucracy to seek a visa extension or a change of purpose in my visit – for "conference," read "vacation" – that would light up all the alarm bells Faku and Nieuwoudt had doubtless wired into my presence in their country: for "vacation," read "spy," "provocateur" or any number of unsavoury, accusatory labels.

I looked up old contacts in the press and diplomatic world who might offer some clues as to the players in this drama, coaxing them under false pretences into meetings – "just to chew the fat", "for old times' sake."

The journalists were older now, as was I. Some had risen to powerful positions – barons of the new order. One of them, Artie van Zyl, had become owner and publisher of one of the biggest, mass-audience newspapers with a predominantly black readership – an incongruous pinnacle of achievement for an Afrikaner who had grown up far apart from the black majority, yet so typical of this newer bond between the tribes competing for, and sometimes sharing, the spoils of freedom.

He was a tall, broad-shouldered man, with blunt, fleshy features and thinning hair the colour of pale straw. He favoured Texan boots and open-neck shirts, with sleeves rolled up over massive, hairless forearms. In his office, where I called to see him, he kept a life-size replica of a black man in the royal blue work clothes worn by most of the country's labour force and domestic staff. At difficult times, in the morning news conference, Van Zyl told me, when he could not decide which scurrilous story should fill his tabloid's front page, he would point to this totem of his news values and ask his staff: which story would *he* prefer to read?

"Works every time," he said.

But the mention of Kobus Theron and the Cooktown Four snuffed out the "hail-fellow" merriment.

"Forget it," he said bluntly. "We've moved on. History is history. Do you know how many generals and colonels and sundry cops are out there, keeping things quiet, drawing their pensions? Do you think they want their lives turned upside down? Do you know how many people in the new government, in business, in provincial administrations have got secrets from The Struggle? Torture camps in Angola. Unauthorised bombs. Settling scores. Do you know how many of these liberals" – he used the term with unconcealed scorn – "these white pussies with their bleeding hearts want to keep quiet about what they really got up to? Couriers for the terrorists, man, I'm telling you! Bombers even! But it's gone now. We're the new nation. We've buried the past. We don't poke into the hornet's nest. I'm not interested in history. Neither is he," he said, nodding towards his god of news.

I found others in dark bars, hiding from the light. Few of my erstwhile press contacts had tenure in their newsrooms now that a new generation of reporters and editors had arrived to replace them. Most had taken early buy-outs on reasonable, no-questions-asked terms, trading decent pensions for discreet exits, especially among those who had been particularly intimate with, or openly sympathetic to, the enforcers of apartheid. The net caught up many who had not fitted either category, ageing workhorses who did the math and figured it made more sense to go quietly to pasture than to scramble for a place in the sweepstakes of a new order where their race was now a handicap.

There was one journalist in particular I wanted to see.

With Artie van Zyl's help I tracked him down to a dingy watering hole called The Rusty Nail, whose décor (and clientele) might not have changed since the 1960s – a polished wooden bar with towels to soak up the spills, a limited selection of essential spirits in a serving rack: cane, brandy, Scotch, gin. The entrance from the street looked as if a signboard had been removed that, I surmised, would once have decreed: "Slegs Blankes" – whites only. Faded by time, gilt lettering above the entrance to a separate room proclaimed: 'Ladies Bar'. There was no muzak, no offering of "pub grub", no raucous slot machines or sports TV. Just booze at reasonable prices, small bags of salted peanuts and potato chips to keep the thirst intact, and cigarettes sold in boxes of 30s.

Outside, the Cape light glittered. Inside, the bar languished in perpetual gloaming.

Shrivelled and sun-wrinkled, skinny as a retired jockey and mounted on a bar stool that seemed too tall for him, Ray Gilliomee had been a star reporter of the right-wing press, breaking any number of stories about divisions within black ranks, misbehaviour among the heroes of The Struggle.

It was he who had obtained the surveillance tapes of a particularly high-profile, mixed-race clergyman and anti-apartheid activist, reaching operatic climax with a white woman who was not his wife – infidelity across the colour bar, illegal in those days on several counts, not only chromatic.

It was Gilliomee who knew in advance that the state of emergency would be declared after Nyati's death. He was the reporter who first glimpsed the police files on the murderous misdoings of the young men surrounding Winnie Mandela. Every story he wrote was big news. And every story worked to discredit the foes of apartheid.

He was also the author of a widely circulated series of glossy works offering the official version of the same struggle as had consumed Nyati and Joubert and the others – except that it had been from the opposite perspective. He had been granted unparalleled access to the army and the police who had stood on the front lines of Africa's last racial war. He had drunk with them, caroused with them, shared hangovers with them and finally glorified them in books that were now mostly out of print, and certainly out of favour in this new nation that was quite happy to concoct its own history.

One of Gilliomee's books interested me in particular – an account of the insurgency in Namibia in which Kobus Theron had fought as a young police officer attached to a shadowy unit called Koevoet before his deployment to the Cooktown region as the top cop in the security police detachment there. The name of the unit translated as crowbar. A blunt instrument, levering away an opponent's protective layers of armour, smashing the soft innards to pulp.

The book was called *The Valor of the Few*, heavy with combat illustrations and printed on high-quality glossy paper that suggested covert sponsorship rather than commercial viability.

"Theron. De Kock. Tough guys," he began after I bought a round of drinks and left a wad of notes on the chipped varnish of the bar. "Merciless. Followed their orders. And then some. Told me things that never went into the rag. Plenty of things. Should I have published and be damned? Maybe, but there was a code. They'd hint at things. Tell you where to be on what day if you wanted the scoop. But the other side of the bargain was that you didn't write 90 per cent of what you heard. Sure there were the horror stories. We knew them. We kept them to ourselves. Who heard of the Vlakplaas farm while it was still operational? Who wrote the stories about gooks being dropped from helicopters? Without a parachute" – he paused and cackled. "Now, of course, everyone thinks they know what really happened. But not all of it. Not by a long shot."

A white bartender polished the same tall beer glass for what seemed like the hundredth time. Something in his bearing reminded me of men like him in the old days with their sun-reddened faces and pencil moustaches whose job was to patrol segregated black townships in armoured trucks, armed with shotguns and *sjambok* whips.

"Then came the TRC. The Truth and Reconciliation Commission,"

Gilliomee went on. "Hah! Some truth! And what reconciliation? We saw all these cops singing like canaries. It made interesting listening. Because we knew that they still weren't telling the whole story, still hadn't stopped telling lies. And we – the old hacks who knew better – we weren't going to say anything either."

"Theron, too? In the Nyati case?"

"You don't want to know." He took a swig of his brandy and Coke, rattling the ice cubes as if he was playing for time while he considered his words, or at least requesting a refill. For the first time in our conversation, he looked me straight in the eye, fixing me with a baleful, bloodshot gaze.

"I don't know what your game is, Kinzer. But if you know what's good for you, leave it. Forget you ever heard the name Theron. Take my word for it. " He tapped the side of his nose with his index finger.

The bartender was still polishing the same glass. I signalled for a top-up for Gilliomee and slid him a plain envelope containing the agreed sum for the purchase of his book – and then some.

He pocketed the cash – all in dollar bills as he had stipulated – with a rapid, fluid movement that seemed well practised.

"Has it changed that much?" I asked him. "Surely the new reporters are under the same pressures."

"Maybe. But they are beginners. Amateurs some of them. Crusaders and all. They are trying to get it right. The whole truth and nothing but the truth!"

He laughed sardonically.

"Some of us like to keep our hands in. Freelance assignments. That kind of thing. Profiles of people we have met in bars. Advance obituaries." He separated the word into component syllables. Oh-bit-choo-eh-ries. "You know what I am saying?"

"Character assassination, you mean."

"At the very least, Mr Ambassador," he said. "Like I said. They are still out there. Everywhere."

It was time to move on.

Outside, the wind had scrubbed the afternoon sunlight bright and clean. Pondering my next step, I realised I had forgotten my copy of Gilliomee's book and re-entered the bar.

The waiter was nowhere to be seen and the polished glass he had tended so assiduously stood on the mahogany counter, in lonely splendour, illuminated by a shaft of sunlight penetrating the gloom, catching motes of blue dust in still air that smelled of stale liquor and tobacco. Somewhere behind the racked bottles of spirits, I could hear the tones of an indistinct telephone conversation that sounded as if it was being conducted through a cupped hand.

As I took the copy of his book, Gilliomee tapped his nose again, nodding towards the source of the telephone conversation and raising his eyebrows for emphasis.

Leaving the bar, it was probably a trick of the searing light that made me think I recognised two men – one black, one white – cruising by in a late-model beige Toyota.

My final – and most difficult – call was to the consulate, which acted as a kind of embassy during the African summer when the ambassador and chosen staff members migrated south for the opening of the South African Parliament in the white, colonnaded building close to the ornamented expanse known as the Company Gardens. The tradition had survived the changes.

Even now, administrative personnel would be preparing for the session of debates and law-making that would open in a few weeks' time. The outsiders would be preparing their switch from the highveld around Pretoria to the balmy, breezy beachfronts of the Cape, planning receptions and dinners to cement their ties with the country's legislators and government ministers.

Since my time, the embassy's diplomatic staff had changed many times over, rotating in and out every few years, but some personnel had remained, weathering the times of upheaval and transition.

One of them, Val Coetzee, had been a senior registry clerk – in effect the den mother of the local hire staff and an unofficial counsellor to generations of career diplomats seeking a path through the maze of official data contained in the mission's files. She acted as PA to successive ambassadors, in effect the embassy's institutional memory, the keeper of many of its secrets – not, perhaps, of those contained in the encrypted communications between the spies and their masters, to which she was denied official access as a non-American but, certainly of the kind of confidences divined from chance conversations, asides around the water cooler, sightings of documents that, technically, fell way beyond her security clearance.

Once, she had even allowed me a glimpse of the dossier relating to Jess Chase – an act of incipient intimacy, never to be consummated, after a breathless encounter at a staff Christmas party.

I was surprised at how little her voice over the telephone seemed to have changed. There was almost coquettishness to her acceptance of my invitation for coffee at my hotel.

"Only coffee?"

When we met she smiled with a beam I remembered well. She wore an elegant, two-piece suit in a light gabardine material, cut close to her slender waist, her hair blonde and short, her skin tanned. She spoke with an accent that led back to her Afrikaans roots through overlays of her employers' Americanisms. The more relaxed she became, the easier it was to hear the lilt of the *platteland*, the backwoods, where she had grown up, blind to the racial cataclysm building around her.

We chatted about our respective trajectories. She had heard, she said with some discretion, about my "voluntary early retirement". Her tone of voice suggested commiseration.

I asked about her life since the time we had "served together" and was surprised to hear a rushed, blushing confession – it sounded unrehearsed – that her marriage had not gone well, that her husband had been the suspicious type and had not trusted her avowals of good behaviour on her absences from Pretoria in Cape Town.

"Of course, you knew he was in the security police," she said.

Of course I did not. And neither had she told me. Even now, such conflicts of interest could ruin a career for someone in her position and she hurried on with her narrative. After the break-up her husband had taken up with the widow of a neighbour killed in one of the South African military campaigns in Angola. For her part, she had raised their children as a single mother. Now her beloved boys had gone their way, both of them working in Britain as waiters with their degrees in engineering and psychology gathering dust in their bottom drawers while their own country sorted itself out. Her job, she said, was what counted now. She could not do anything to jeopardise that. The current ambassador was a stickler for procedure, she said. No peeking at the files anymore. She smiled as she spoke, but the message was clear enough.

"And the archive?"

"Gone," she said.

"Onto micro-fiche, diskettes?"

"Just plain gone," she said. "I was sure you would have known this. After Mandela's release, we weren't the only ones. A lot of embassies did it. Men from Washington came in and boxed everything up. All the old files. The whole lot."

"But you always had a good memory, Val."

"That depends on what I'm supposed to remember and what I'm supposed to forget."

"I'm interested in a bunch of young white people. It's for a conference report. Historical stuff. They lived outside Jo'burg in a place called Old Deep. Zoë Joubert was one of them."

"Wasn't she the student leader? Married to a poet. Rod. Rod Harris. Rodney Harris. His poetry was banned, of course. There was a file. A cross-reference to someone else."

"Solomon Nyati?"

"How did you know?"

"A guess. Kobus Theron? Ring any bells?"

She looked sharply at me. The humour drained away from her voice, replaced by a wariness I could not quite explain.

"My ex did mention that name. Terrible things. Terrible. And there was something in the files they took to Washington." She glanced at her wristwatch.

"I have to go – *tempus fugit*," she said. Her accent became more clipped, like a suburban housewife trying not to speak too sharply to a clumsy maid.

"Did the file say anything about Nyati's death?"

"I really wish you would not ask me. You know there are orders sometimes that you don't just go around disobeying. You of all people should know what happens."

She took a business card from a crocodile-skin purse and wrote a cell phone number on it. She smiled in a way that was half warning, half invitation.

"Call me if you want to just chat. But no more questions, hey, Thomas? Promise me. Things have not changed here as much as you might think – or as much as Mr Mandela might think. You are treading on thin ice."

When I returned to the hotel room, the phone was ringing and Zoë Joubert was talking to me.

"I have an answer of sorts for you. We're having a party," she said. "Why don't you come along and meet my friends? And be a friend, Tom. Just a friend... Can you do that for me?"

Of course I could, I said, crumpling Val Coetzee's phone number into a ball in the palm of my hand. My life seemed to be filling up with people who wanted to set very clear markers. Conference purposes only. Conversation without questions. Friendship without prospects.

As I lowered the phone to its cradle, it rang again. I thought it might be Zoë Joubert calling to change her mind.

"Now don't you go ..."

"Don't go doing what?" Lily Nyati said.

Nine

THE MAIN HIGHWAY TO PLETTENBERG Bay, the N2, leads through towns with main streets wide enough to turn a span of oxen – across the Breede River to Riviersonderend, Heidelberg and Riversdale, then on, over the Groot Brak River, bypassing Mosselbaai and George until the final stretch on what they called the Garden Route, alongside the great lagoon at Knysna leading through a turbulent passage called The Heads, into the Indian Ocean.

My plan was to see a different, less manicured part of the country, along the dirt roads meandering through indistinct places in the Overberg, where the dust devils rose to herald the approach of distant vehicles and you wondered whether the single telegraph wire, strung on spindly roadside poles, carried any signal or intelligence at all.

Was there some vestigial notion of tradecraft in the instinct to avoid the obvious route? (During my time as ambassador, my security detail had always spent what seemed a disproportionate amount of time devising unpredictable itineraries.)

Or was the decision to take this more circuitous approach simply a way of preparing for my reunion with Zoë Joubert, allowing me to compute my options, steady my nerves?

The tiny settlements in this great, broad expanse boasted names that suggested a fantasy world, as if strange things had happened and would happen again without clear explanation. One hamlet was called Baardskeerdersbos – beard-cutter's bush – another Wolvengat, the Wolf's Lair, where an artistic colony had established itself, offering sculptures, reflexology and vegetarian Indian cuisine. Strange creations in iron and stone rose in fields fringing single-storey homesteads with old tin roofs. It was easy to ask: why here? Which wolves were prowling now?

I had flown over the region many years earlier and had been struck by its white beaches and curling surf and its long, uninhabited stretches where flowers blossomed in the local undergrowth, the *fynbos*.

The guide books told me that, at Cape Agulhas, a plaque had been unveiled by President PW Botha in August 1986, informing visitors that they now stood at the southernmost tip of the African continent. I wondered how Botha felt that day, looking south across the blank fury of the ocean while, at his back, his country burned with fires set by those who had taken Solomon Nyati's mantle after his murder?

My journey would proceed on unpaved roads, touching Cape Agulhas with its lighthouse hooped in red and white, and odd places like the Malgas Ferry, where a small crew of boatmen pulled a pontoon across the Breede River on the unpaved by-ways between Napier and Swellendam.

I had planned to travel alone, but, Lily Nyati persuaded me otherwise.

"You can give Celiwe a lift," she said over the phone, after we had completed the formalities.

"Happily. If she wants to."

"She wants to, I know," the mother said. "She wants to meet anyone who met her father. She was too young."

"Is she going to Plettenberg Bay?"

"Ha!" Lily Nyati laughed at the very suggestion of her daughter at such a place. "Plett! Jo'burg-by-the-sea! Apartheid-without-the-guilty-conscience! You will see. Not too many formerly disadvantaged South Africans go to a place where the formerly advantaged still have their place in the sun."

She laughed, but without malice.

"Drop Celiwe at the Intercape bus at the Shell station there and she will go on to PE and then Cooktown. You will save her time and money and you can talk."

"You have seen the newspaper?" she said, changing the subject abruptly. I admitted I had not. Too intent on my own private inquiry, I had ignored the public prints.

"You should be alert, Thomas," she said in her stern, school-ma'am voice. "If you want to find out you must be on your toes. You should read the story about the statute of limitations."

She pronounced the term with lugubrious irony. I caught the school-room inflection. S, underscore, L, underscore. "Perhaps they have got wind of you already. Now they are saying there will be a statute of limitations. Soon, in our Parliament. The people's Parliament."

She laughed again, this time with the same bitter tone as had suffused her speech to the conference gathering on the lawns of the Mount Nelson Hotel.

"So the Parliament of the people will pass a law – this week, next week, whenever – to say that the unsolved cases from the TRC will just disappear. And the people's Parliament will let the people's oppressors go free. You do not have much time. But time to take my daughter closer to home."

Celiwe Nyati arrived at my hotel a little while after I had checked out, impatient to be started, already annoyed at falling behind schedule so early in the journey. She was wearing the same skirt and T-shirt, both freshly laundered, as when I first met her in the gardens of the Mount Nelson Hotel. She carried a small, inexpensive tote and a Pick n'Pay supermarket plastic bag containing what she called *padkos* – food for the road – which Lily had insisted she bring along.

A bell-hop offered to carry her bag, but she hissed something in their shared language and he stepped back as if scalded. A floor manager – a white man, as it happened – asked whether she had a reservation and found himself facing a look of such scorn that he apologised and called her 'madam'.

"Madam is a term used by maids," she said haughtily, this time in English. The man gasped. His underlings sniggered. "Are you a maid?"

As we began our journey, she settled into the car, lighting a cigarette without consulting me. Sensing my disapproval, she opened the car window a fraction to allow the fumes to escape.

What would you expect from a daughter of the revolution if not defiance?

She was studying African Development and Politics at the

University of Cape Town and spent much of her time, she told me, in student politics, demanding better conditions, higher grants and improved accommodations – the legacy of her father's martyrdom. How pleased he might be to know that his battle had been won, allowing his heirs to hone the terms of victory.

"But the main target of our struggle," she proclaimed, "is corruption. The corrupters who have betrayed my father's struggle."

We drove along the rocky, breezy inlets of the coast to the resort town of Hermanus, past the village of Stanford and then on to Gansbaai before turning inland. I tried to ease the strained atmosphere by chatting about her mother's courage, but the overture met with a tart response. Her mother, she said, was simply the public face, the public conscience of the new dispensation.

"She is being used. She thinks we can still change our nation, our leaders. She knows in her heart that power has merely been handed from one small group of men to another. The skin colour is different. That is all. Not the gender. Not the structures of control."

I said that seemed a harsh judgment. "Look at the new houses, the democratic choices. Elections. Freedom."

"Do you really think the people have power?" she said. "Do you think power is not still in the hands of a few rich men?"

"But they are African men, black men."

"They are men, not women. Whatever their colour. In my country it is the women who are abused and the men who give them AIDS."

She switched the conversation to my previous experience in her country. Her questions were sharp, angry: what had the Americans known about the apartheid regime, how much had they kept back, how much had they collaborated in the system and its perpetuation?

"We were maybe misguided, not malicious. We wanted change," I said, ignoring the uncomfortable evidence implied by Val Coetzee's account of the bundling of the apartheid files.

"And did real change come? Or just change that kept the big companies in charge of our minerals, our wealth? Was it short change for the masses? Who owns the gold, the diamonds? The people? I don't think so. When I was at school I used to wonder why the biggest company in the country – in all of Africa – was called Anglo American. But now I know. It is obvious."

She turned to me.

"How did you meet him, my father?"

It was a question I had been hoping she would ask, one for which I did not need to prepare a legend.

The encounter was one I had never forgotten or sought to erase, a moment that, for a young diplomat, explained far more than any embassy cable. It had been in the modest family home in the arid reaches of the Eastern Cape with its long horizons and ochre soil under an azure bowl of sky. We sat across from one another at a coffee table adorned with a pot of plastic flowers. I was expecting a kind of African Che Guevara. But Solomon Nyati seemed an unlikely warrior – bespectacled, trim, with the merest wisp of a neat beard, clad in grey flannel slacks and a white shirt, as if he were not too long out of high school himself, a 10th grade Lenin.

I recalled asking him if there had been a single event that had inspired him to seek change, convinced him he could make a difference. He looked at me and removed his spectacles, rubbing his eyelids and squeezing the bridge of his nose.

"It's a long story."

"We have plenty of time."

"You, perhaps. In The Struggle, time can be very short."

"Did he tell you the bicycle story?" his daughter said, interrupting my reverie as I piloted the rental car onto the loose and treacherous surface of the gravel roads that latticed the Overberg.

"He told everyone that story, my ma says. It was his party piece!"

"Would you prefer not to hear it?"

"No. Go on, go on. Tell me the bicycle story."

As an adolescent, in his hand-me-down school uniform, on a rickety, black, sit-up-and-beg Hercules bicycle, Solomon Nyati had been pedalling home along on a dusty track, bouncing on the worn, unsprung leather saddle as the wheels bumped on the corrugations left by the local grading machine that came to repair the damage of the rainy season.

He was in his mid-teens, intellectually precocious, an achiever, but still obliged to wear short grey trousers and a matching uniform blazer with cow-hide patches where the elbows had worn through.

On this day, particularly proud of himself, he had passed an important examination that, under a different racial dispensation, would have qualified him among the top percentile of university entrants. The bicycle was old and heavy, with no fancy gearing to speed him home, so he pushed on the pedals all the harder to reach his destination.

He was in a hurry to break the news of his triumph to his parents. Robert Nyati, a school teacher with little more than rudimentary qualifications, followed his son's achievements closely, hoping that Solomon would one day secure the place at Fort Hare University that poverty had denied to previous generations of the family. The sweat collected in mercurial beads on the lower rim of his spectacles. He kept his eyes on the road for he had always been a cautious boy, never one to risk the crazy games with spears and dares that the others played with the snakes and crocodiles.

"Did he tell you that? About snakes and crocodiles? Or did you invent it?"

"He told me that. He told me all of it."

"And you remember it all?"

"I was a good listener. And it made a strong impression on me."

"Go on."

He had tied his books in their satchel onto the rear carrying-rack of the bicycle – Shakespeare and Higher Mathematics. The books were written in languages other than his native isiXhosa. That did not trouble him.

The richness of centuries-old English thrilled his soul and, in any event, the themes of love and loss, battle and tragedy, were universal, as familiar as the sagas of Maqoma and Shaka and Dingaan. ("The villains, in those days, were the British, before you Americans even came on to the scene," he said with a light smile, "So Shakespeare was a case of: know your enemy.") By the same logic, he saw no harm in extending his mind to embrace Afrikaans – even if it were the language his people came to associate with barked, inchoate commands, the prelude to gunfire.

I broke off to ask her a question.

"You said he always told this story. To whom?"

"To people like you. People like you who needed to understand what it was like to be black."

"But it is different now. To be black, I mean."

"Do you think so?" she said. "Do you think there are not people who still do not want to understand? Who think they got away with the crown jewels and must not pay? Do you think they care about the bicycle story?"

At the roadside, somewhere near Baardskeerdersbos, a pickup truck towing a long, blue, inflatable boat with a scratched fibre-glass keel and powerful, twin outboard engines was parked at the roadside, canted at an angle where a tire had burst on its trailer. Two men stood next to it, one of them speaking on a cell phone.

"Should I offer to help?"

"Are you crazy?" Celiwe Nyati said. "*Skollies*. *Tsotsis*. The new South Africa. Smugglers of perlemoen."

"Perlemoen?"

"Abalone. They dive for it illegally and trade it for tik."

"Tik?"

"Tik. Drugs. Methamphetamines. The perlemoen goes to Asia. The tik comes here. Do you know nothing about this rainbow nation of ours? Ha!" She lit another cigarette.

The road wound onwards, towards the small settlement called Elim where Moravian missionaries had built a settlement in the 19th century. It boasted the only monument in South Africa erected to commemorate the abolition of slavery. Under the tires, I could feel the corrugations where the graders had scraped away the surface bumps and drifts of dirt. I wondered if the road on which Nyati had set his story was real or more a movie set, a notional trail that foreigners would understand from visits to safari parks.

We drove on, more peaceably now, the powerful odour of *fynbos* blending with the smell of Celiwe Nyati's tobacco. Far behind, a plume of dust betrayed the position of a vehicle closing in, a warning that I would be overtaken and engulfed in its contrail.

I thought fleetingly of Zoë Joubert driving in this same direction just a few days earlier along a different road with her teenage daughter. Had she, too, been interrogated about some historical moment? Was this what parenthood was all about? Would she, too, be thinking back to her first encounter with Nyati? She had been present, by her own admission, at his last, known public gathering before the murderous drive back to Cooktown, to the homestead he would never reach, to which his daughter was now heading.

But, in her narrative, as I recalled it, Zoë Joubert had not mentioned when, or how, she first met him. Was she the one who led the other white liberals to him? And, if so, what had been the antecedents of their relationship? I was reminded suddenly of the scar on her arm.

"Tell me everything," Celiwe Nyati said, as if resentful of my silence, interpreting it as mental redaction or censorship.

"Tell me everything he told you about that place."

The dusty plume behind us seemed much closer.

He reached a fold in the green hills where a sharp, downhill corner would bring into view his parents' settlement just back from the banks of the Grootvisrivier – the Great Fish River – nestling between the ripening stands of corn.

From the bend above the river, safety was only minutes away, past the general dealer's store with its paraffin lamps and hoes and dried fish, past the small chapel visited by the touring priest on his bicycle, past the sometimes noisy primary school near the makeshift sandy soccer pitch. Soon he would see the small stone house with its raggedy thatched roof and, parked outside, the old jalopy his father used to attend mysterious meetings in Queenstown and Port Elizabeth.

Sometimes, the country bus would bring home cousins and brothers from far-flung mines and cities and there would be the slaughter of an offering for the prodigals, a goat usually, and millet beer would be passed in a round gourd polished with frequent use, hand to hand, mouth to mouth. Sometimes the visitors would be more secretive, arriving after dark and leaving at first light, their presence unacknowledged, unrecorded.

Most times, the settlement would seem to slumber in the midday heat at the end of the first shift of the school day.

As he approached, heralding his arrival with the rusty bell fixed on the handlebars of his bicycle, his mother would appear with a huge white apron around her girth and a half-smile on her lips, as if fighting back a hidden sadness from the many untold worries that she carried to and from the chapel and the hymn singing that seemed her only real solace.

This time there was something wrong.

"You know. My ma can tell that story down to the last detail," Celiwe Nyati said. "But if I ask her if it's true, she just laughs. Every hero has his stories, she says. But I have been there. To the old house where my grandparents lived and there is a road like that."

We were approaching Elim, driving between wild expanses of spidery plants and tiny blossoms in mauve and yellow. The vehicle following in my dusty wake was a white pickup truck with an amber light on the roof, flashing as it approached us. I was driving at around 80 kilometres per hour – a recommended safe limit for roads such as these, lined by shallow ditches and culverts that could be treacherous if they caught a tire. The pickup seemed to be travelling much faster.

He rounded his favourite bend, his legs stretched out from the pedals, his thumb itching to ring his bicycle bell. But then he saw his mother, Matilda, standing outside the family home with her white apron held to her mouth and stained with vivid red specks. Neighbours had emerged from doorways, hesitant, staring at his parents' house. Further afield, his sister, Priscilla, had dropped a big, blue, plastic water container she had been carrying from the borehole and was running full-tilt towards their mother.

Two police vans, the kind whose rear compartment had been converted into a cage for prisoners, headed towards him. Behind them, moving more slowly, a big yellow truck rumbled away from the village, armed men peering from the high rim of its armour-plated steel flanks.

The pickup in my rear-view mirror had closed in now, its headlights flashing, hovering off the rear fender of my rental car like a stunt pilot flying wing. I nudged in towards the roadside culvert but held my speed at around 80 kilometres per hour, reluctant to abandon my story or my position on the dirt road.

The police van in the lead rounded a bend with red dust rising from its wheels. As it passed Solomon Nyati, its driver twitched the steering wheel, spinning him off the road into a drainage ditch. He cartwheeled through the air. As he fell, he caught a glimpse of his father, bloodied around the mouth, nose and forehead, gazing in surprise from the iron grille of the second van – his face seeming to register a blend of rage and entreaty, as if he were calling for vengeance but did not know quite how to say so. Solomon Nyati landed in the ditch, his bicycle crashing on top of him, its pedals and cogs and broken, sharp spokes finding tender parts of his flesh to stab into.

At first he thought that the men following the police van carrying his father would stop to help him clamber out of the ditch. But, as he looked up – they looked down on him from the great height of the truck's armoured rim – all they did was laugh. Black pools of sweat stained their blue uniform shirts, and the sunlight caught the silver-blue sheen of gun barrels.

The white pickup had begun to overtake, rattling alongside, spewing dirt and gravel, its flashing light blinking rapidly. In the driver's seat, I caught sight of a man with a beard, a battered, narrow-brimmed sun hat jammed down on his head – a familiar enough sight in these parts. He pulled past. I thought for a second that he had miscalculated because he seemed to swerve across in front of us.

"Slow down!" Celiwe Nyati said. She yanked on the handbrake

between us and the rental car began to slew until I released it, obeying some distant memory of dirt-road lore: never touch the brakes.

"Couldn't you see what he was doing?" she exclaimed.

Her father had paused in his narrative so that I could absorb the image of a young black boy on the cusp of manhood lying in a ditch. But that was not the crime, he said, or rather not the only crime. His mild, myopic eyes had lost their soft edges. The men who laughed at him were not all white, he said. Some of them were black, black stooges, cooperating in their own oppression, laughing at one of their own.

Only later did the men from the settlement come to him and lead him to the river bank, in a safe place where the cattle drank and the crocodiles did not come, and they told him that his father would not be returning from the big concrete building in a far city where many brave men entered in hoods and manacles and none emerged.

The white pickup had pulled ahead; my windscreen filled with its dust. I had slowed down considerably now, without using the brakes, stick-shifting through the gears and declutching cautiously to prevent the rental car from sliding towards the hazards of the roadside.

But still it seemed that the cloud of rusty dirt ahead of me had not begun to dissipate.

"Look out," Nyati's daughter cried.

The white pickup blocked the road just short of the neat rows of cottages lining the high roadside banks in Elim. Its orange light flashed balefully through the settling clouds of dust.

The driver had clambered out and was standing to one side of the road waving a ragged red flag. He was wearing khaki shorts and a short-sleeved shirt in similar colours – once the uniform of southern Africa's white warriors. This time, there was no time for fancy manoeuvring. I slammed on the brakes and the car skidded broadside, forcing me to steer into the slide to prevent a full spin.

Celiwe Nyati was running clear almost before the car stopped. I followed her, striding angrily to the man who had blocked the dirt road.

"What in the hell do you think you are doing?"

"Subsidence, *meneer*," the man said. "The roads these days, you know. Poor maintenance."

He gestured to a section ahead where a deep hole with jagged, crumbling edges ran across the carriageway as if the planet's crust had chosen to split at precisely this place and this time.

"You must be careful," the man said. "There could have been a terrible accident. Terrible."

Ten

WE WERE ON THE LAST LEG OF our journey together, driving between stands of exotic blue gums and indigenous forest. On a long high stretch back from the coast, a squall blew in from nowhere. Usually the summer weather marches along the ocean-front resorts and settlements from Cape Town, but this time the wind had come from the south-east. It darkened the sky without warning. Bullets of rain burst across the windscreen in a deluge that the wipers could not clear.

I slowed and switched on the headlights, their beams spangling the downpour as it bounced off the tar. A tattoo of hailstones pummelled the roof. The traffic slowed to a crawl, trucks groaning in low gear as the highway snaked down towards the Knysna lagoon. A slick veneer of icy particles spread across the green roadside foliage.

And then, equally unheralded, the sun burst through and the clouds hurried on towards distant mountains and the highway began to steam in the heat. She was still rattled.

"Don't you see it was a warning?"

"From whom? That guy saved us from driving into a mighty big hole in the road."

"And who dug the hole there? So naïve. You really are such an American. A naïve American."

"It's one of our best features," I said with false joviality, but I was thinking of Molly Blackburn, the Black Sash activist who had called to tell me of Nyati's death. She had died in what was officially listed as a tragic mishap, an accident on the highway involving a driver who had lost control of the vehicle that struck her Kombi head on. Road accidents had once been part of the repertoire of state terror. Maybe they still were. If Nyati's daughter had not pulled on the hand brake, I could all too easily have careened into the white pickup across the road ahead of me.

Knysna had once projected itself as a genteel bastion of whiteness, a retirement and vacation settlement with dainty restaurants on Leisure Island, connected to the mainland by a causeway that carried the maids and other domestic staff to and fro at dawn and dusk – the metronome of what apartheid's planners called separate development. But since the early 1990s, reality and demography had combined to synchronise the place with the new political and economic realities. Hawkers and peddlers flourished on the main thoroughfare and black faces far outnumbered those of whites.

To the east, the N2 highway clambered up from sea level in gracious curves, fringed with an irrepressible growth of shacks and shanties. Children dodged trucks as they crossed from one side to the other. A rogue cow meandered along the black-top, unattended.

Further on, the road signs advertised Bed and Breakfast accommodation and bric-a-brac stalls, yellowwood furniture stores and places selling cheese and wine. Closer to my destination, where Celiwe Nyati would leave me to travel on alone, I espied a place that had not been there at all in my earlier days. Kwanokuthula was a brand new township of breeze-block, matchbox houses and overhead electricity supply lines, stretching back geometrically from the roadside to accommodate people drawn to the jobs of the resort. Technically, it offered homes in something other than unplanned and unlawful settlements.

But already you could see impromptu extensions erupting in the tiny yards of the formal housing. Mini-buses hurtled back and forth in an endless shuttle, crammed with paying passengers, as impossibly laden as their equivalents in Kenya or Zimbabwe. New ways had surged south, their tide pressing into every fissure of what the whites had sought to preserve as their exclusive sanctuary, their redoubt.

Celiwe Nyati had chosen this final moment to nap. In rest, her features lost their anger and she looked younger and less ferocious than the persona she assumed on the barricades with her bullhorn and her slogans.

I tried to imagine life from her perspective, growing up in the final days of apartheid, when the men in the police trucks still wielded absolute power over their comings and goings, just as they had in her father's day, ensnaring the people in a web of oppressive bureaucracy and physical control, reinforced by the ever-present threat of state violence. Perhaps, in her earliest years, it had seemed that the weight would never lift, that she would be condemned forever to entering stores from separate entrances, living in segregated townships, attending poor schools with none of the abundant sports fields and well-equipped laboratories as at those reserved for whites.

But then, watching on television as Mandela walked free with his wife Winnie Madikizela-Mandela, at his side, she would have shared the thrill that pulsed across the nation and around the globe: finally, irrevocably, freedom had been sealed by the presence of this man, reclaiming his land after 27 years of incarceration. No longer would her skin colour relegate her to third or fourth class status. No longer would the pigmentation of the Race Ogres enthrone them as the overlords.

The songs and refrains and slogans – Free Nelson Mandela – had built to this moment of his release, like the storm on the highway, purging the past. And here he was, in the flesh, the great redeemer. A nation's wish had been granted.

At her father's funeral, cocooned in a blanket on her mother's warm back, how could she or anyone else have known that the martyrdom of Solomon Nyati and all the others would bring the land to such a momentous turning point?

The emergency decree, proclaimed within hours of his burial, was the admission by the Race Ogres that they had lost the initiative, the momentum of oppression, and could rule no longer by anything approaching consent. Power was slipping, oozing irrevocably away. After his release, Mandela himself had journeyed to the monument erected to honour her father and his comrades. And he had called them the true heroes of The Struggle.

But then, as she grew, as she heard the legends, as she absorbed the horror of her father's murder, how could she have squared his heroism with its legacy? In Cooktown township, the shanties were just as bleak, the tubercular coughs just as wracking, AIDS victims just as grey and skinny. She had lost her father. For what? So that men would still stand in lines on roadsides begging for work; so that her mother would yearn for release from her private suffering? No one had ever asked her permission for his sacrifice.

I wondered how she felt when the hearings began at the Truth and Reconciliation Commission and Theron, the killer, began his grim reprise – the manacles on her father's wrists; the drive to the dunes; the single bullet through his skull before the incinerations. And this same man walked free while her father would never again take her in his arms, help her with her studies, or bring her a gift from a journey and share quiet, special times.

A shell of rage had been grafted onto her and she was trapped behind it. Anger came much more easily than trust. Formally, her land had moved on, but I wondered whether she had made that transition, too.

Celiwe Nyati stirred awake as we began the approach to Plettenberg Bay, blinking into the brightness, checking her cell phone for messages, stifling a yawn behind a balled hand. I felt an unfamiliar sense of my own inadequacies: I doubted I would have a child of my own to accompany on that voyage from innocence to adulthood. The years had advanced too far for that. But how lonely that voyage must be – the daughter of the martyred hero, the public face of her cohort – struggling to locate herself in a world of peril and uncertainty without Solomon Nyati's wisdom, resenting fate's theft of her father ever more keenly. Many had fallen in that cause, not only her father. But where was the solace in freedom's failing, in the betrayal of his Struggle?

"You know, if you ever want to come to Washington ..." I heard myself saying.

After the Portuguese discovered Plettenberg Bay for Europe, they called it Bahia Formosa, the Bay of Beauty. The first foreign settlers were 100 mariners stranded for nine months after a Portuguese vessel, the *San Gonzales*, went down with the loss of many hands in 1630. The town took its name from Joachim van Plettenberg, the Dutch East India Company's governor of the Cape Colony in the late 18th century.

On the websites I consulted before I embarked on my journey from Cape Town, the annals seemed to focus more on these intrusions rather than on any indigenous populations after the first evidence of habitation in the Middle Stone Age. But that may have been simply because the outsiders had left a greater trove of written records. Of course, history's lessons are rarely confined to the past – a phenomenon I had observed in other places of elemental conflict, from the Balkans to the Middle East, where much energy was devoted to establishing prior claim to the narrative attached to this piece of territory or that.

From the 1960s, the town grew into a premier white resort town, a place that people reached by a long drive south in cars laden with surfboards, towing boats with powerful engines – a modern reversal of the Great Trek. Even settlers far to the north, from lands that would be renamed Zambia and Zimbabwe after their ceremonies of independence, embarked on journeying along strip roads and across dry riverbeds to bathe and tan and relax here.

Vacationers constructed big villas, vying with one another for the most grand, the best-designed, and the most (or least) tasteful. Smaller places of only three or four en suite bedrooms grew like seedlings in the shadows of the great mansions with the prime ocean views.

Developers built condos, golf courses, polo pitches, cheek by jowl with tumbledown squatter camps. At the height of the resort's prosperity, the airport – a single, low building with wheeled trolleys to carry the luggage from the dirt strip – could not cope with the number of private planes clamouring for landing rights.

Even now, with the softening of hindsight, it was hard to shake my own guilty memories of that era – witnessing the fiery funerals and the protests in cramped, miserable, higgledy-piggledy townships. Then returning home to find friends using the pool and tennis court in the two acres of lawn and flower garden that seemed a natural adjunct to every home in my new neighbourhood; plunging baptismally into the chlorine tang to wash the smear of teargas from my hair and skin; driving out from the plump affluence of my suburb to the raw hillsides of tilting shacks and land scraped clean of all flora and fauna that made up the so-called homelands where the government banished millions of black people; then back to my luxurious stockade, my gilded prison, while those I had met hours, minutes earlier enjoyed no such release.

At the Shell gas station as we awaited the Intercape bus, Celiwe Nyati's eyes set again into the hard gaze she had cast over the hotel staff in Cape Town. I had pulled in to fuel the car. I knew enough of her by now to guess that she was seething at the sight of her kinfolk doomed to perform the same menial tasks as ever before – pumping gas, cleaning windscreens, checking oil and water, running the cash tills – while the people they served took the great racial and economic imbalances for granted, as if they had been given a "Get out of jail free" card.

"What has my mother told you to do?"

"Just to ask around. Make inquiries. Quietly."

"Then please find her the answers she wants. She is burning inside. She is trapped in her own past. If the answers will release her, then please set her free. But soon."

"And then?"

"And then we will punish the perpetrators."

"We?"

"The People."

"Like before? In The Struggle? People's courts?"

"An eye for an eye."

"That seems very harsh in this new nation of yours, for a new generation."

"You are forgetting who I am. You are forgetting that I was robbed of my father and the killer has not been punished."

I tried to couch my response as gently as I could. "Don't you think that he fought for a new nation where people talked out their differences instead of fighting? Don't you think he fought for peace, forgiveness?"

"Do not presume to tell me about my father. One story about a boy on a bicycle and you suddenly know everything that is to be known. No – don't interrupt me! My father was a revolutionary, a fighter. He took comrades out of the country for military training. He believed what Mandela said at his trial that the apartheid regime had left the people with no choice but to take up the armed struggle. He was not some Western liberal. He was a communist! You are surprised to hear that? Why do you think there were so many red banners at his funeral? He was a commander! He believed in the power of the gun barrel. I am his daughter. It is my duty to carry on the fight until the last vestiges are defeated. Until we have truly created the land he fought for without corruption and nepotism. Until then there can be no forgiveness. We are the wretched of the earth. 'Let us waste no time in sterile litanies and nauseating mimicry.' – That is what Frantz Fanon said."

"But your father faced a different enemy," I said. "He faced the apartheid regime. He faced the men with guns and Casspirs who came into Cooktown and arrested and tortured people. He did that to make a new land for you."

"The enemy was and is oppression. The battle is not over. He did not fight so that women would be abused and politicians would get rich and the apartheid killers would walk free. Look here. At this place. Who is driving the cars? Who is cleaning the windscreens and filling the tanks? Can you see that nothing has changed? My father will – and must be – avenged."

The Intercape rumbled in, debouching bleary-eyed passengers with backpacks and bulging travel bags bound with twine. She clambered aboard, taking a seat on the upper deck. Just as the bus pulled out, she glanced down at me. I thought she might be about to offer a wave of farewell, a smile to acknowledge our shared journey so far. But her fingers curled into a small, tight fist, and her face set into its mask of anger.

"Welcome to Plett-on-sea," the gas attendant said cheerily. "Oil, water, tires, okay?

Eleven

A CROWDED ROOM. YOU ARE THE stranger, the interloper. Tolerated, not embraced. People are introduced to you, then move on. Their eyes betray suspicion. If they linger, their questions are barbed. They seek motives, not answers.

For much of my professional life, my social rhythm had been set by the embossed invitation cards that mark the stations of the diplomatic cross. I had gone forth into crowds of strangers. I had manoeuvred my way around grand salons, below chandeliers, navigating a path between liveried attendants and bemedalled generals and unctuous officials to close on my target – a particular under-secretary, an ambassador with discreet connections – to press a specific point of policy.

I had progressed from Junior Attaché (Press and Information) to Ambassador Extraordinary and Plenipotentiary, mixing confidently with kings and presidents, clothed in the vicarious mantle of a power that none could equal.

Here, on this wooden deck above a vast moonlit bay, I was the alien, the Other. This was the cabal of which Zoë Joubert had spoken in Cape Town, the assembly of almost-40-year-olds who had minted their credentials in The Struggle and who now sought their niches in the new dispensation, far from the tin roof of Old Deep.

Among them were some who had been present at Nyati's last known meeting before his death. Among them was the Judas.

A barbecue sizzled with fresh-caught fish – Cape salmon and yellowtail, prepared in luscious marinades of oil and garlic and spices.

Cold bottles bobbed in a zinc bathtub filled with water and ice. A table bore hard stuff: tequila with salt and lemon, vodka, Scotch. Chatter fizzed, sparkled, subsided in knowing smiles – conversations borne on dark currents that sometimes broke the surface in ripples of intimate laughter, shared memories.

...and Gerry, of course, thought she was waiting for him...

... and in The Struggle we all suffered, though relatively, and you, were you, you know, recruited?

When she introduced me to her friends, the names brought faint memories of manila files, seen at the embassy in the old days – requests for comment on Fulbright scholarships, visa applications, some rejected on the grounds of suspected communist sympathies, a catchall for undesirables. Here they were: Nils, the lawyer and Clarissa – gosh, another lawyer – and Jenny, the reflexologist married to Colin, the singer, and Rod Harris, the poet, my ex, actually. Father of Mills. A blur of names: Dave, the impresario and Johnny, the film director. Producer, actually. Martie. Neil. Riaan van Rensburg. Cathy and Rachel and Ferd.

And this is Tom Kinzer. A friend. No history offered. No rap sheet. A rogue male from another herd of a different stripe altogether. Even my sense of appropriate casual clothing seemed, well, inappropriate – neatly pressed chinos and laundered polo shirt, obviously different from the preferred combo of baggy pants cut to calf length and loose-fitting, quasi-Hawaiian shirts. My hair was too short, my skin too sallow.

People who bothered to take a second look at me sometimes divined a Semitic or Mediterranean background – Lebanese, Israeli perhaps – although my grandparents had converted long before they fled Germany and the South Tirol for New York in the late 1930s.

I remembered the curious patter of their conversation, laced with phrases of German and Italian and Yiddish, as if they sometimes awoke from the American dream to seek some linguistic connection to the old world they had left behind. When I left for South Africa with my degree in law and my State Department credentials, they called me *meshugganah*, crazy.

I took a beer from the icy bathtub, scanning the crowd, but

detected no questioning looks, no surreptitious glances to confirm recognition.

The heat was moist, close, begging rain and thunderclaps. The teenage children of the celebrants – not Zoë's daughter, I noticed – clustered under the palms in the garden below the deck to build cigarettes from the local marijuana. The parents rolled their own: Durban poison, Malawi gold. I thought, too, that I recognised the surreptitious rituals of cokeheads, signalling with a raised eyebrow, a casual nod, that a line was being prepared in some locked side room with a glass-topped table.

As the hostess, Zoë Joubert – taut, bobbed, chiaroscuro in a loose-fitting black muslin robe over her trim athlete's body, a slight, quizzical wrinkling at the corner of her eyes – was busy ensuring that people had drinks, food, company. She moved effortlessly between friends, contacts, men who clung to her with unfinished dreams in their eyes that their wives pretended not to notice. She left happiness and longing in her wake.

I sensed tripwires, faultlines known only to the intimates – Colin and Rod and Clarissa and Riaan. Being among her friends redefined her through a prism of old secrets to which I would never be privy. Watching them mingle, I felt her slip away.

"And what line are you in, Thomas? Tom?"

It is a man introduced to me as Riaan. Riaan van Rensburg. He is younger and taller than I but has allowed himself to run to seed. A belly swells and heaves beneath a loose shirt with bright patterns of green palms and orange flowers – camouflage. He is holding a bottle of Castle Lager, beaded with condensation. The red and yellow label has slipped slightly where it has become unstuck in the water of the bathtub.

He has been in charge of the barbecue – the braai as it is called – and there is sweat on his forehead, collecting in corrugations of thick worry lines. His hair is black, formed into a widow's peak, with bold slashes of white at the temples. His brown eyes, slightly bloodshot and bulbous, remind me of a badly trained Labrador, supplicant but deaf to the most simple commands.

"This and that. Analysis. Talk shows. I have a consultancy in Washington. Risk assessment, I guess you would call it." There is no point telling him that the consultancy consists of one person and is run from a top-floor eyrie in an otherwise empty house.

"Corporate clients?"

"Some. Banks. That kind of thing. Corporate, I guess." He is probably thinking: Goldmans, Carlyle. I can only wish for such patrons.

"And you were a diplomat?"

"Ambassador."

I feel as if I am being fitted into an identikit picture of the military-industrial complex, the sinister American to complement the naïveté Celiwe Nyati had discerned in me. I surmise, too, that his motive in seeking me out is to gauge the nature of my relationship with Zoë Joubert: men always intuit – or invent – their rivals.

"And you, Riaan?"

"NGO. Promoting investment in the former so-called homelands, the bantustans. Small loans for tools, seeds. Grassroots. Microcredit. The best kind." Then, switching tack: "So what do you think of our rainbow nation?"

He seems to be sneering, but whether it is at me, or his country, or his country's failure to deliver greater rewards for him, I cannot immediately guess.

"I'm impressed. I was here before, you know. In the apartheid era."

"A visitor, were you? A temporary sojourner? Come to punch the liberal card in the evil empire?"

"Not really. A functionary. American Embassy."

His eyes light with malevolent recognition.

"Constructive engagement. Isn't that what you called it? Set The Struggle back years. Typical American. Thinking you're the cavalry. Hey, over here with that thing, man."

He turned to draw on a large, well-constructed joint doing the rounds.

And then across the crowd on the warm deck above the bay at the start of that hot summer, I glimpsed another face, a woman's face. Zoë Joubert was shepherding her towards me, an uncertain smile playing across her lips like a shadow cast by clouds, saying: have you met Jessica de Vere?

Twelve

I WAS STANDING AWKWARDLY WITH my back pressed to the wooden corner of the deck. The balustrade flexed and was flimsy where it should have been solid. Jessica de Vere – once plain Jess Chase – was not helping me feel comfortable, glancing over her shoulder towards the door, as if planning to bolt, or welcome a third party she had not yet introduced into the conversation. Around us, people danced with the pantomime awkwardness of age mimicking youth. The music – Mango Groove, Bob Seger, Johnny Clegg, old days stuff – was loud enough for intimacies to seem discreet.

"Does she know? Zoë?"

"Know?"

"About us, dammit, Tom. Us. The past. Ancient, dangerous history."

She did not quite fit the memories. There were diamonds embedded in white gold jewellery decorating her ring finger, earlobes, neck; skin glowed with preparation and care; seal-sleek hair without a blemish of silver seemed to bounce on inner suspension; fine edges suggested scrupulous self-maintenance. She had always used conversation to protect privacy, vulnerability. But, on the rickety deck that night, her talk seemed more like Kevlar.

The Jess Chase I remembered wore shabby clothes, asked impertinent questions of ministers and diplomats, dodged police roadblocks on her motorcycle. Her newspaper articles stripped away pretence and untruth. She witnessed, first hand, the brutality and meanness of the townships. She lived among her subjects, breaking the Race Ogres' laws to spend weeks under cover in Soweto and Khayelitsha and Cooktown.

And then, in hotel rooms in Port Elizabeth and Durban and Bloemfontein, I would wait restlessly as she composed her article on what passed in those days for a laptop – the pre-harddrive Tandy 200, the "AK-47 of laptop computers," she called it – flicking back and forth through the pages of her notebook, muttering phrases to herself as she sought the precise language she required to frame the day's anguish in columns of print, making calls to sources who recognised her voice and did not give their names over the unreliable hotel phone networks.

She would write with rapt intensity, hungry for the glory of the page one byline, fired by righteous rage. When she hooked her computer to the phone line with alligator clips or curious headphone-like cuffs, she seemed oblivious to my existence, cursing profanely when the line went down or when her editors said her story had disappeared into the ether in those early days of technological experimentation before the internet changed everything.

Only when she had transmitted her dispatches – "filed," as she put it – to the newsrooms she served in London and New York, did she permit any contact between us. Only then would she reach into the ice bucket I kept ready to charge a glass with chilled wine. Only then would she awaken to other needs. Her skin dark and her topaz eyes bright, as if the adrenaline could not be sated by word alone. Her hair short, black and spiky.

In her formless work gear she seemed to be without proportion. Beyond its disguise, she nurtured a physique moulded by whatever it was that drove her to excel in everything she did. If you were looking for adjectives to describe her, you would light on words like elfin and inquisitive, enigmatic, edgy, elusive. Nothing about her smacked of sentimentality or soft focus. Nothing about her, to use a diplomat's weasel word, was "appropriate" to my status, my ambitions to achieve high rank.

Each time I headed out with her and her colleagues, trading my suit and tie for a photographer's fishing vest, I took one more step away from the circumspection expected of me as a diplomat. Each bout of love-making, each ingestion from her stash of powerful local cannabis exposed me to the possibility that my ambassador would discover this secret life I led outside the embassy, and punish me for it. The risks were legion and I was besotted enough to ignore them all. It was the kind of love that brushes aside thoughts of self-destruction, maybe even feeds on them.

Each clandestine visit to the rough township drinking houses called *shebeens*, each meeting with people known to be "banned" as subversives took me a little further away from the bland, half-smile of the diplomat and towards the passions of those who were "involved" – that worst of professional indictments.

In her company, I skirted the world of The Struggle and its enforced choices. A chance mis-statement, an ambiguous look, the 'wrong' response at a police roadblock or a comrades' *indaba* would change the course of your life forever. I remembered a woman in a township near Johannesburg whose daughter was a revolutionary and whose husband was a cop. "You just live like birds," she said. "You cannot sleep."

My secret half-hour with her embassy file had barely ruffled the surface of the cross currents that formed her.

Her childhood had unfolded in a former railwayman's cottage in the Backlands – the name we gave to the black-ruled states to the north. A delusional British mother misfunctioned in loose tandem with a buccaneering American father, a Walter Mitty whose gold mines never produced gold, whose private yachts never sailed, whose stories never quite extended beyond the prologue.

He came to the attention of a Backlands Station Chief after he enlisted in one of the white-led armies – not the kind of thing Uncle Sam wanted its citizens doing, but there was nothing anyone could do to stop them – misfits, ne'er do wells, Vietnam vets washed up on the Africa mercenary circuit. In one particular fire-fight, according to a military prosecutor's notes prepared for a court martial, he refused to advance when ordered to do so and, instead, took cover in thick bush, emerging with an empty magazine to prove he had indeed behaved as a warrior.

When the investigators went back the following day, they discovered 20 pristine, unfired rounds, emptied into the dense scrub. His discharge – not exactly honourable – followed pretty soon afterwards, as did his disappearance from the Backlands. That left a young daughter with a mother who insisted on being addressed as Ma'am, reinforcing her claim to descent from some aristocratic house. (The title had not checked out when she made a citizenship application – rejected – at the local US embassy, citing her marriage to an American national.)

It was never quite clear to me how this odd couple had washed up in Africa and Jess Chase showed no inclination to enlighten me. Even her most intimate offerings of autobiography drew a veil over her childhood, just as I maintained my reticence about the file on her in the embassy registry.

Her break with me was equally unexplained.

Returning from the embassy to my villa sometime after Nyati's death, I found she had left the set of house keys I had given her along with a handwritten note on a half-moon table of burnished cherry wood in the entrance hall, caught in a shaft of bright light from the open door.

"I cannot see you again. Do not come after me. Jess."

"I heard that you quit early because they wanted to give your job to a political appointee. So you stamped your foot and threw out the toys."

"And your byline seemed to disappear as well."

"I married."

"And stopped writing?"

"It was the deal."

"Must have been a hell of a deal."

"It was. Is. It's called love. He's here. You might know of him. Chris de Vere."

"Finance. Venture capital. Diamond money magnified. He was written up in *The Journal*."

"He didn't like that."

"I always thought you'd go back home. To the Backlands."

She looked at me sharply.

"This is my home now."

"So you finally joined the aristocracy."

"That's what people seem to think. What are you really doing here?"

"I met Zoë in Cape Town. That's it. Isn't that enough? Boy meets girl."

"Hardly a boy. Or girl."

"Ouch. And how do you know these guys, Zoë and company?"

"Oh. Back then." She waved a hand backwards over her own tanned shoulder, as if dismissing a life she had outgrown. "In the reporting days. They were a good story. Old Deep. ODAC. White liberals. Angst. Sex. Police raids on the servant's quarters. Detentions. A prison suicide. I stayed with Zoë and Rod for a couple of days to get the feel for it – you know, sex under hot tin roofs, barefoot servants. And we became buddies. In fact, she introduced me to my husband-to-be. "

"You never told me."

"It was later."

"When?"

"Whenever. Around the time I introduced the Old Deep set to Solomon Nyati. Making my contribution to history, racial harmony. Although it didn't quite work out that way. You feeling alright?"

"You introduced them to Nyati?"

Behind her, an outer door opened into the living room that led onto the deck. She turned and slipped rapidly through the crowd, linking arms with a tall, slender, silver-haired man who scanned the room from patrician heights, finding it all too predictably inadequate.

"I didn't know you knew her." Zoë Joubert had emerged from the throng, as if stepping from a dense jungle.

"From the embassy days. I was doing press work. That's how I met her. Journalists. You know the kind, some of them at least. Couple of gin and tonics, a long lunch and get Uncle Sam into the paper in a good light. Find out what they're up to. Pick their brains. I guess it was cynical. But she was in a different league."

"Well, 'twas in another country," she said with a laugh that did not quite reach her eyes. "But this wench is very much alive."

"So you keep in touch?"

"I can see you need a lesson in the caste system in dear old Plett.

Plett 101? There are two kinds of people that you will meet here, white people that is, people who get by quite comfortably, like me and this lot" – she gestured fondly to the crowd on the deck – "and seriously rich people like Chris de Vere. We rent houses. They own them. We throw parties like this where everyone brings food and drinks and their kids snog in the bushes. They have staff to fix lunches and cocktails. Snogging is conducted more decorously. And once a year when we all come to the seaside, we cross the lines. Chris and Jess come to my parties, I go to theirs. In fact, I expect you'll be getting an invitation for lunch from Chris fairly soon. He likes to keep track of newcomers. Likes to know who's sniffing round the harem."

"Harem?"

"Figuratively speaking, of course."

She stepped back into the throng, disappearing into the crowd, the babble. I felt like a fly fisher who sees only the perfect ring of water where the quarry surfaced before sliding away.

I struggled to reconcile the timelines. I knew for a certain fact that Jess Chase had been at my villa – in my bed – when word broke of Nyati's death. But she had never mentioned her contact with Zoë Joubert and her comrades-in-arms. So, if Jess Chase had been talking clandestinely to Solomon Nyati about the Old Deep set, how much more of her life had she kept secret? And if Zoë Joubert had introduced Jess Chase to Chris de Vere, had that been during, before or after my own relationship with Jess?

"You look like you're trying to remember the theory of relativity," Riaan van Rensburg said. He had that skill acquired by very serious drinkers of reaching a plateau of advanced inebriation which, to the casual eye, resembles extreme sobriety.

"Have you seen my wife?"

The painter and sculptor I had been introduced to as Vanessa van Rensburg with her flame-red tresses and emerald eyes had disappeared some time earlier into the thickest cover in the walled garden. Minutes later, another woman – short, cropped-headed with ear and eyebrow piercing – had followed.

"My third. Third wife. Vanessa. All-purpose genius. Mother of my sons, and of my step-daughter. Love of my life."

A bitter cackle rumbled up from his chest like bubbles in swamp water and ended as a protracted bout of coughing. He pulled a packet of the local Gunston cigarettes from the pocket of his flowing shirt and lit one, inhaling deeply.

Below the deck, his wife emerged from the bougainvillea, smoothing down her dress and drawing the back of her hand across her mouth. Riaan van Rensburg fixed his gaze on the bejewelled night sky.

When people are new to one another, thrown together without time for inquiries or due diligence, they have a golden moment to define themselves in their best light, to turn the kaleidoscope so that their flaws are presented in acceptable symmetry, the constructs free of inconvenient questions or contradictions.

They are creatures without history, granted brief licence to compose their narratives to their advantage. So I wanted it to be with Zoë Joubert.

For my stay in Plettenberg Bay, I had splurged my moderator's fee – and then some – on a suite at the resort's premier hotel with its vista across Lookout Beach and Keurbooms Lagoon to the serrated ridgeline of the Tsitsikamma Mountains. Now, at her party, I was thinking how I might detach her from her guests – from the web of shared history that bound as surely as chains and manacles – and persuade her to step into my stranger's world.

The party was winding down. Jessica and Chris de Vere had left quietly, folding themselves into a smart, silver two-seat sports car, a Mercedes or BMW, for the return journey to their part of the resort. As Zoë Joubert had forecast, Chris de Vere had sought me out and invited me – or, rather, ordered me – to join them later in the week for lunch at his villa (he called it their beach cottage.) 1:00 for 1:30. Casual, of course.

I guessed he was 10 or 15 years older than I, immaculate in a yellow sports shirt with an expensive logo of the kind favoured by serial golfers, fashionably creased blue linen trousers and Gucci loafers worn without socks. His hair had begun to thin, running in silver waves that softened the uncompromising lines of his tanned, hawkish features. He had the look of a man used to winning contests whose real prize was not so much victory as the loser's humiliation.

The sky began to lighten on the stragglers tackling the worst of the damage – congealed steaks, half-eaten skeletons of fish, ashtrays piled with cigarette butts and exhausted reefers. I joined in the ritual gathering of glasses to be deposited in the kitchen where a dishwasher whirred with a first batch of stained offerings. A maid hired for the season would doubtless arrive in due course to complete what we had begun.

Other late-stayers were sweeping shards of broken glass and filling black garbage bags with the detritus of our libations: the paper plates and burned-down candles that had become mounds of wrinkled white wax streaked with black; the bottles drained to the lees.

In deck chairs, in quiet corners, the overwhelmed, the drunk, the defeated and the abandoned dozed in heavy, fitful slumber – Riaan van Rensburg among them, his wife long departed. I had seen her leave, darting quickly out of the door, followed by her brush-cut companion. If Van Rensburg had noticed, he made no attempt to pursue, challenge or restrain her. Beneath the floral shirt, his stomach rose and fell in time to his snores. From the kitchen I smelled fresh coffee.

"You guys always party like this?"

"Partying is one thing these guys do best. And they never seem to slow down."

We were alone in the kitchen. The scar tissue on her shoulder produced an irresistible desire to touch it.

"War wound," she said, mimicking gruffness, like a Purple Heart Marine deprecating personal valour.

She put her arms around my neck and I slid mine around her waist. She drew her body close to mine and I pulled her closer. Then, inexplicably, her embrace slackened.

She took my hand, leading me to the rickety balustrade of the deck. I noticed that Riaan van Rensburg had vacated the deck chair where I had presumed him to be sleeping. We looked east across the bay, towards the mountainous ridgeline beginning to detach itself from the bruised vermilion of the dawn. Soon the sky would flare into striations of orange, lime, scarlet and indigo.

"Don't ever say we never saw the sunrise together," she said with a smile.

"How about sunset, too – morning, noon and ..."

"Slow down, Tom. Friends, we said. Remember?"

"But ..."

"No buts," she said.

Thirteen

I AWOKE MUCH LATER THAN planned. The day had already advanced far beyond my usual hour. I threw open the drapes and recoiled from the acid intensity of the light. The sky was cloudless and below it, the view I had seen by moonlight seemed all the more breathtaking, as if the sun had etched every detail, every curling crest of surf, every sweeping line of dune and mountain.

A stretch of white beach, now flecked with bright parasols, led to a gap of perhaps 100 yards where a treacherous tide rushed in and out of the Keurbooms Lagoon, forcing its way through a curving channel, washing over the shallows that skirted it.

Through my field glasses – a gift when I first left for Africa from friends who apparently believed I would be on some kind of permanent safari – I scanned a more distant shoreline, where a man cast a line into the surf and stood back, holding aloft a long fishing pole. A child dug a hole in damp sand. Both wore shorts and wide-brimmed sun hats. A woman in a yellow swimsuit stretched out beside a blue tent – tanning and reading next to a red cooler box. Otherwise the entire beach, miles of it, was deserted.

On the lagoon, pleasure boats – inflatables and compact cabin cruisers with outboard engines – churned the waters into pristine wakes, or bobbed at anchor, fishing poles sprouting like the antennae of oversized crustaceans. Closer to me, just below the hotel across gorse-covered rocks, a beach restaurant was starting up for the pre-lunch crowd, its tables filling under dark green canopies designed for shade. Waiters and waitresses in black pants and white shirts wove a slinky-hipped way through their clients bearing jugs of beer and pots of grilled shrimp.

Looking at them through binoculars, still clad in a hotel bathrobe, I felt oddly embarrassed, as if I might be accused of voyeurism.

A few hours earlier, as I left her villa, Zoë Joubert had invited me to join her and her friends for a picnic at a beach they called the Robberg. I would need beach clothes and sun lotions.

The late hour left me little time for the morning's errands.

I walked up quickly from the hotel towards Main Street, past a curiously English-looking church – St Peter's – in rough brown sandstone, set in a stand of blue gums. The gate to the churchyard was a virtual replica of those bucolic lych-gates you would expect to see in an old movie set in Dorset or Devon or some other place in England in the 1940s with Spitfires or Lancaster bombers roaring overhead. A signboard set out the timetable for the forthcoming Christmas services – midnight mass, family Eucharist.

In the town I had seen fliers advertising carols on the beach, by candlelight no less. Such fervour amid the pagan decadence, the sun worship! I imagined the church in the off-season – boarded-up, its notice board empty save for a couple of forlorn drawing pins, its pews and altar dormant, dusty, awaiting the recall to life as the visitors of the African summer rolled in from the goldfields farther north, their Mercedes and BMW SUVs bulging with offertory.

More likely, of course, the church would be open for its regulars all year round – quietly, modestly – its priests living in a mixture of fiscal joy and spiritual dread at the thought of the seasonal worshippers swelling the collection purses and transforming the line of communicants into God's traffic jam.

Now, as I walked on, past the Steers burger bar with its population of pre-teens, towards the CNA bookshop and Foschini's fashion store, I thought of those believers – Tutu and Mkatshwe, Chikane, Naude, Boesak – who had taken their crosses to the barricades. I had once been present, purely by coincidence, when security officials in Johannesburg's Jan Smuts Airport (as it was then called) sent Desmond Tutu back and forth through the metal detector as he sought to board a flight to Cape Town.

He was the only person the police body-searched. He was the only black man in the line, the only Nobel Peace Prize Laureate, the only man to trigger the metal detector with a pectoral cross.

Did they think it was a weapon, he said to no one in particular. (Of course, with his interpretation of the faith, the cross was indeed the greatest of weapons.) In his lecture accepting the Nobel, Tutu had proclaimed: "Let us work to be peacemakers, those given a wonderful share in Our Lord's ministry of reconciliation. If we want peace, so we have been told, let us work for justice. Let us beat our swords into ploughshares."

The line for security clearance at Jan Smuts, offered the rejoinder.

I made my purchases – a cooler box, outlandish surfing clothes, smoked trout, wine and beer – and returned to load my plunder into the rental car. A hotel concierge in an unseasonal dark coat stood over it, as if on guard.

"*Skollies*," he said. He pointed to the tires. All four of them were flat. One had been clumsily slashed and the others apparently deflated.

"We are very sorry," he said. "It has not happened before."

Was it just a coincidence after the episode on the dirt road at Elim, or, perhaps, a warning shot for straying beyond "conference purposes only"? Or, like the man said, just plain old vandalism, the kind you got everywhere? Even in places where the plots never thickened.

The concierge offered to be in touch with the rental company to have the car replaced or fixed. I handed him the keys and started down a wooded path past signboards telling walkers to beware of thieves and other skulduggery.

As I turned to look back at the hotel, I thought I saw in the distance a beige Toyota pulling away. But South Africa was full of beige Toyotas.

The Robberg Beach stretched towards a hump-backed peninsula bearing the same name, a curve of sand and surf abutting rocky redoubts where seals flubbed and flopped and honked on cliffs above the sea, fighting for the high ground occupied by the great cantankerous alpha males while lesser creatures perforce contented themselves with lower shelves of sand-coloured rock, closer to the water where they sometimes provided sustenance for Great White sharks.

Zoë Joubert had chosen a picnic location at the far end, easy enough to reach by car, but a slog on foot. I felt I might just as well have been setting out to cross the Sahara for all my chances of arriving on time.

The promontory formed the southernmost horn of the great bay from which the resort took its name, stretching from the tip of the peninsula back, past the squat ziggurat of the Beacon Island Hotel towards some distant point beyond which lay another resort called Nature's Valley.

Even further, visible only in the imagination, lay the wild coastline leading on to Port Elizabeth and East London and Durban and, ultimately, as Africa's cartography curved north, to Mozambique and Tanzania, Kenya, Somalia. Since delving into the transcripts of the Truth and Reconciliation Commission, my mental GPS had marked another waypoint – Crystal Sands, where Nyati died – but I did not dwell on the thought.

Rising sharply from Robberg Beach, thick ramparts of brush held the dune in place against the wind and the rain of the off-season. Narrow wooden staircases and paths with handrails provided discreet access to the rows of mansions occupying the front line between the land and the sea, between Africa and ocean.

High above, with echoes of the Hamptons, were the villas of the local aristocrats, Chris de Vere among them, where the elite unwound as staff members made beds and cleaned rooms, laundered clothing, marinated prawns, unloaded comestibles, set out buckets of ice, filled fridges with bottles of white wine, sliced limes and lemons and collected errant newspapers and mislaid coffee cups and glasses smeared with lipstick from low poolside tables.

Jess was ascending towards a substantial residence, painted in white with bright blue shutters. She had turned to look back at the relentless, cresting surf. She was wearing a short, white blouse over a dark, wet bikini – the strap had left a visible water mark across the back of her shirt.

She carried a rubberised, black swimming cap in one hand, a

beach towel in the other. Her black hair had sprung loose. Her tanned legs still glistened from the sea. The lower part of the bikini clung to taut buttocks that I remembered with a physical jolt. I waved and she made as if to return the gesture, then lowered her hand abruptly and turned away, resuming her ascent of the stairs, quick and busy. She did not look back to see what had become of me in my ludicrous disguise, my cover as a vacationer of no sinister intent, with cooler box and baggy shorts to prove it.

My gaze followed the line of the stairs, up through the delicate, intricate vegetation of the *fynbos*. The path contoured around, below a battlement of hedge and lawn outside the big house. The blank monocle of a brass telescope peered directly at me, as unflinching as the barrel of a tank cannon. I could not make out who stood behind it in the shade of a white canvas awning. The whole episode was over in a matter of seconds, but it crystallised as a moment of foreboding, a harbinger, somehow, of hazard.

I found the night's revellers re-established in a colony of beach umbrellas, towels, kikoyis, cooler boxes, drinks cans, wine bottles, paper plates, children and the flat body-surfing equipment called boogie boards that allowed the more athletic to catch the waves and hurtle towards the shore. Some of the exchanges, I imagined, would be the codas to last night's conversations, themselves merely the latest reworking and revision of themes broached decades earlier.

Old Deep was an impenetrable, uncharted terrain of liaisons, cross-references, subliminal connections. Without a compass or guiding star, outsiders intruded at their peril. But I had blundered in now, for better or for worse.

Zoë rose to meet me, looking quizzically at her watch. I apologised for my lateness, rubbing the stubble as if the gesture offered some kind of explanation.

"I thought you weren't coming," she said. "We missed you."

"How could I not come?"

"You walked? I'm sorry. I could have given you a lift."

"I'll remember that next time," I said. It seemed inappropriate to go into long explanations about the rental car. All that mattered was that she – or some undefined *we* – had missed me. Missed me!

"Swim?" she said. "You look as if you need it. In a nice way, of course."

I lowered my paraphenalia onto the sand and spread my towel on the fringes of the group, making camp beyond the protective perimeter. Following her advice, I headed for the waves, but on the way to the churning, pounding water, the sand was so hot it burned my feet.

I thought for a moment of turning back but was persuaded to continue when I heard the croak of Riaan van Rensburg's voice singing an old Beach Boys classic. He had reached a line, urging me to find a new place and was guffawing. I thought some others in his group were laughing, too, presumably at my unfamiliar attire – long, loose-fitting shorts and a tight, protective top accentuating the paleness of my skin. Or, more likely, at some insider joke they had shared many times.

I ploughed on, diving, finally, into the surf and relishing the brisk shock and scrub of salt water. Zoë Joubert followed me, hand in hand with the same girl I had last seen reading a magazine in the hotel room in Cape Town, who now interposed herself between me and her mother, entwining her arms around her and turning her back to me as the waves lifted them to their peaks and lowered them to their troughs.

Zoë Joubert looked down at her daughter with loving eyes and then she looked at me with what I took to be a plea for understanding. I never saw the wave that caught me and pushed me down into the seabed so that I came up gasping for air, my hair full of sand.

"You know," Riaan van Rensburg said when I returned to my towel and cooler box, "it's much quicker if you drive. Something wrong with the car?"

Fourteen

WE WERE SITTING CLOSE TO ONE another on beach towels. The ocean tang mixed with other odours – suntan cream on warm skin, wine, cigarettes, and marijuana. Someone – a straggler tardier even than I – brought the day's morning newspaper which arrived around noon from Cape Town. I espied a headline:

"Nyati Widow Rejects Probe Curbs."

Lily had gone public with her opposition to the statute of limitations.

The article explained that the legislative proposal had the support of a high-ranking group of political leaders and wealthy business types who had prospered from a programme called Black Economic Empowerment designed to expand the white monopoly on corporate wealth. A new law would draw a line under the Truth and Reconciliation Commission's findings. "In the interests of racial harmony", there would be no further inquiries, no right to re-open cases deemed closed, although pre-existing criminal cases would be heard.

A vote was scheduled in Parliament within days. "Analysts" – those mysterious figures beloved of reporters seeking anonymous attribution for their own gut-feelings – forecast that the law would win easy approval. No one wanted to raise the phantoms. No one except Lily. And, by extension, Thomas J Kinzer, her unofficial, unannounced ghostbuster.

The topic was one that would naturally interest the Old Deep set – one of them in particular: if the law was approved, it would no longer matter who had betrayed Solomon Nyati.

Back at the hotel, before my sortie to the beach, I had planned to use the stash of stationery purchased in Cape Town to open files on each of my suspects using codenames to shield identities from prying eyes. It was, I suppose, a reflexive gesture and the names were none too subtle, or flattering: Fatboy (Van Rensburg) and Rugby-boy (the lawyer Ferd), Poet (Rod Harris, Zoë's ex), Cobra (Kaplan, another lawyer) and Professor (an academic from Durban called Porter). Certainly Jess would have to be in there, and Zoë, too. (Codename "Venus?") But what about me? Was I somehow a player, too? Codename TJ?

Rugby-boy was a tall, powerful man with broad shoulders and a big chin that needed a shave – the sort of fearless, hail-fellow type you would choose as a companion for a long, unpredictable voyage into uncertain territory.

Cobra, slender, saturnine – better met at the end than the beginning of a precarious journey – had been a young lawyer with an uncanny knack for the high-profile case that brought the television cameras along with the dry, legal hearings, turning the fierce spotlight of global publicity onto the sins of the regime.

He had a look of unbearable arrogance and I wondered if his friends found this appealing or simply tolerated him as the unfortunate adjunct to his effervescent wife. Cobra – Maurice Kaplan to his clients and colleagues – had a habit of tilting his head backwards to scrutinise his interlocutor through hooded, half-closed eyes. (The inspiration for his codename was not hard to figure.) He spoke with a languorous drawl. And, like Rugby-boy – Ferdinand Walker, a.k.a. Ferd – he had no objection to responding to the honest inquiries of an earnest American: no one can resist re-telling the final version of their finest hour, particularly when gilded by selective memory.

Throughout my professional life I had believed that curiosity is the greatest flatterer; that sincere questions disarm even the most guarded interlocutor. So what was it like, back then? How did you get by when the system was stacked against you? But how many of these versions were camouflage, false trails to cloak betrayal?

Even Zoë Joubert leaned forward to catch the exchanges between us, though she must have heard the rationales and exculpations a thousand times. As she did, she smiled at me, seeming happy that I was so fascinated by their common history. My spy's guts squirmed in shame.

"You see, Tom, you had to make your mind up whether you would stand up and be counted," Rugby-boy was saying.

"Think of pre-war Germany if the Germans had collectively said no to Hitler, or the Romanians under Ceauşescu. Think of your civil rights movement – if you say you have a dream then you have to take the risks to make it come true. You know, most people didn't stand up – not in our society, not the whites. It was too easy not to, too easy to take the bait – the houses, the cars, the security. Apartheid was a welfare system. The whites, the Afrikaners especially, got the jobs on the railways, the mines, the post office, the whole state infrastructure – police, army. But that was only one side of the coin. Apartheid produced a national schizophrenia, true separation not just physically but in the mind, the soul. The result was that life and death took on different meanings for both sides. I'm talking about black lives, black deaths. Steve Biko, Hector Pieterson, Matthew Goniwe, Solomon Nyati. There was a white politician, Jimmy Kruger, who said the death of Biko left him cold. Cold! That was not just callous, not just indifferent, it was blinkered, blind stupidity, as if you were on the Titanic and you said the iceberg left you cold. Which it did of course."

Cobra took up the refrain, speaking with a particular intensity, his eyes widening hypnotically.

"You could make your choices, but you had to put them into effect and that was the hard part. Of course we all opposed apartheid, hated it. But how were we to oppose the system in a meaningful way? Where could we make a difference? There's a sense now, especially for you foreigners, that The Struggle was all black–white, but it was never that simple. There had always been whites like Helen Suzman or Beyers Naude and Helen Joseph. But they were pretty high profile. What about people like us? Young. Students. Would-be professionals. When we tell people now that we fought in The Struggle, too, they look at us as if we are crazy. But we earned our place."

Cobra paused to run the tip of his tongue along the adhesive strip of a Rizla paper in which he had rolled a blend of tobacco and marijuana, placing a thin curl of rolled cardboard at one end and twisting the other into a fuse.

"So, yes, we could defend people – pro bono of course. We could ensure that what little law obtained was used. We promised legal redress, even achieved it sometimes. But was it enough? Not all of us were lawyers. How could we associate ourselves with the real opposition, the comrades, the ANC? Throw bombs? Fire Kalashnikovs? Go for training in Moscow and East Berlin? Angola? Do you remember the necklace executions – death by incineration with a car-tire around your neck after a summary decision by a people's court and sometimes not even that courtesy, just the mob demanding the same conclusion as the hanging judges of white justice? The modalities varied. The instinct was the same. How could we join a struggle in a less violent way?"

Cobra lit his cigarette and the odour drew a few more intimates into our circle. From the perimeters, the Professor – John Porter – had been eavesdropping and chose to spoke.

"The necklace was a question of perspective," he began, probing for a response. "Remember: we weren't all fighting the same way at Old Deep. A lot of people – Zoë especially – were looking to politicise the whites, stir their conscience. Some of us crossed the lines" – his remark met with grunts of assent and demurral. Cobra rolled his eyes, as if at an oft-told tale.

"On the day of Nyati's funeral, when we heard that the emergency was coming that night, we drove back to Jo'burg at 200 clicks an hour to grab what we could. They came to our offices, just after we left, and smashed everything – presses, printers, copiers. And that was the nub, really. That was our value to the comrades. We had the mobility. Even after the emergency, we could move around the place. We had cars. Kombis. Being white was an ID in its own right. They didn't expect you to use it against them. But they really hated those that did."

It crossed my mind to inquire how he had heard of the imminent emergency when only people like the cop-friendly reporter Ray Gilliomee – and the security forces themselves – were in the loop.

"And you were there, at the meeting in PE, the night he died?" I ventured.

"No, no. I had another gig."

Rod Harris, Zoë Joubert's former husband, joined us, moving a small folding chair and a parasol to be closer to our sub-group. He was accompanied by a slender young man of Asian descent, introduced to me as Ricky Rajbansi.

Harris wore long, loose pantaloons in black linen and a black shirt in the same fabric, covering his eyes in small, round, impenetrable sunglasses and his head in a gaudy cap that somehow reminded me of the Caterpillar from Alice in Wonderland. With the ending of The Struggle, he had lost his raison d'etre as a poet of protest and had turned his hand to other forms of self-expression.

As an installation artist, he had erected the letters G, O and D in steel on the pontoons of a disused road bridge near Plettenberg Bay, obliging motorists to consider whether divinity lay in the swamps and bird colonies of the Bitou River Estuary.

He was well entrenched on the cultural lecture circuit, a regular at the Grahamstown Festival. He had edited collections of African poetry and had taught alongside Coetzee at Cape Town. At one point he had appeared at a conference in the Netherlands, sharing a platform with a noted agent of the apartheid security police who had once hounded him – reconciliation as performance.

"Rod wrote about the necklace, right?" The young man – Ricky, who I took to be a student or some kind of acolyte – gazed intently at the older man. Rod Harris waved a loose hand as if to chase away this adulation. Rummaging through a bright, woven beach bag in black and red zig-zag stripes, the young man produced a copy of the most famous volume from The Struggle years: *Powers of Emergency – Selected Poetry from the Frontline of Apartheid* by Rodney Harris.

Ricky Rajbansi had found the page he was seeking and coughed.

"Necklace 1985," he began, looking around at his audience as if to warn them from the title alone that this would not be a pleasant experience for any of them.

Dutifully, we fell silent.

If we are to be free we must be pre-free, ready
To launch on wings not yet feathered
Or built to be
Flown on, aflame.

If we are to be free we must see freedom
As one
For all
Our phoenix freedom burns in another's fire,
Our freedom rises from the traitor's pyre
Where we alone would not search for it.

Freedom born not of blossoms but smoke and rock,
For we are slaves of our own hearts
And we must break and burn our own hearts
To be free.

Hounded, grounded, necklace-bound and burning,
 the Judas finds no salve of prayer
no thirty pieces
 to buy this moment, his moment back,
to end the agony.
His flames
Are our freeing and dying, he redeems.

"Still think that way, Rod?" Cobra focused on the poet with a condescension that had been a hallmark of his courtroom technique, his tradecraft. His thinning hair stood in tufts. His eyes, reddened from the sea and the cigarette he had rolled, panned slowly to the slender young man who had read the poem. His voice took on a cavilling tone, almost braying with scorn.

"It was needed. At the time? A necessary phase," the young Rajbansi said, looking to Harris for support.

"And you were there, hey, Ricky? In The Struggle? In your diapers?"

"Leave it, Kaplan, for God's sake."

"Touchy, Rod, are we today? Rough night?"

"I said leave it, man."

I wondered when the conversation had really begun.

The beach was filling with the post-lunch crowd. People in wetsuits and surfer tops like mine paddled out to find The Wave to end all waves, skimming back to the beach on their flat, Styrofoam boards, laughing at the thrill. With hi-glo orange, life-saver rings on their upper arms, children sloshed around in the boisterous, frothy shallows, watched over by parents and, here and there, plump nannies in pale green uniform, the blackness of their skin all the more remarkable for its infrequency in this particular enclave.

Teenagers bobbed in lines as the waves foamed over and around them. On the beach, sons and fathers lofted oval rugby balls, larger than American footballs, mimicking their national heroes from the Springbok team. Families played noisy games of tennis using wooden paddles. If you went to the beach in this country, you did not go to slumber over a thick novel, or to baste yourself with sun oil.

Just overhead, no more than 100 yards from the shoreline, motorised gliders on pleasure rides skimmed the waves, held perilously aloft by their broad wing-span. Farther out, you could see the powerful tourist boats scudding across the swells towards the Robberg Peninsula. Sporty catamarans traced wild zig-zags as the wind caught their sails, propelling them on a single pontoon as their crews leaned out to prevent them from capsizing.

Just beyond the surf line, quite suddenly, grey, triangular fins broke the surface. I inhaled sharply and pointed, my mind running through the computations of swimming children and sharks.

"Dolphins!" Zoë Joubert cried and ran helter-skelter to the water, her daughter at her side, arcing perfectly into the surf at the point where the breakers threatened to slow her progress. Others followed – Kaplan and Ferd and Porter and Ricky Rajbansi. Even Riaan van Rensburg lumbered towards the waves. From a distance they might have looked like they were members of some arcane sect seeking terminal marine fulfilment.

"And Nyati?" I said to the poet when all the others had scampered off to the water, towing children and partners with them towards the dolphins – six of them, I counted, gliding within the glassy walls of the outermost swells. "Did Nyati approve the necklace?"

"Why Nyati?"

"Just an idea for a post-conference article. No poetry, of course. Just 2,000 words to appease the organisers."

"Well, read the transcripts of the TRC. You'll see that Nyati talked two games. One to white folks like us. One to the townships. And the townships message was war, blood, fire."

"So he approved?"

"It was never so much approved, among the top echelon. More like: 'who will rid me of this troublesome priest?' Sometimes you don't have to give orders to make things happen. Sometimes there's no point standing against the flow and the comrades, the street-fighters, the grunts as you would say – they liked it a lot. It felt good to them."

"You sound as if you were convinced."

"Look. Kinzer. It's history. We've moved on. Maybe it's not all perfect. Maybe it's corrupt, getting like the rest of Africa, but it's ours. We don't owe it to anybody. Not to America or Britain or anyone else. This wasn't decolonisation – lowering the flag when some prince or queen told us we were allowed to run up our own. This wasn't Zimbabwe: now here's the new constitution, Robert Mugabe, and don't break it! We did this ourselves and the rest of the world reacted – sanctions and so forth. I was never a great believer in what a few whites could do. It was not our Struggle. What were we struggling against? Our parents? Our protectors? Ourselves? The system that gave us everything? But in the townships, they knew what to fight against. They felt it every minute, every day. They started it and the necklace made damn sure that everyone with any sense stayed onside. It was no time for wavering. You were either with The Struggle or against it. You made your choices. Necklace or not. Commitment or punishment. Loyalty or pain. And it gave us what we have today – peace, harmony. Not perfect. But ours. And a damn sight better than before. The end justified the means. I should imagine that Americans would understand that after your civil war. Nyati certainly did."

"You met him?"

"Sure I met him."

"That last night in PE?"

"You ask a lot of questions. What is this? The third degree? John Vorster Square all over again?"

"Just interest. You know, I was in the country at the time. But I never met the Old Deep set. I knew your name of course. You'd gone to Lusaka, as I recall, met the comrades – Oliver Tambo, Thabo Mbeki. Not many people did that."

"You have a long memory."

"It must have been tough when you came back. I mean, the police must have given you a hard time."

"I was called in. Sure. We all were."

"And they'd want to know if you had been recruited."

"They certainly did."

"And were you?"

"That's not something I talk about."

"Even now?"

"Even now."

"And the last night in PE With Nyati. The meeting. You went to that?"

"Sure. We all did. But I'm more interested in the present."

"Meaning?"

"Meaning that maybe your motives are none of my business. But Zoë is. Mills is, too. So be careful, right? No destructive engagement."

He looked out to sea and I followed his gaze out to where the swimmers seemed to be surrounded by grey fins.

Fifteen

Zoë and Camilla, Riaan, Ferd and Kaplan came back from the water, laughing, breathless, and glistening with the surf. Riaan van Rensburg took Zoë's hand as they walked across the beach. The gesture seemed intended as brotherly, companionable, but it reinforced my first impression of Van Rensburg's true motives, his yearning for contact.

I turned towards Vanessa van Rensburg to gauge her reaction, but found her watching me with a half-smile on her face. She had swum earlier and her red hair fell in stiff wavelets, almost in the manner of a Botticelli, framing a remotely aquiline face that had none of the angelic detachment of the paintings.

"Don't worry about Riaan," she said. "He has always felt that way about Zoë. It's just that she never has about him."

"And you?"

"Oh, my feelings are just a little – what shall we say – complicated. But inclusive." She leaned across me to raid the cooler box. A warm, damp bikini cup brushed my arm.

The dolphin worshippers fell back on their beach towels.

I touched one; I wanted to grab its fin and let it take me to Antarctica; it felt as if they had come to say hello to us; they made me feel special; cool.

"You really missed something there. With the dolphins."

Riaan van Rensburg squatted beside me, his heavy, tanned gut falling over the rim of baggy black shorts. Uninvited, he fished a Castle Lager from my cooler box, twisted off the cap and drank deeply. When he lowered the bottle, almost empty, his laboured breathing suggested a taxing excursion into the waves.

He gave no indication that he had noticed his wife's physical contact with me – or particularly cared. With the salt water flattening his black-grey hair to his head, his baleful eyes seemed to protrude even more, emphasised by the dark bags below them. Water dribbled off his shorts onto the sand, like urine.

"Too busy spooking were you?"

"I was talking to Rod about Nyati. About that last night in PE."

"How would he know? He wasn't there."

"And you were there?"

"Of course I was there. I was driving the Kombi. Zoë's Kombi. The blue one. We all went down from Jo'burg. And what's the big deal for you about all that? Come to that. Never mind Rod or anyone else. How did you meet Nyati?"

I don't think he expected an answer, but I told him anyhow. I fancy I narrated the story well. A small audience gathered, Zoë Joubert – I was pleased to note – among them. My text was close to the version I had offered to Celiwe Nyati, conjuring once again the image of a boy on a bicycle, tipped into a ditch. I offered a postscript from our conversation that I had withheld from his daughter.

The boy never did see his father alive again. The brief official notice of death arrived in a brown manila envelope sent by second class post, informing whoever it may concern that a body could be collected from a distant morgue.

By then, he said, it was too late to ask the questions that all good sons want to ask their father before they are parted forever: was I worthy of you? Were you proud of me? Did I fulfil the dreams you dreamt for me?

"And did he tell you that his father ran guns and explosives for the freedom fighters?" Rod Harris broke in. "Did he tell you that the old boy had blood on his hands? No, I thought not. You got the sanitised version, the version for the journalists and diplomats. Nyati knew the risks. And so did his father."

The picnic finally broke up around seven. I remained on the beach with the last swimmers, the just-one-more-wave surfers. I had contrived to spend some time in semi-private conversation with Zoë Joubert. Disappointingly she told me she would not be able to see me until the following day because of a custom whereby she and other friends from her college years partied privately.

Once a year. Girls' night out.

We left the beach in a shambling crowd, laden with furled parasols, sand-blasted boogie boards, cooler boxes rattling with cans and bottles drained of every last drop. Somehow, in the melee of loading beach kit and children, Riaan van Rensburg ended up escorting Zoë Joubert and her daughter, occupying the passenger seat of her Volkswagen convertible like some huge protective hound. His teenage children filled the rear seat, squeezed in with Camilla Joubert. I found myself driving an old Jeep Cherokee with Vanessa van Rensburg at my side.

She had not changed her attire, save for wrapping a flimsy cotton cloth around her waist. It fell open at the fork of her thighs and the sunburn on her belly highlighted the merest hint of a fine, pale, gingery down, like the skin of a peach. The car smelled of marijuana, salt, sand, mixed with a hint of beach towels left too long. The rear seat was taken up with a folded easel and neatly bound clusters of brushes and pencils.

"A project? Work in progress?"

"There's always something in progress. Whether it's work or not is a question of definition. You drive this old buggie to your hotel. Then I'll take it on from there. If you like," she said.

I pulled out ahead of the Volkswagen. The Jeep's rear-view mirror showed Zoë Joubert and Riaan van Rensburg together, he with his great, bulbous head turned towards her in supplication and she laughing at some joke or other, eyes sparkling below the tennis peak she wore to protect her skin from the sun. With their teenage children, his and hers in the back of her car, they could almost have been an organic couple, a stereotypical, never-sundered, always-happy family – perhaps the couple that Van Rensburg craved. Why not Zoë, too?

Was this the partnership she wanted after her marriage to a man who then brought young men to her parties, a complete man-and-two-sons arrangement simply awaiting her occupation? Then the

VW pulled past and sped ahead, with Zoë and Riaan both waving back to us. I thought Camilla Joubert flashed a look of triumph in my direction but I dismissed the idea as unworthy.

On a quiet stretch of road, Vanessa van Rensburg asked me to pull over and, with remarkable deftness, chopped white powder into two lines on a vanity mirror in her lap, using a rolled 100-rand banknote to take the first, thicker line. She offered me the second and I declined, as she had probably suspected I would.

"Waste not, want not," she said.

I pulled quickly back onto the road, knowing that she would be laughing at me.

"Don't you ever wonder you'll get caught?"

"By Riaan?"

"No. By the cops. For the white stuff."

I peered dramatically into the rear-view mirror, partly to make a joke of my squeamishness about travelling with illegal substances – a leftover from the diplomatic days when discovery might have led to some kind of demarche or similar embarrassment.

She swivelled in her seat.

"What cops? That old Toyota behind us? I don't think so."

When I looked in the mirror, I saw only the tail of some vehicle or other disappearing down a side street.

The way she told it, Vanessa van Rensburg had been one of the backroom players at Old Deep, not exactly a groupie, but not one of the frontline, headline-grabbing activists either.

It was easy to imagine her as the artist of the revolution in her paint-spattered smock and torn, blue jeans. She had attended the meeting with Nyati, she said, laughing as she related how she sat at his feet like a disciple as if he were Gandhi, sketching him as she hung on his every word.

"You seem very interested in us all, the Old Deep days."

"Just Nyati, really. That last night before he died. For a conference paper. You know the kind of thing: Apartheid and the liberal dilemma. You guys seem to have been the last people to see him alive."

"Like in a murder thriller. Hercule Poirot. So you were the last to see the deceased" – she mimicked a Gallic intonation and I smiled – "therefore you are suspect. Non?"

"Riaan was telling me he was there."

"He wishes he was there. You were no one if you weren't there."

"But he said he drove the Kombi."

"For sure. He drove the van from Jo'burg down to PE. He refused to let anyone else take the wheel. I wasn't with him then. It was during my very brief Kaplan phase. Well, Kaplan-plus, I suppose you would call it because there was a lot of confusion under all those sleeping bags in the back of the Kombi. Porter was there, too, whatever he says now. But Riaan was driving. Most of the time I can remember him hunched over the wheel. Zoë was asleep in the passenger seat. It was quite a journey. Road trip. Down through the Free State, along the Lesotho border. Things sort of got out of hand around Aliwal North. Lots of lips, elbows, stray fingers, sticky fingers. But old Riaan just kept on rolling along."

"What did Rod make of all that?"

"Rod wasn't there and Zoë didn't join in the other stuff. Rod had stayed back at Old Deep. Something about finishing a big poem. The Epic of The Struggle. So Riaan was the big hero, Alpha male, escorting Zoë, doing all the driving. But then when we got to PE, he lost his nerve. Decided the whole venture was crazy. What was it to do with us? It was their Struggle, the blacks. Let them have it. Let Nyati go it alone. He was scared. Because nothing happened without the security police knowing. Anyone who went would have had a file opened on them, even if they didn't have one already. And you never knew when the police were up to some dirty tricks or other. So Riaan handed over the wheel. Zoë ended up driving. Riaan always says now that he was at the meeting with Nyati. And no one contradicts him but we all know. If anything it's the shame of his life – well, one of them. At the very moment he was supposed to take a stand, he copped out. He's been living with that ever since. Remind me to tell you the whole story some time."

"You don't seem to like him very much."

"Are you crazy? I love Riaan. I think that in a perverted way he loves me. But we neither of us love exclusively. We're not capable. That's all.

You saw us today. Kids on the beach. Picnic with our friends."

"And then night falls."

"Exactement, Monsieur Poirot."

"And he doesn't mind? The women? The men?"

"He's used to it. It gives him his freedom. He doesn't like it. But he understands that I can't be the little housewife. He prefers it if it's women – less of a threat – but he doesn't like it whichever way."

"So why has he done this? He almost pushed me into the car with you."

"And you don't like the idea?"

"Too old-fashioned. Sorry."

"Or too smitten. Too smitten with Zoë Joubert. Like you all are. That's it, you see. He knows I will behave badly and if he can make you behave badly with me, it might keep dear Zoë away from you so he will have a chance."

Sixteen

Hurrying through the hotel lobby, I caught sight of myself in a wide mirror across a circular, glass-topped table held aloft by stone carvings of three fish. My hair was caked and spiky from the brine, my skin mottled by the beginnings of sunburn. I was wearing a T-shirt with salt lines where my protective surfer top had dried underneath. My garish shorts were still slightly damp and I had pulled on my sneakers without bothering with socks. In one hand I carried a beach towel wrapped around my Tilley hat and in the other a cooler box, now relieved of its contents.

During my time in the Foreign Service, I had maintained a tailoring account at Brooks Brothers in the belief that appearances matter – a view that prevailed among a certain breed of diplomat. I had shirts made at a place in Jermyn Street in London that kept my measurements on file and would dispatch its handmade Egyptian cotton creations across the globe.

Over the years, through diet, exercise and – I suppose – more than a hint of vanity, I had contrived to ensure that my measurements barely changed. The fine woollen suits tailored in my 20s and 30s had not required alteration. When I appeared as Ambassador Extraordinary and Plenipotentiary, I did so in the knowledge that the studded cuffs of my shirts and the dark glow of hand-lasted Oxford shoes by John Lobb of St James's Street reflected the dignity of my office.

But now I represented no government, no nation, no policy. The only loyalty required of me was to my suddenly haphazard self.

Since arriving in South Africa, I had paid court to a stranger and re-found a former love. A married bi-sexual woman whose husband coveted the new woman of my dreams had hinted at her availability. Had I chosen, at this very moment, I could have been striding arm-in-arm with a bikini-clad Vanessa van Rensburg towards the boudoir of my suite.

The lure of availability – mine and hers – sent a visceral thrill through me. I felt a perverse sense of gratitude to Lily Nyati. My pursuit of her truth had triggered an accidental liberation of my own. No matter what I did, the results would be on my personal account. I alone would seek out the traitor, the informer who had knowingly sent Solomon Nyati to his death. Was I not the captain of my soul?

I tipped a concierge who approached from nowhere with the keys to my repaired rental car, re-shod with four new tires. I sprinted upstairs, two at a time. My mind was racing ahead, to the entries I would be able to make into my new filing system, my case notes.

Then the alarm bells began to jangle.

The door to my room was slightly ajar and a light was burning. A whiff of cigarette smoke seeped into the corridor outside.

Whoever had broken in was making no secret of the fact. I steeled myself. Crime here was often terminal, with the clatter of automatic rifle fire and witnesses left in pools of blood to tell no tales. As a diplomat I would have retreated, called security, weighed options. In my new recklessness, I braced for confrontation and pushed open the door with a sneakered foot.

"You look awful."

She had been sitting in an armchair and rose to face me.

"Don't get ideas. There are things we need to talk about."

"What on earth are you doing here, Jess?"

"Chris is with his drinking friends playing poker. Annual event. Boy's night out. Girl's night off. I have questions to ask and you have the answers. I apologise for the break-in. Easily done if you pretend to have locked yourself out. And I hope I haven't disturbed any romantic plans."

I showered quickly, shaved off a day's stubble and dressed in the privacy of my bathroom, reverting to predictable chinos and a plain blue Oxford cotton button-down. By the time I emerged, my hair slicked back, the reek of sea and sweat expunged, Jess Chase had telephoned a dinner order and thrown open the windows that framed a vista made pungent by *fynbos*.

She had positioned a small table at a point where we could benefit from the evening breeze and a degree of privacy. When the room service attendant tapped on the door, she darted across the bedroom, past the king-size bed with its white cover and into the still steamy bathroom.

My suite – Room 65 – was decorated in muted tones of eggshell blue and dove grey. It was the kind of accommodation that explained why the hotel qualified for its five stars. Original prints of various species of iris, exotically titled in Latin, adorned the walls. Bright, modern drapes offset older, mellow furnishings from much earlier times in the Cape, crafted from yellowwood and the almost black stinkwood.

My papers had found discreet lodgings in an antique dresser that I had used as a desk. I wondered, briefly, if Jessica de Vere had reverted to the instincts of Jess Chase to rifle through them, but dismissed the idea as counterproductive. If she had, I would soon know. If she had not, my thought had been unworthy.

I was tempted to recall our previous hotel time together after she composed her articles. There had been the soulless chains, Holiday Inns from Ulundi in Zululand to Bloemfontein, tawdry small-town pensions run by severe Afrikaners, the stellar hostelries of Durban and Cape Town. Once, way out in the east, during a massive downpour, we had lodged at a place called the Hydro Baths Hotel, little more than a series of thatched-roof *rondavels* scattered in the scrub near the border with Mozambique.

On arrival the owner warned us against allowing a black retainer – identified as James, no second name offered – to join us in the car as he showed us to our hut. To our enduring regret, we watched him through the slosh of the windscreen wipers, guiding us on our way, caught in the headlights as the rain soaked him to the skin.

When I returned to the reception to inquire about food, I was told we would have to wait for sandwiches because "the ladies are watching 'Dallas'". But, I was assured, James would be on hand to bring them just as soon as the TV schedule permitted.

Jess had changed too much to encourage light-hearted reminiscence, or familiar reference to her youthful indiscretions in remote mud huts. (Her presence in my room, though, suggested she had not lost all her dare-devil mischief). Her hallmark worn Levis and bland, baggy T-shirts had been supplanted by a black sheath tracing the lines she had once kept hidden. Thin straps settled across tanned, unblemished shoulders, offset by a platinum necklace crusted with ice-blue stones. The earrings matched the necklace in carats and sparkle.

Around her eyes no trace of heaviness or pouching betrayed the years' advance, as if the process had been discreetly reversed. The muscle definition on her arms suggested workouts and tennis under personal, professional supervision. Her hands – and you could always tell by the hands and neck, my dear – offered the only clues but they, too, were camouflaged by gold and diamonds.

We settled at the table. I served the crayfish tails and salads she had ordered for us, poured the wine and eased the bottle into its bucket of ice. She had chosen a Chassagne-Montrachet – way beyond my usual budget, but perhaps a deliberate marker of the circles in which she now moved, of the gulf between us.

The pounding of the ocean carried into the room, a relief from some of the resort's other acoustic offerings – the insistent bass thump of Flashbacks Bar that filled the nocturnal Main Street, the heavy period rock of Larry's Bar, the crescendo of gossip at Cornuti's, a pizza joint. (Didn't they understand that the Italian meant "cuckolds", or was that part of a joke I had missed?) Jess ate as if she had been fasting, dissecting the crayfish with minute attention, ensuring that no single trace of sweet, white meat was lost. She buttered a bread roll to dip into the light vinaigrette of her salad. She reached for the wine bottle to recharge her glass.

"What a day. "Tennis at dawn. Ocean swimming. As you know. Were you stalking me? Then golf in the afternoon. Eighteen holes at Goose Valley. Didn't see you lurking behind the bunkers. Then bridge. Then drinks on the terrace. Who said leisure is easy?" Her day's activities came out in a rush, a prelude to what she really wanted to say.

"What are you in fact doing here, Thomas J Kinzer?

I have a bad feeling, a premonition about all this. The old hack instincts die hard. As I recall, you used to love that Bogart line – "of all the gin joints, in all the world, she walked into mine." So why mine? Why my gin joint?"

"You know why."

"I know what you have hinted at. I know you are following Zoë Joubert as if she were in oestrus. But there's something else, isn't there? Always the hidden agenda. What is it this time? I fear you have no concept of the damage you could do. Still on Uncle Sam's unauthorised missions?"

"I thought part of you was American," I said, more as a rebuke than a riposte for I have little tolerance for those who wrap themselves in Old Glory when they need its protection, then burn it for reasons of political expediency.

"Nice suite," she said. The light splintered on her jewellery. "I remember you always liked your comforts."

"Preferably when someone else was paying. Aren't you taking a risk, being in another man's room?"

"Aren't you taking a risk that Zoë Joubert might come calling and find me here?"

"Touché. But it's more of a risk for a respectable married woman. I'm a bachelor, remember."

"A calculated risk, yes. But rather this than being seen in public, or not knowing whatever time bomb you might be setting off."

"I'm on vacation. Struze bob."

The expression was from my lexicon of southern African English. Struze bob, struze fact – terms perverted from "true as" to insist on the veracity of a statement. Other usages: flat dog – crocodile; floppy – slain, black freedom fighter; lekker, meaning tasty; ou, pronounced oh and meaning a man; cherry, girl or chick. Hence, the lekker ous only get the cherries, hey! – the slogan from a long-forgotten TV advertisement. Struze bob!

As she lit a cigarette, I asked her, as casually as I could, about Zoë

Joubert. Her reply seemed almost scripted. Another legend to be filed under "Venus." Or maybe "X" for Jess Chase, the ex of all times.

"Zoë, Zoë. What do we know about Zoë? Trust fund girl, essentially. Only child. Very wealthy, very nice parents. Her father, Benny, supplier in the mining industry. When men dig for gold, sell them the shovels, he used to say. So he did. Made a fortune. Tin roofs for mine hostels. Building contracts for pit heads, compounds and offices. Everything you needed to prosper, short of getting your hands dirty. Quit when the going was good and went into VC – private equity as you Americans call it. Bought into one or two big-time internet winners – Data Solutions, Safezone. Wasn't too greedy. Didn't get burned. Made his second fortune and still keeps his hand in. Bit of this. Bit of that. Very cultured man. Very protective wife, Yvette, runs his life brilliantly, which is what we are supposed to do. Houses in London, Jo'burg, Sardinia. I think they had ideas for Zoë – joining the firm, founding a dynasty, protecting the legacy. She went to the best schools. Ran with the horsey, polo set. African summers in Plett or Hermanus. Spring skiing in the Alps. Mediterranean yachting. Monaco. Cap d'Antibes. Lots of parties. Suitors among the gilded elite. The last thing Benny wanted was for some gold digger to run off with everything he had built up from his father's general dealer's store."

"You didn't lose your reporter's touch."

"I got to know them all quite well. Later, of course. After you left."

"I left after you went first," I reminded her. The breeze from the window caressed her, raising goosebumps, hardening her nipples. She reached for a pashmina shawl and pulled it across her shoulders and bosom.

"Do you want to know about her or not?"

"Okay. But how on earth did she get into The Struggle?"

"Of course she had to go through all the stations. PPE at Cambridge, post-grad at Harvard Law School. A media course at Columbia. And then she came home. Slap bang into The Struggle. Up until then she was more or less on track. But seeing her own country after she had spent so long in the home of the brave brought out everything she had been bottling up about how Benny made fortune number one, how the system exploited the blacks, the majority. She went back to college for the politics. Did African Studies to make the point. A brilliant leader. On the barricades, with her bullhorn, marshalling student protesters. Looked like a cross between Joan Baez and Joni Mitchell. Left her cottage on the family estate, got arrested a couple of times. Moved to Old Deep. Married Rod the God. That's when I met them. One minute they were the power couple, struggle-chic. The next it was over. Zoë took it quite badly. We were closer than we are now, but she didn't tell me the whole story. She went through a crazy patch, which you'll probably hear about from other people before too long. Then she swung the other way. Abstinence. Commitment. Months on end living in the homelands on doomed development projects with a baby in tow. No nannies. Just the two of them. She had one serious relationship. He was a photographer for one of those agencies in Paris. Jordan McBride. Big name guy. Won lots of prizes. Then the story moved on and so did he. Bosnia. Afghanistan. Whatever. He had talked about getting married, moving out together, starting over in Europe. But when it came to it, he just cleared off with his flak jacket and his cameras. Zoë was devastated. But she didn't go haywire. She just worked harder. Conferences. Projects. Research papers. Then, all of a sudden, here you are, pursuing her to her bolt hole in the sun. In front of all her friends who've watched her go through all this stuff with handsome foreigners once before. So don't be too surprised if she doesn't seem too keen on your idea of play-play."

"And her daughter?"

"My, my. We are being the assiduous suitor, aren't we? Funnily enough I could never see you as a father. Too self-absorbed, I guess. The daughter – Camilla, Mills – is incredibly bright. Protects her mother like a Rottweiler, and Zoë lets her. She can't seem to let the child think anyone could be as important as her. I sometimes think Zoë lives her whole life through her when she's not at the coalface with her research and papers. The shrinks call it co-dependency."

"And you? What happened to you?"

She pulled the wine bottle from the ice bucket and poured a glass, jerkily enough to spill a few drops, the way people do when familiar constraints fall away and they drink more quickly than is good for them.

"I did keep track of you, you know, after you left. I had friends in the embassy and they told me your news: fast-track promotion to First Secretary, Cairo, Counsellor in Rome. I heard you married well. French nobility, right? Then what was it? Icarus? Daedalus? Too close to the sun? My embassy gossips told me you got to Paris as Ambassador – the full Monty for a career diplomat. Unprecedented. And so young. Right? Then something or other went wrong. White House sent in a political appointee, campaign contributor. Offered you Berlin but Madame wasn't interested. You left. She stayed. You fell off the circuit. She remarried. Oil money. Sounds a trifle harsh, Tom. Even by my standards."

"I thought we were talking about you."

"Since you ask, there was a choice and I was happy to make it. You know I was nominated for the big P – the Pulitzer – and the George Polk. And there was my book on Mandela. Two weeks on *The New York Times* bestseller list! Two weeks of fame! So I had been there, done that. I wanted a rest. I'd had it with biting my nails for a story, and nights fighting deadlines. I wanted roots where I understood things – not, before you ask, three years in this mission and four years in that and all the packing and embassy wives and reception lines. I'd had enough of hurtling around like a deranged worker bee, sipping a little nectar here, a little there. It was hive time, so to speak. Time to become the queen bee. Get a life with some fun. Travel without taking a notebook and laptop along – and Chris was offering all that. He was – is – funny, warm, loving, attentive, kind, you name it. But these guys don't come without their circle, their connections, their safety net. You marry the man – but you get the history, the tribe, the cross-references, the portfolio. For all the bridge afternoons and golf mornings and jaunts to Sotheby's and what have you, they still don't accept me completely. Some of his friends are married to real bitches – but they're our bitches, if you get my meaning, from the right kennels. Chris looks after me, and I love him for it – don't look so pained! He's very proud, not to mention jealous, possessive. He'd kill me, and you, if he knew I was here, and I am taking a big risk.

Remember that. It makes me nervous. Maybe that's why I'm talking so much, running off at the mouth. He would not understand that I'm trying to protect us both."

"From whom?"

"From you."

"He seemed very interested on the beach, with his telescope."

"I thought you might notice. He's a tad obsessive. Successful men expect things of their wives. They expect them not to let them down in front of other successful men, to talk the talk and walk the walk, whether it's wearing Dior or discussing the new Philip Roth or bidding for a Picasso or knowing the score at the Opera, so to speak. You have to decorate the homes and run the staff and amuse your guests and keep track of the diary at the same time as looking like a million bucks 24/7. It was what people like Zoë Joubert were brought up to do. Above all, you don't embarrass anybody. You don't have lovers from the past popping up and spoiling the show. As for me, well, one day I'll tell you about my learning curve, but not now, except that it was vertical. What I do want to say is that I have built all this up. I have secured it. I don't want to lose it. I don't want to lose Chris. And experience tells me that when some loose cannon starts bouncing round the decks, the best thing to do is to batten down. So, with nautical metaphors mixed, over to you. Time to sing for your supper."

She sat back and lit another cigarette. I gestured for her to pass one to me. I had not revived the habit to the extent of buying my own packs of Camels or Chesterfields, but I was happy in my new, unwired way to beg or steal. She looked surprised but lit a cigarette from her own, passing it to me with a smear of red lipstick on the filter.

I was probably more open with my reply than necessary.

I told her about the letter from Lily Nyati, about her speech at the conference in Cape Town.

I told her about Lily's insistence that the truth lay in the identity of one person who did not attend the meeting with Nyati in Port Elizabeth. I said we could be crossed off the list of suspects as we provided each other's alibi. She lit another cigarette then left it to burn and expire, leaving a long grey caterpillar of ash across a white porcelain ashtray.

She was silent for what seemed a long time. "Don't go there, Tom. Please. If anything we had ever had any meaning for you."

Her face was pale underneath its tan and her hands were clenched.

"I have to go there, Jess. I have promised Lily Nyati. I promised her once and did nothing about it and this time she's called in the bets. I have no choice. It's a question of honour. The Jess Chase I knew would understand that."

"Well, Jessica de Vere is asking you – begging you – to drop it, fly back to Washington. Anywhere. What honour? One man's vanity or an honourable history that has been written, accepted? You have no concept of what is at stake. What is it with you? The Avenging Sword? That's it, isn't it? The 5th Cavalry charging over the hill. The presumption that there's a simple, one-stop solution. Truth, democracy, the healing power of freedom? It's history, for God's sake. The TRC spelled it all out. The killer admitted it. Chapter and verse. Look at the transcripts. They're out there on the internet. Page after page after page. Cross examination by George Bizos, full disclosure. How they stopped the car, how they separated them and killed them and burned them. Where, when, how. The planning. Who gave the order. What it said. Permanent Removal from society. The accomplices. What more does Lily want? She knows what happened. You say she wants to know the name of some informer or other. How do you know there is only one? How do you know what you'll stir up? You say you are looking for the guilty man, or woman. But who's going to decide guilt or innocence? You talk as if you are judge and jury. But you're neither. You're an outsider – like you always were – trampling the grass. Now take me home. Quickly. It's late and I don't want to call the driver."

Beachy Head Drive – Millionaires' Row, as most people called it – was virtually deserted, the cars and the people locked away securely behind high, white walls. I stopped outside the house she indicated and waited as she let herself in through a heavy wooden door that looked as if it might have been imported from Tunisia or Morocco.

Before it hissed closed on hidden, hydraulic hinges, I caught a glimpse of a courtyard arranged around a pool and open area looking out over the moonlit ocean. She did not turn. I heard her heels tip-tapping across tiles.

I retraced the route, skirting Central Beach and the Beacon Isle, up the sharp rise past Cornuti's. On Main Street, the teen set was just getting into stride, the music booming, the drinks pouring with hours to go before the procession of parental SUVs and hired mini-buses arrived to gather up their rubber-kneed charges. I turned down Church Street towards the Plettenberg. As I passed the crossroads near the stone church, another vehicle – a black Range Rover – pulled out of the side street leading to the party house. Through the dark-tinted windows, I caught a faint glimpse of a profile that seemed vaguely familiar. Only when I parked my repaired rental car alongside the ranks of more august vehicles outside the hotel did I notice that my passenger had dropped her gold Cartier lighter. It was engraved: "To Jess, with enduring love, Chris."

Seventeen

THE CASE AT THE TRUTH AND Reconciliation Commission boiled down to this: to secure amnesty, Kobus Theron had to make a full and complete confession, proving that his actions in killing Solomon Nyati were inspired exclusively by the political struggle – warfare, not murder.

It was not at issue that he and his crew had killed Nyati and his comrades – Lucas Zinto, Sipiwo Ngalo, Happy Mboniswa.

But under the commission's mandate, the question to be answered was whether all four targets had been part of the insurgency against white rule in the Eastern Cape, or had one of them – a driver – been a person of no known revolutionary status, an accidental player, collateral damage.

If that death was proven to be gratuitous, amnesty would be refused. Poring over the testimony – all the more grisly for its matter-of-fact tone – there was another line of inquiry that fascinated me just as much.

In the darkest of his bloodstained dreams when – if – he relived the moments of gunfire and burned flesh, had Theron ever thought that this moment would come? Could he believe that the world had changed so much, that Captain Kobus Theron had been brought before a public tribunal, with the sound of the tumbrels rattling in his ears?

Yes, I gave the order to De Kock and the others.

Yes, I devised the means of beating and stabbing and burning.

Yes, I executed the plan, as was my duty. For I was a soldier. A soldier assassin.

In one way, Jessica de Vere had been right: the Truth and Reconciliation Commission had heard in exhaustive detail what happened on that awful night. The killer's recital was in the public domain. Why stir the bones, unearth the ghosts? But she was wrong in another way. The Commission had heard nothing to identify the traitor mentioned in Theron's testimony. The story was critically incomplete, and the prospect of a statute of limitations being imposed within days meant that it might well remain so forever.

I could not delay either. When it came to the business of getting to grips with the evidence and the personality of Theron, I had postponed and prevaricated for long enough. The deadline set on the visa page of my passport – "conference purposes only" – was fast expiring.

In Gilliomee's study – propaganda would probably be a better word – the photographs, and the not-so-subliminal message, bore some comparison to movies like *The Wild Geese* showing valiant white men on devious but fundamentally noble missions in Africa, mercenaries with hearts of gold who emerged from the battle as heroes, while the bad guys got their comeuppance. And, when the filming was over, everyone wiped off the blood and muck. Those were not the ground rules in Namibia.

The images showed Theron and his men dressed in tight-fitting camouflage shirts and shorts, accompanied by loyal, black trackers who helped them follow the spoor of their prey – insurgent nationalist guerrillas barely into their teens.

In the background, you could see large armoured vehicles, or a helicopter gunship or a troop-carrying, old Dakota airplane. On some of the vehicles, the bodies of dead insurgents had been lashed to the big front mudguards like hunting trophies.

In one photograph that fascinated me in particular, Theron kneels alone, his squad out of focus in the background, to examine an indistinct footprint. He leans on an automatic rifle painted in camouflage colours as if it were his staff. It is the dry season and the trees behind him are brittle as twigs. The ground is powdery, bleached to the whiteness of bone. He wears a forage cap, a gingery pioneer's beard obscuring his face. There is not an ounce of fat on him. He seems separated from his men by the burden of command as much as by physical space.

The caption identifies the location as Ovamboland, long before his arrival in the Eastern Cape. He is leading a "stick" of police special forces, some Namibian, some Angolan, some black, some white. They will run all day through the sparse, sandy bush, weaving between skeletal trees, shadowed by their lumbering Casspir armoured truck with its mounted .50 cal. machine gun and supplies of water and food. (When the trucks hit landmines, they sometimes ignite like beacons in the bushlands, offering conflicting messages to the combatants on each side.)

They bring their adversaries to ground. They force a firefight which they usually win, kneeling to shoot as tracer rounds ignite the dry foliage. When the fight is over, they will collect the enemy's captured weapons – Kalashnikov assault rifles, rocket-propelled grenade launchers, landmines – to be photographed and taken as booty – perhaps for use in subsequent dirty tricks manoeuvres when it is necessary to leave forensic traces of the enemy, to ascribe blame for a particular massacre or atrocity. In the firefights, the police special forces have no body armour, no protection other than their wits, their superior firepower and their ability to out-manoeuvre their foe.

They prefer agility to encumbrance. They gather up captives and prisoners, to interrogate and recycle into the fray as turncoats. If they win one skirmish, they soon have to fight another: their adversary has the numbers to replace its dead, while Theron and his men do not.

They win battles but lose wars.

Kobus Theron was born on the outskirts of Windhoek, the Namibian capital. His childhood was no different from that of other white youngsters raised at a time when racial separation seemed built to endure, when white leaders offered their followers no reason to doubt that supremacy would last, as one of them said, for a thousand years.

The habits and manners Theron grew up with were just as much part of the fabric of his life as a Yankees game for a young New Yorker or a night's clubbing at a trance party for a teenager in London. But his generations' destiny was to fight a string of hidden campaigns to maintain the protective shield enfolding their people, to guard the perimeter of privilege.

In those days, there were few points of comparison with the outside world. Television was not even introduced to South Africa until 1976 – the year, by coincidence, of the Soweto uprising.

At home as a child – I came to understand – Theron had befriended the son of the family maid who lived in a shack in the dusty backyard of his small detached home in what would have been a de facto "white" suburb, despite the presence of black menial workers in their much smaller quarters. You can imagine them, barefoot boys, Tom and Huck, indifferent to skin color, in ragged shorts and oversized khaki shirts, spindle-shanked and giggling, one tow-headed and unkempt, the other crowned with tight, dusty black curls, inventing games to play involving pebbles and dirt and arcane scores, much like children anywhere in the forgotten epoch before Play Stations and Game Boys and electronic distraction. How many times, travelling in southern Africa, did you hear that white refrain: man, I grew up with these people; I know them. And how many times did you doubt the validity of that claim to a deeper wisdom?

Youngsters like Theron – and their black playmates – soon arrived at the point where their destinies diverged. It might be in a segregated church or cemetery, or walking down a street where black people were booted from the sidewalks if they strayed onto them. It might be when laws apportioned them to different store entrances, different neighbourhoods, different schools.

Theron would learn that his young playmate was the son of a different tribe, subservient to his in the natural order. His playmate, too, would know that this was how things would proceed henceforth, unless he took steps to change it, excluded from the benefits his white friend took for granted. It is quite conceivable – although there is no record of this – that, in later years, in the bush of Ovamboland, they would take their places on different sides of the same firefight, Theron intent on preserving the life he grew up with, his playmate battling to destroy it.

The origins of Kobus Theron's commitment to counterinsurgency, his roots as a bush warrior, as a murderer, remained stubbornly hidden.

According to a faded newspaper clipping folded into Gilliomee's book, Theron's father had been the sub-manager of a small bank, cautious and deferential, with little cause to draw attention to himself. And for most of Theron's teenage years, his mother was an invalid, struggling with blackouts and surgery that sapped her strength even as he grew into his manhood.

In his teenage years, poring over the selected, filtered offerings at the small public library, he read widely about Africa of the 1960s – the beginnings of The Struggle in South Africa and the Rivonia trial that sent Mandela to prison; the upheaval in the Congo and Kenya; the decline and bloodshed that seemed to accompany Africa's freedom elsewhere on the continent; the visible involvement of the Soviets and Chinese in supporting the struggles against white domination.

Afrikaners traced their African heritage to the 17th century, when Johan Anthoniszoon – a.k.a. Jan – van Riebeeck landed at the Cape in April 1652 to establish a victualing station for the Dutch East India Company's mariners rounding Africa on their long voyage to Asia. He was just a few days shy of his 33rd birthday and was already a veteran of the company's far-flung operations. Among the tasks set for him and the followers who arrived with him aboard three ships was the building of a fort.

For Van Riebeeck's descendants, theirs was the Covenant with God that guaranteed their civilising role in Africa; and theirs was a sense of supremacy that shielded them through all their tribulations, delivering them, finally, into the highest offices of the land in 1948 to build a state defined by racial separation. In the darkness they attributed to their adopted and subjugated continent, though, their candle soon began to gutter, buffeted by what Harold MacMillan, a visiting British prime minister, called "the wind of change".

When his mother died of brain cancer, Theron was just 18 years of age, a draftee in the South African Defence Force. But his preference was for the police, actively fighting insurgents on the outermost frontiers of South Africa's stockade.

He discovered a liking for the hard life of the bush, the nights under the stars cradling an automatic rifle as the crickets fell still in the chill towards dawn. He relished the elemental battle for survival, eyes and ears alert for the crack of a snapped twig to betray an enemy's approach. But how could that explain the callousing of the soul that permitted him to devise and oversee the stabbing and incineration of Solomon Nyati?

Nowhere in his testimony at the Truth and Reconciliation Commission did Theron acknowledge any particular racial hatred, although I doubt that he would have killed whites with the same clear conscience as he killed blacks.

Perhaps, given the lessons of his childhood, given the high tensions of the bush wars in which he fought, killing on behalf of his beleaguered people might come to be seen as a mere extension of the inherited order, a holy war before the term acquired the connotations it did. And the Covenant endured.

Four times Theron was riding in Casspir armoured trucks that hit landmines and four times he survived – proving to him that the stern God who received his people's prayers had some purpose in keeping him alive.

In South Africa, he traded the camouflage fatigues for a collar and tie, or a safari suit hung from his slender, muscular frame. Squash, jogging and swims in the surf replaced the more ardous regime of Ovamboland.

In the townships of the Eastern Cape, with his unregistered weapon and his warrant card and his underlings and informers, the job held fewer perils for him, but just as many for his adversaries. The outcomes were no less lethal.

I glanced up from my reading, blinking into the light. In another world, platoons of early bathers had secured their beachheads, armed with parasols, cooler boxes, lotions, refreshments. Youngsters bobbed in their wet-suits behind the backline. Sharks, presumably, cruised below but abstained from attacks. Paradise had not changed demonstrably overnight.

The newspaper article describing Theron's voyage from bush war to urban insurgency was surprisingly detailed and well-written, clearly based on a lengthy interview in which Theron had been allowed the luxury of explaining himself. I assumed it was written before the killings of the Cooktown Four. I had also assumed that it was written by Ray Gilliomee, but, in place of a top byline there was merely a set of initials at the end of the piece: JC. Of course, many reporters shared those initials, but I knew only one: Jess Chase.

Sitting at my impromptu work station I felt a vague unsteadiness, as people do in the aftershocks of tectonic convulsions, as if many of my assumptions had suddenly become untrustworthy, unsound.

Did the initials mean that Jess Chase now qualified for inclusion on the list of suspects along with Van Rensburg, Porter, Harris and the others? How qualified was I to pursue my inquiries if her alibi lay in my boudoir? Or were those precisely the doubts that Ray Gilliomee had intended to sow by folding the newspaper article into the book he had sold to me?

The excerpt from the transcript sent by Lily Nyati said the Judas was one of the group who had been absent from the meeting itself. But what could the motives have been? Jess did not qualify technically as one of those representing the Old Deep set, but she had set up the encounter and must therefore have been familiar with its coordinates.

As far as I knew, she had no reason to wish to betray a man she had beatified in print. But – if she was indeed the author of the article – where and how had she acquired such detailed knowledge of Theron's biography? Where did that leave my suspicions about the events and the players on that fateful night in Port Elizabeth?

Riaan van Rensburg had dropped out at the last moment, according to his current wife at least. So that might mean he had gotten cold feet after meeting his contact, making his call, marking a pre-arranged wall or phone booth with white chalk, or however the tradecraft had been arranged. Alternatively, his decision might simply denote the failure of courage, as his wife had suggested – his bold lurch into direct action undermined by quavering inner voices counselling retreat.

Porter was different, a steely revolutionary, an organiser, deeply committed, who had served his time in prison and under banning orders – hardly the profile of a traitor. Except that he had not been where he said he was when the meeting took place.

And that left Rod Harris, Zoë Joubert's former husband, the poet of The Struggle. Why would he betray everything he had made his sacrifices for, unless it had all been an elaborate invention, a fiction, a mole's ploy to allow him to tunnel into the opposition? When he visited the Backlands had he really been anointed by the leaders of The Struggle, or, as so often happened, had he been turned by agents of the regime, sent back into the fray stripped of his former loyalties?

Perhaps I was looking at everything blindly, from a false perspective. What if the root cause of betrayal was not volition but coercion? What if one of my suspects had been vulnerable to pressure, blackmail, forced to provide information to protect themselves? Seen from that angle, any one of them might have been subverted, even Jess. Why else had she reacted so sharply when I told her of the mission entrusted to me by Lily Nyati?

What had Zoë Joubert said? Jess Chase knew everyone on all sides. So how deep did that knowledge go? How far had she slid into the trap of knowing too much, crossing the line between observer and player?

If she had interviewed Theron, had she been at least figuratively seduced by the soldier's magnetic absolutism, the memory of total, uncompromising violence behind the blue eyes – the very resolve her own father had so conspicuously lacked? Perhaps the betrayal had been inadvertent, a slip of the tongue, a whispered conversation betrayed by an eavesdropper, a careless lapse in the precautions she routinely took to shelter her sources.

I returned to Van Rensburg. Doggedly loyal to Zoë Joubert, why would he provide information that was almost certain to harm her great project to breach the lines of colour? If he had been coerced, how could he have not understood the implications of betraying Nyati's movements?

Surely, anyone providing information about such a prominent figure had to assume potentially terminal consequences – especially given the record of the times – Biko, Mxenge and all those who fell anonymously from the high windows of John Vorster Square police precinct in Johannesburg while "attempting to escape". Would Porter have wished that? Or Harris? Or any of them?

I wrote down the names on a page of the A4 yellow legal pad. I ticked one name – my preliminary prime suspect, but without any evidence. I placed Jessica de Vere's Cartier lighter on top of the dossier as a paperweight. It caught in the sunlight spilling through the open window. The lighter was one of the few baubles I might have afforded to purchase, had we stayed together. The rest of Chris de Vere's financial offering was way beyond my pay grade.

I turned again to the transcripts, trying to marry the dry exchanges at the Commission with memories I had coaxed from the Old Deep set.

Eighteen

ACT ONE: A DESERTED ROAD, late at night, soon after Zoë Joubert and her delegation returned enthusiastically to their hotel rooms, incandescent with excitement at their encounter, at Solomon Nyati's vindication of their Struggle, his anointment of them as freedom fighters.

Finally, they have tied the Gordian knot. They are whole, children of light emerging from the darkness. Imagine them, irrepressibly happy, determined not to discuss the encounter within earshot of the listening devices almost certainly planted in their hotel rooms, raising fingers to smiling lips, signalling silently to meet in the noise of the bar, the quiet of the parking lot, bursting with joy at their revolutionary act, celebrating, perhaps, with a spliff of cannabis or a few beers, their yearned-for admission to The Struggle.

But how ironic – pathetic, really – to think of them in light of what we know now, squinting into the rear-view mirror, looking over their shoulders, taking their half-baked security precautions when every last detail of their plans had been betrayed.

When they arrived to meet him, Nyati was waiting, ensconced at the home of a white activist, the chairs set out around the walls in a circle for their meeting. They shook hands – awkward, awed – and took their places. He asked their names and made each feel special with a remark that suggested he knew their work, in law, in protest.

I assumed that he addressed his remarks to Zoë Joubert as the natural leader, but not exclusively, his eyes roaming across the group as he praised their courage in wanting to cross the lines. The host brought in sandwiches and cold drinks – the last supper – and they spoke for 90 minutes.

What, they asked, could they do? How could they bring themselves into alignment with the revolution of the townships, but without the violence? Was there some Gandhi-esque middle road? Solomon Nyati pondered their bemusement with a light smile playing across his face, his bony fingers stroking a wispy beard. Well, you could hear him saying, it was simple enough. They should play to their strengths. No one was expecting them to throw rocks and petrol bombs.

But campus demonstrations, pro bono lawsuits, organisational work among the labour unions, setting their example among fellow whites – all that was within their remit. Newspaper articles to keep up the pressure. Peaceful demonstrations. Multi-racial structures.

Of course, there would be risks: If the security police reviled black protesters, imagine the feelings they harboured towards traitors within, whites eroding the very laager that shielded them.

He was not, Nyati said, the person to come to if they wanted to do more for the cause – intelligence work, sabotage training. He could not – would not? – help them there. For that they would need to take different routes which he was not about to divulge – by-ways that led into exile, night-time flights across the border, safe houses in Lesotho and Swaziland and Mozambique, contacts with bombers, engineers, commissars.

If they took that route – and he was not counselling them to – their skin would mark them out as potential infiltrators, spies. They would need to prove themselves. They would be given perilous tasks. They would have a hard time of it. And when the regime got wind of their involvement, as it almost inevitably would, they could expect the worst – torture, prison, maybe even assassination dressed up as a suicide, a car wreck on a distant highway.

But, if he sometimes saw them at the funerals, along with the women from Black Sash and the priests and the people, Nyati said, then he would be heartened. Perhaps, he said, they would attend his funeral. Then he laughed when their faces fell so precipitately at that unimaginable prospect.

He told them what they wanted to hear, and he knew it. And they told him what he wanted to hear – that The Struggle was broadening, that it went beyond the small settlements, the crucibles of protest, into the white homesteads, the tennis courts, the fragrant gardens.

Take the message, he told them, and tell it to your people – the business people, the cricket players, the people looking the wrong way, blinded to the truth. Make them see what their land would be and could be. Tell them we are not monsters. We do not eat your babies or rape your women. We will not burn your homes, even if you burn ours. There will be no slave revolt. We seek only peace. The armed struggle has been forced upon us and we would rather talk than shoot.

Towards the end, Nyati inquired whether there had not been more of them scheduled to see him. Down the road, Theron settles in to wait, his machine pistol – his beloved Skorpion – resting easy in his lap.

Act Two: Nyati and his comrades pile into their Honda for the return trip to Cooktown, perhaps uneasy that the young whites had not arrived in the promised numbers, but not too worried. Three of the activists in the car that night were teachers suspended from their jobs, and all of them had learned that moves were afoot to reinstate them.

The testimony laid out in the transcripts of the Truth and Reconciliation Commission made clear that the white authorities were divided, contemplating two solutions to the same problem.

One was to bring the teachers back into the fold, give them back their jobs, co-opt them into the system through promotion and status. The other was the method endorsed by the security establishment at the highest level, summed up in four words: "permanent removal from society". But, piecing together the events, what shocked me most was the dry, almost clinical recounting of meetings within the security police elite, offered as if this formal record were some kind of fig leaf over the topic under discussion: assassination by death squad.

During my diplomatic days in South Africa, I had occasionally been required to act as an embassy observer at trials in which security officers gave testimony. Their manner was usually casual, vaguely insolent, with their weight on one leg, the other cocked at a jaunty angle, hands brushing jacket pockets to ensure that the pack of Chesterfields or Lucky Strike Filters was in place, waiting faithfully for the adjournments. There was no suggestion that, one day, they would be called to book.

Theron and his men saw themselves holding the slender line, their armour confronted by those whose only power was to resist, denying themselves a life if that was the price of victory. It was a battle of force against martyrdom, with each side possessing overwhelming superiority in their chosen tactics: the authorities had the guns, their enemies had the numbers, and the ability to make the land ungovernable.

And here, at the Truth and Reconciliation Commission, was the reckoning – the too-hot hearing rooms, the notetakers, the reporters with their pens scurrying to revise the national memory, so distant from those times of racing adrenaline, banging, booming gunfire, the blaze of tires over prone bodies, framed by the arcing parabola of Molotov cocktails. This was the last battle, for exculpation, closure: confession as a tool of escape.

Theron: *"Colonel Van der Merwe summoned me to his office and told me that the situation at that stage had become so critical that there was only one way in which to try and stabilise these areas, and that was by means of the elimination of Mr Solomon Nyati and his closest colleagues."*
Question: *"You have already referred to the situation which existed. What exactly was the situation at the time?"*
Theron: *"As I have said, we spoke again to Colonel Van der Merwe about the situation. He informed us that final permission to proceed with the elimination operation had been received from Colonel Snyman, who was the Commanding Officer.*

Myself and Colonel Du Plessis, or the then Mr Du Plessis, went to Colonel Snyman's office where a submission was made to Colonel Snyman by Colonel Du Plessis about the situation. This was no news to Colonel Snyman and he then stated that he agreed with us and I think his words were that we should do what would be in the best interest of the country."

Question: *"Thank you. Colonel Snyman tells you that you should do what is in the best interest of the country, what happens then? How did you understand or interpret this when he told you to do what would be in the best interest of the country?"*

Theron: *"I understood it that it would be final approval for the procedure of the elimination."*

Imagine them at police headquarters in the Eastern Cape. They check in for work, drinking sweet tea and instant coffee in the canteen, smoking in a collegial way. They go through the cables, the traffic.

Sometimes, they arrange a meet with an informer; perhaps take a call on a secure line. They read the transcripts from the interrogation centres, the phone taps, the bugs. They pore over their files, using typed flimsies to fill out their picture of who went where, who said what, who slept with whom, who plotted to overthrow the government. They authorise informers' payments, perhaps creaming off a little for themselves. They report on progress in recruiting a double agent, a mole, turning a treacherous ANC guerrilla back into The Struggle in their own cause as a thug, an interrogator, a fall guy for their conspiracies.

They send their recommendations to a higher level and await a reply through the appropriate channels. They draw weapons and sign for unmarked cars and drive to remote townships – Cooktown, Cradock, Cookhouse – and burst into small houses at 3:00 am and drag people away to be beaten mercilessly, offered a choice between informing or incarceration. And at some stage, they receive the orders they know they will receive from the way they framed their "evidence". Elimination. Permanent Removal. Best interests of the country.

Theron: *"Mr Chairman, at that stage we knew all the suspects and political activists in the Eastern Cape quite well.*

At that stage I had returned from a border duty in Ovamboland, not too long back and I was fairly aware of the activities in the Eastern Cape.

I would like to explain further. As a result of my conversation with

Major Du Plessis at the time, I gave very intensive attention to these activities, specifically in respect of Mr Nyati and the people whom he had contact with especially in the rural areas as well as in Port Elizabeth.

During this time, a considerable number of names of suspects or people came to the fore, it included the names of the four deceased and these names came from various parts of the Eastern Cape.

After having familiarised myself with the most effective of these activists, in other words, the activists who posed the biggest problems and threats for us in the sense that they were responsible according to our information for the destabilisation and chaos in these areas, I spoke to Major Du Plessis again."

And then, it becomes an operational matter, a question of practicalities, technique, cover stories, planning.

Theron: *"The commanders proposed or gave the order that the attack should appear as if it was a vigilante attack, black-on-black. In other words we should use sharp objects to eliminate the individuals and that we should burn their bodies with petrol."*
Question: *"That would be the method that would be followed. Did you then begin to investigate the 'how' component of the operation?"*
Theron: *"That is correct. We felt that with our information that we had at our disposal, the best method would be to place them in a deserted road. They moved around a lot. Because of their activities, they were often travelling. Otherwise, it would be impossible to eliminate them in a concealed fashion."*

And remember. These cool, calculating words, these practical, professional debates – akin, perhaps, to a judge contemplating a thorny point of law, or a plumber discussing a blocked pipe – were conducted at public hearings of the Commission, in the presence of Lily Nyati and the other widows of the Cooktown Four. While the lawyers and the ex-policemen considered these technicalities, the women sat and listened with their eyes welling and their hearts entombed.

And the timing?

Question: *"I think we were last at the point where you had begun planning the method of the operation. Your aim was to intercept the individuals on the road. The where and the when, could that have been included in the planning at that stage? We have the how, but now we need the date and the place? At that stage, would that have been included in the planning or would that have happened on an ad hoc basis?"*

Theron: *"That would have occurred on an ad hoc basis if the opportunity presented itself."*

Question: *"So you have mentioned that the activities of these individuals had been monitored intensely in order to collect information regarding a proposed conference in Port Elizabeth. Could you expand?"*

Theron: *"That is correct Mr Chairperson. Information was received that a number of activists would be in Port Elizabeth. This was confirmed on the day that they were actually in Port Elizabeth for a conference or a meeting. The persons who were with Mr Nyati were identified by means of informers during the day. The informers — the main informer – was not in the meeting group. And I reported to Mr Du Plessis that that evening we would make an attempt or investigate the possibility of undertaking the operation."*

Entr'acte. On the eve of the funeral, we are sitting with the widows, Jess and I, and they are wrapped in their blankets, guessing at what might have happened to their husbands, suspecting the police but not certain, carried along willy-nilly by the preparations for the burial – the visitors, the planning, the provision of food, the arrangements for public sanitation, the songs and marches, the secret emissaries from the Backlands moving like shadows between the small neat homes.

The women must nurse the children, too, the infants. Like Celiwe Nyati, sitting in her mother's lap as we visit, bewildered, wide-eyed, unsure what all the fuss is about, asking when her father will come home to explain it all, to make it all right.

With the crowds assembling, the buses disgorging the comrades from the Transvaal and the far north, from Cape Town and Mpumalanga, we are all caught in the huge, powerful stream whose source sprang forth so long ago in these same lands in the Eastern Cape and is now broadening and widening, gathering power from tributaries and storms and waterfalls as it hurries onwards, ever onwards – a Nile, a Zambezi, a Congo – towards the white-crested ocean we know to be liberation, freedom.

But we cannot begin to imagine that, one day, after the moment of triumph, the enemies will be offered a chance to redeem themselves, to tell their stories truthfully and to convince the world that they acted as soldiers in a political struggle.

For this is what Theron is doing in these transcripts. He is fighting still to prove that he is a solider, a combatant, not a murderer. And the widows must hear it, sitting in the hearing room in Port Elizabeth, long years after their husbands died, the events reborn, conjured from the words of the man who killed them, who recruited other men to help him, who instructed them.

The first death. Nyati himself. Already dead.

Theron: *"They all stabbed the corpse using knives. They then took petrol from my vehicle, it was in a petrol can, they poured it over the body and set it alight. From there we drove back to the point in the Crystal Sands area where Nieuwoudt and De Kock were waiting with the other three activists.*
We were driving in that wooded area and we then got the second one to get out of the car. One of the black members then hit him with a rubber truncheon over the neck or on the neck or head and the two black members then stabbed him with knives whilst he was lying on the ground."

Then this:

"We then left the corpse there and returned to where Mr Nieuwoudt and Mr De Kock were waiting with the other two activists. Sergeant De Kock and some of the black members then took one of the activists

and they walked away from me with him. When De Kock came back he reported to me that he had knocked the activist unconscious and that the black members then stabbed him to death."

And then:

"When Sergeant Faku took the petrol from me, they then told me that they could not get the cuffs off the body and that they had to remove his one hand to get the cuffs off. They then poured petrol over the body and in a short radio broadcast to Lieutenant Nieuwoudt I told Nieuwoudt that they should set alight the other corpses and they did that and we then left."

"They had to remove his one hand." I read the line again and shuddered. Something else struck me.

Faku. Nieuwoudt. Surely not uncommon names in those areas at that time, not uncommon for black and white men to work side by side against the anti-apartheid forces. And, perhaps these days, to oversee the airport immigration lines. "Conference Purposes Only."

The bureaucratic loose ends:

And then I returned to the office where I arrived at about seven and I reported to Mr Du Plessis that the operation was concluded and Mr Du Plessis and I went to Colonel Snyman's office and we reported to him that the operation was concluded.

I riffled through the transcript, skipping pages, to look for the final ruling on Kobus Theron's application for amnesty.

"In the result we are not satisfied that the applicant has complied with the requirements of the Act. Consequently the application for amnesty in respect of the murders is REFUSED."

So where was he now, this security branch policeman who was perhaps the only person who knew definitively about the informants, the moles, the Judas of the Old Deep set? He had admitted – in the most gruesome detail – a truly appalling suite of murders.

Yet there was no record of a trial. He was, as far as I could understand, a free man, one of those who would benefit from the proposed statute of limitations to avoid prosecution. He had lived and worked and – for all I knew – retired in the Eastern Cape, in these lands that stretched from the ocean to the arid interior.

But where?

I flicked again through the sheaf of testimony in case there was some record of a law company representing Theron, or even an address for him. Instead, two familiar names leaped from the jumble of confession and cross-examination, the long, labourious and exhaustive record of the proceedings.

It was a passage I had not noticed in my earlier perusal of the transcript and I went over it again to be sure I had understood what it said, that I had not misread it. The paragraph came in a lengthy exposition by state investigators of the broader political context of the Nyati killing and the factors taken into account by the security police as they weighed their decision to order his "permanent removal".

Advocate: *"I present as evidence a document that was drawn up by the security police on the basis of their surveillance at the time when the authorities were preoccupied with Mr Nyati, and wished to know the nature and identity of those consorting with him. In the period immediately before his death, his visitors included the following persons: Miss Jessica Chase, Mr Thomas Kinzer ..."*

Nineteen

I LEFT THE PAGES OF PRINTOUT AND legal pad jottings in a concertina folder of black cardboard, tucked away in an unlocked drawer in the antique dresser of my hotel suite. The only document I took with me was the article from Gilliomee's book. Looking back, it is clear to me that I should have used the small safe in the closet, but hindsight is always the wisest counsellor.

A breeze, softening the heat, carried the sounds of surf and ocean. Men and women, families and children, strolled past the hotel towards the beach, ignoring the signs that warned them to beware.

The TRC transcripts had embedded a procession of images in my mind – truncheon on bone, knives slicing into flesh, drawing a sluggish flow of venous crimson or spurt of arterial scarlet, evidence of what outsiders like to depict as Africa's atavistic violence.

But was this place so much worse than others? Were its battles all the more bloody for being black on white, white on black? In numbers, wars fought by Europeans and Americans and Japanese far exceeded Africa's tallies, including the worst genocides of the Great Lakes.

Twenty million Soviets! Six million Jews! Whole cities razed with remote technological precision; epic battles of artillery and airpower. The World Wars, 1914–1918 and 1939–45 – so enormous that we comprehend them only by reference to heroes and symbols: plucky British Spitfire pilots over southern England, Soviet snipers at Stalingrad, GI Joe pushing doughtily across Europe and Asia, raising the Stars and Stripes at Iwo Jima, just as Comrade Sergei lofted the Red Banner over the ruined Reichstag in Berlin. But our heroes cannot explain to us the emaciated victims of Dachau and Auschwitz, the mushroom cloud over Hiroshima, the ash of Dresden, the rash of brutal camps stretching from the Kwai River to the Soviet Gulag.

Then, take these African wars in faraway places, in thatched villages without phone lines or electric power or pumped water where the soldiers are always the first to arrive and the last to die.

The white security officers like Theron and De Kock who had flooded the Eastern Cape in the mid-1980s had merely moved on, transferring their war to a newer theatre among factories, highways, airports, fastfood outlets. So who could be surprised at its outcome?

I drove my re-shod rental car, as arranged, around the corner from the Plettenberg Hotel to Zoë Joubert's villa with its creaking deck and grand, sweeping view over the bay. As I ran up the steps to the front door, she was already leaving the house, dressed this time in white linen slacks and a tailored yellow top that showed off her sleek, tanned lines but hid the scar on her shoulder.

For the first time since our first meeting in Cape Town, I noticed jewellery, a thick gold chain and pearl earrings, and make-up on her eyelashes and lips. No rings, though. Her hair was held back in a lacquered, oriental clasp, stressing the haughty rise of her forehead and high cheekbones. Her eyes sparkled and she offered me a kiss on both cheeks as we met. There was no sign of her daughter.

My own marriage had been without children. Various physicians had examined us both, finding no particular biological hindrance. Yet conception had eluded us. And when our sacred vows crumbled in Paris, when the futility of questing for compatibility overwhelmed us both, it had been a relief to exclude issues such as custody and weekend visiting rights from the attentions of the lawyers.

But childlessness breeds its own primness. When friends came to visit with their boisterous broods, it must have been obvious that I had placed cherished ornaments far from view. They caught my quick glances as a child wobbled, holding a glass of cola like baptismal fluid over a pale carpet, or experimented in re-organising the elaborate jade solitaire I had acquired by long haggling in a Cairene souk. Children seemed drawn to delicate china, sharp Yemeni daggers, square-cornered, glass coffee tables that collided with toddlers' delicate heads. They left open refrigerator doors and tripped on antique kilims. They jammed videos in video players and re-entered the house from the garden having dipped their sneakered feet into the only un-scooped canine deposit in miles.

In Washington, I had begun to live like a monk, or a prisoner, obsessed with the neatness of his cell. A monk with a navy blue Jaguar Roadster gathering dust, and no one to invite for a spin.

I had little preparation, thus, for the demands and duties of the rambunctious extended families I confronted in Plettenberg Bay: the kids need a ride to/from the disco/the waterslide/the monkey park/the tennis courts/the white-water rafting place/the bungee-jumping station on the Storms River canyon; the kids have gotten lost at the beach party or been stung by jellyfish or want to dig holes and build castles in the sand. The kids – how I hated that word with its reminder of goats – were out getting pizza. The kids had gotten drunk/stoned. Again!

I did not see myself as a potential soccer pop, giving up my free time to ferry young teenagers from appointment to appointment, from sports field, to debating society to sleepover to party. I could barely imagine myself in the role of the fretful, 3:00 am parent, reaching for the phone to inquire as to a child's whereabouts, haunted by the recurring nightmares of doom and disaster that stalk the custodians of the young. Was it too late to change, or was I thinking way too far ahead?

Without any attempt at persuasion from Zoë Joubert, I had begun to toy with a different way of looking at the relationship that might be within my grasp. Instead of seeing a child in terms of self-sacrifice, should I not be thinking that a surrogate daughter would enrich my life, bring pride and love, force open the trap door of my hermit cell to let in a little sunlight, a little life?

"Is your daughter not joining us? I hope it's not because of me."

"I know you find Mills a bit a difficult. She has grown up with me, you see. I guess you would call her territorial. Most of the time, it's not an issue. When it's just the two of us, or we are with old friends, there is no hassle. Newcomers are something else."

I nodded my acknowledgement. She was saying: I come with conditions attached: they are not negotiable.

"I suppose part of it is my fault. We are very close. I have always tried to bring out her brightness. Nurture her. Make sure she goes to the best schools, excels. She plays the cello in the orchestra and is school tennis champion. At 13, dammit. But I seem to have paid less attention to preparing her for sharing me."

I pulled up outside the De Veres' vacation home.

"Been here before?" Zoë Joubert asked.

"No. Why?"

"I just wondered how you knew the address."

"Tradecraft?" I laughed.

I realised I had left Jessica de Vere's gold lighter at the hotel. I could hardly turn back, still less explain why I might need to.

In a garage I thought I saw the outlines of a silver sports car and a darker, larger vehicle, an SUV or some such. The big double door where I had last seen Jessica de Vere was ajar. Zoë Joubert led the way with the ease of familiarity.

"Be prepared for House & Garden meets Conde Nast Traveller." She squeezed my hand then went on ahead as if we were not much more than strangers.

The house was in a different league from Zoë's rented villa. The reference to glossy magazines was an understatement. The place was immaculate, as if in a permanent state of readiness to welcome the most demanding of guests. You could not imagine a newspaper left to flap in the breeze or a rogue tennis shoe left to peek from beneath a sun-lounger. I was aware of tiled steps and walls of white offset with blue shutters.

The house had nine bedrooms and an equal number of en suite bathrooms, their proportions disguised by the same architectural cleverness you see in those labyrinthine rock dwellings in Yemen or Turkey.

An inner courtyard had been designed around a small pool with its mandatory Kreepy Krauly cleaning device. Beside the pool, to the right, a long table had been set for 10 people close to a huge hatch leading into a kitchen where an indeterminate number of people busied themselves around hobs and surfaces of polished steel. Whoever had designed the house had done so with perfect taste.

Zoë Joubert led the way to an arched, indoor seating area that gave way through wide-open, glass doors to a shaded veranda with white, cane furniture covered in pastel-blue cushions. Beyond, a triangle of emerald kikuyu grass jutted over the *fynbos* like the prow of some mighty ocean-going vessel: on its tripod, a powerful telescope pointed seaward.

I could understand why Jessica de Vere might not want any of it jeopardised.

Christian – Chris – de Vere leaped up from his guests and embraced Zoë. His wife approached me with an outstretched hand.

"Chris. Did you meet Ambassador Kinzer?"

"I gather you spent some time here a few years back." Chris de Vere had one of those practised, personal trainer handshakes designed to break bones. "Can't say I recall meeting you."

"Different circles," I said. "I remember your wife, though."

Jess shot me a quick look of refrigerated caution.

"We used to read her articles at the embassy to find out what was really going on." I offered the remark with a flatterer's easy smile.

"Well, Ambassador. It was all a while back. Different times. Different country. We're the rainbow nation now. And a great relief it is, too."

He introduced me to our fellow lunch guests – a South African entrepreneur who had survived the liberation struggle as a downtrodden labour leader, and a titled couple from an indistinct European royal house, immaculately groomed and coiffed – he in a summer-weight double-breasted blazer in navy blue with white, Sulka shirt and a silk cravat, and she in a two-piece hound's tooth suit whose skirt stretched over thighs of pneumatic plumpness.

There was no suggestion in the lines of their attire of anything so crass as a wallet or cell phone. The true sign of wealth, some people say, is never to be seen carrying cash or chattels. The gift of royalty is the unshakeable belief that someone else will always pay.

Another couple I vaguely recognised from the gossip sheets came from the entertainment world – a woman who had starred in movies that once drew crowds but whose name now floated on the soft-focus fringes of memory; a man who had staged award-winning shows on Broadway and in London's West End.

She was dressed – labelled might be a better word – in a cascade of Escada and Dior that offset tanned skin and determinedly blonde hair. He wore a matching shirt and slacks in pastel blue, Cartier sunglasses and white loafers from Fratelli Rossetti. The softness of his handshake reminded me of a pale glove in fine Italian leather, adorned with a golden ring that would not have looked out of place among Tutankhamun's funeral offerings. His watch was one of those Piaget objects designed to resemble a sovereign but costing so much more than any simple coin or timepiece. Their conversational references presumed a certain familiarity with yachts and mansions.

Was this where the wild and cynical Jess Chase now belonged as Jessica de Vere? She glanced in my direction and I fancied she knew exactly what I was thinking.

Clad in a green golfing shirt and broadly checked trousers, Dube, the entrepreneur, had a look of sleek well-being. In his earlier days, on the barricades, he had been a lean, revolutionary figure, his head shaven and his rhetoric powerful. Even now, there was barely a hint of spread around the waist. And the watchfulness around his eyes had not left him.

The royal couple had recently made the headlines when they were allowed to return to their Slavic homeland for the first time since the communists turfed out their family after the Second World War. With her reporter's instincts, Jessica asked them how well they had been received on their first visit – an event that had been chronicled in the news magazines with much attention to the vast crowds lining the streets and the general enthusiasm and the cavalcade entering the royal palace.

"Then at the end of it," the prince said, "when all the courtiers had retired and everyone had gone for the day, we were alone together in the royal palace for the first time anyone from our family had been there in 50 years."

"And we couldn't find the kitchen!" the princess chimed in with perfect timing.

"And it turned out to be exactly 78 yards away," the Prince said, glancing around the gathering to ensure he had full attention for the punchline. "And through a tunnel so that you couldn't smell the cooking!"

I could no more imagine them looking seriously for a kitchen than I could envisage them knowing how to boil an egg.

Watching Jessica de Vere move so fluidly and reassuringly among her guests, I felt a rare hankering for what might have been. Her graciousness made it all the easier to imagine her in the role of a diplomatic hostess, flattering ministers and power brokers in gilded salons, with her devoted spouse – the Ambassador Extraordinary and Plenipotentiary – at her side: the power duo of the diplomatic circuit.

She had come a long way from the wrong side of the tracks in the Backlands. I wondered how much of her story she had told Chris de Vere. He would surely have recognised the blend of artifice, ambition and opportunity that had propelled her on her way, if only from his own ancestry.

In the mid-19th century, the founder of the De Vere clan – initially known as Jack Bramford, a poacher and brawler – had fled his home in the county of Hampshire in England. He was one quick step ahead of the constabulary investigating a jewel theft from a large mansion on the banks of the River Test during which a member of the domestic staff had been sexually assaulted.

Bramford had taken ship from Southampton, South Africa-bound, his first-class passage paid by his loot, with a sizeable amount locked in his steamer trunk to stake his future. He embarked as Bramford but disembarked in Cape Town as Michael de Vere – inspired by the name of his Hampshire village, Micheldever.

The official biography – the kind you found in sleek corporate brochures – made no reference to those episodes. The family myth – the early stake in the diamond mines, the partnership with Rhodes, the establishment of Anglo Vere Mining Corporation – had been written and circulated as if Michael de Vere stepped ashore fully formed as a member of some new aristocracy. Honoré de Balzac once said that every great fortune hid a great crime. It was never clear to me whether the De Veres' discomfort at their history related to the truth of this statement – or the tawdriness of Jack Bramford's particular crime.

Now, the De Veres had constructed a more cultured legend – the art collection at the family seat on 25 acres of prime real estate in Johannesburg, the apartments in Paris and New York, the sponsorships at the MOMA and the Musée d'Orsay.

Chris de Vere himself had been one of the very smart, very few businessmen to see the great transformation that was to come, making the mental leap into pole position for the race to riches in the new South Africa. He spoke out against apartheid before it became the vogue to do so. He met in secret with Oliver Tambo and Thabo Mbeki even as the government sought to outlaw any contacts with them.

"If we hold onto everything now, we will lose everything," he had famously proclaimed. "The moral imperative is clearly in favour of change. The global mood urges change. And I implore you, as citizens and business representatives, to consider this one single argument if no other: without change we remain locked in a single, shrinking market at the tip of Africa that has become too small for all of us; political change is the key to a much greater market, both at home and abroad, that will be to the benefit of all in this great nation of ours."

Jessica de Vere moved in a world quite remote from anything I might ever have offered her. The official residences I had enjoyed – including, briefly, in Paris – might have seemed spectacular at the time with their art collections and tapestries and long, dark banqueting tables. But they were all on loan from Uncle Sam, debts that would be – and, indeed, were – called in abruptly at Washington's whim.

Chris de Vere and his wife stood four-square on the more solid ground of title deeds and ownership in a world that bore no relation to the circumstances of most of the planet. Jess presided over it as if she had never known any other way.

No one around her table felt anything but flattered by her attentions, her memory of their children's names and greatest triumphs, her ability to debate political initiatives or the latest off-Broadway hit with the same ease as she might recommend a masseuse or a tennis coach. How could she not be admired, coveted, cherished? It seemed inconceivable to me that De Vere would not have had Kroll or some other high-ticket investigator trace the timelines and cross-references of her past before he committed a portion of the family fortune to her pre-nuptial ambitions. But, knowing his own history, he would doubtless have concluded that great bloodlines sometimes need a roguish gene to flourish.

Chris ran the occassion with easy authority, ensuring that those meant to feel relaxed did so as he tended to their wishes for pre-lunch drinks – beer for the entrepreneur, who barely sipped it, Punt e Mes for the prince, white wine for the rest of us. In navy blue slacks and matching silk blouse that offset the dark tan of her skin and her lustrous black hair, his wife appeared from the kitchen escorting a black maid in pale-blue gingham uniform carrying a huge platter of fresh oysters on ice.

I took the opportunity to stroll out onto the lawn, pausing to peer through the telescope. It did not surprise me to find it focused on the same area of beach where we had picnicked a day earlier.

"That was not too smart – knew your wife, read her articles et cetera." She spoke quietly through a cocktail-circuit smile I found hard to recognise from our earlier days. "He knows a lot. He doesn't know about us. For reasons I will leave to your imagination, let's keep it that way."

"I wanted to tell you something. About the meeting with Nyati. It seems the authorities knew."

"They knew? Of course they knew. How could you be so naïve as to imagine they would not know? Getting cold feet? Please say you have had second thoughts and we can all get on with our lives."

"I'm not cutting and running." I had lowered my voice in a way that made me sound like a conspirator.

"Because Americans don't? "

"Because this American won't."

She rolled her eyes.

"Can't you drop this this witch-hunt? Please." She, too, was speaking in little more than a whisper.

I took the clipping of her Theron interview from a pocket and unfolded it.

"Did you write this?"

She glanced at it and nodded.

"Did you meet him?"

"I was not in the habit of making up quotes. Who gave you this?"

"I'll ask the questions, please. Did you stay in touch with him?"

"Possibly."

"Do you know where he is, for Chrissakes?"

"Maybe."

"Maybe? What kind of an answer is maybe?"

"Maybe the only kind you are going to get if you go on bullying." I took a deep breath.

"I need to meet him now. I need to go to the source. The one person who knows. Kobus Theron. The killer. He set it all up. The whole thing. And you knew he set it up. Goddam it, Jess, you interviewed him and never told me."

"There were plenty of things I couldn't tell you."

"Couldn't or wouldn't?"

"However you want to phrase it. Dammit, Tom. Have you forgotten what was at stake? You were America. You were the embassy. I had to play my cards close."

"Please, Jess. An address. A cell phone. An e-mail for Theron. His lawyer. One call and I'm out of here. I'll even give you your lighter back and not tell your husband where you left it."

She glanced over my shoulder and took a step away from me.

"Monopolising the hostess! How very undiplomatic! Still. I should be used to it." Chris de Vere had approached almost stealthily. Now, he looped a proprietorial arm around his wife. She smiled, bright and loving.

"Five minutes à table." She pronounced the last words in the French way and headed back across the lawn. Zoë Joubert rose to meet her and said something that drew laughter. De Vere followed my gaze. His eyes flickered between the two women.

"So you knew Jess back then. Zoë, too?" His voice was harsher now, the boss-man in him elbowing aside the host.

"Not at all, in fact. My job was press, so, of course, you had to be aware of the star reporter in town."

"And that was it?"

"That was what?"

"You know what I'm saying, Mr Ambassador."

"I don't think I do."

"I'm asking a simple question. I know a lot about relationships. I have had many. Once a man and a woman have slept together they maintain a certain claim on one another."

"And you want to know if I have a claim on your wife? For what it's worth, the answer is no. If it makes you feel any better."

"Lunch everybody," he said, tuning back to his guests.

Twenty

I WAS SEATED ACROSS FROM Strikes Dube and next to Princess Irena in her squirmy mini skirt. We ate in a companionable cocoon spun by our host and hostess with questions and anecdotes. Children? How many? Teenagers? What can you do with them? Join the SKI club! Spend the Kid's Inheritance! Laughter at the very thought that anyone in this charmed circle would do anything so un-dynastic.

"Strikes," the princess said. "That is an interesting name."

"A nickname," the entrepreneur said.

"Nom de guerre, more like!" Chris de Vere interjected with a snort of laughter.

Dube's baptismal first name, it turned out, was Gabriel but he took his more familiar nickname from the weapon he once deployed frequently as a labour union negotiator against the mining magnates like Chris de Vere, calling out thousands of workers to support pay claims and political strategies.

His association with his former adversary had made Strikes Dube extremely rich extremely quickly, opening the doors to the BMW dealership and the realtor's offerings of galleried mansions and en suite bathrooms.

He took easily to the designer loafers and gold watches and fine whiskies of his new persona: his humidor contained nothing less than Davidoff and his cellar was filled with the finest vintages. Even in the old days, I seemed to recall, he had a reputation for ordering old single malts by the double when others were paying. Now he could afford entire distilleries if he so chose.

Solomon Nyati had died fighting for the country in which this had all become possible, but I had my doubts whether he would have approved some of the material by-products of The Struggle while so many remained jobless and hungry.

"You talk of our tribalism, but you too are tribalist," Strikes Dube was saying. "Look here. At this table. You have a De Vere and a Joubert. English and Huguenot."

Zoë blushed and De Vere came to her rescue.

"Strikes, I am ashamed of you," he said with a complicit grin. "Zoë may have a Huguenot surname, but she is, as we all know, detribalised. And as for myself, my Englishness was absorbed by history a long time ago. I am as much an African as you are!"

"So you know how it is to live without shoes?"

De Vere shot his lower leg from the cuff of his trousers to reveal loafers over tanned skin.

"Without socks, even!"

"Chris, you are impossible," Zoë said.

"Blame Strikes. He started it."

"That's what you always said in the old days, too."

"And what is it you are doing here, Ambassador?" The Princess said.

"Well, a bit more than I figured," I said. "I came here for a conference and now I'm staying on for some other reasons."

Jessica de Vere and Zoë Joubert both looked at me sharply.

"You know," I went on, as casually as I could, "I was here many years ago and one of the people I met was a guy called Solomon Nyati. You remember him, Mr Dube?"

Strikes Dube was midway through lighting a cigar, making a show of the platinum cutter and long matches that ignited a perfect circle of fine tobacco.

"And I figured I would just look up his widow and a few other folks because I guess there's a lot of unfinished business from way back then. Loose ends. Maybe even guilty consciences."

It may have been the heavy smoke from the Davidoff cigar, but Strikes Dube began to cough and his wife, Pumla, glanced quickly at a dainty Rolex. "My goodness. Is that the time?"

"Nyati?" the Prince interjected. "Wasn't he some kind of terrorist?"

"Freedom fighter," I replied. "Fought against entrenched privilege, that kind of thing."

"Now I've heard everything," Chis de Vere said, making it sound like a joke. "A diplomat with a conscience."

"Former," Jessica de Vere said when the laughter subsided. "A former diplomat. Right, Tom?"

As the lunch guests offered their farewells, the big double-doors leading to the street opened and Mills and a boy in his early teens entered, clutching tennis rackets, their white shoes stained with the rust-brown dust of a clay court.

"Tom, meet my son Charlie," Jessica de Vere said.

A son!

Somehow I had never thought of her having children. The boy looked at her, as if inquiring whether he was expected to know me.

"Charlie, Tom's an old friend. A diplomat."

"Oh, right," the boy said. "Mills has been talking about you."

It was easy to guess what she had been saying.

"Hi, Charlie. Who won?" Chris de Vere interrupted.

"We didn't keep score, did we Charlie? Just a knockabout," said Mills.

Jess Chase had moved behind her son so that she could rest her hands on his slender, somewhat drooped shoulders. The boy had his father's blonde hair, flopping across his vision in a long fringe, crimped where a sweatband had held it in place.

"Just a knockabout?" Chris de Vere said. "No such thing, is there Strikes? Only winners and losers. That's how life works, boy, and don't you forget it."

"Well, actually, Charlie won, but he's too much of a gentleman to say so," Camilla Joubert said. She moved towards her mother and their hands joined together.

"Ready, Mama?" she said.

Zoë had told me that she and a small group of her friends planned to undertake an expedition on foot across the gap at the base of the Robberg Peninsula and on to the rocky point where, finally, the last of the land fell away into the Indian Ocean. She would be accompanied by her daughter. Riaan van Rensburg would act as guide and protector. Who else?

As I made my farewells, Jess Chase shook my hand and palmed a scrap of paper into it.

She was waiting in the public area below the stairs of the Blue Wing, where my suite was located.

Vanessa van Rensburg beckoned to me to join her on a sofa in the entrance hall beneath a huge, marine-themed oil painting in blues and greens. I sat next to her. Playing by the rules of some arcane game of her own devising, she placed a hand on my knee. By my Victorian version of the same game, I removed it.

She was wearing an opaque orange sarong and – as far as I could see – only an opaque orange sarong. The rim of her left nostril was very lightly powdered in white.

"It's about Riaan. But not the way you think. He has gone into some kind of rage about you. He thinks you are out to destroy us all, the Old Deep set. He thinks he knows why. He says you have been asking too many questions."

"I'm sorry he feels that way. It's not true."

"He feels that way because he's vulnerable."

"In what sense?"

"In the sense that his contacts, back then, in the old days, were not what they should have been. A lot of people were taken in. They were complicated times. Sometimes you couldn't tell friend from foe."

"I'm not sure you want to be telling me this. I'm not some kind of prosecutor. I'm just an ex-ambassador with an interest in history. No more. No less."

"Bullshit!" Her anger flushed her cheeks crimson. "You come here out of nowhere. Nobody knows who you are and suddenly you are everybody's friend. Don't think I wasn't listening to you wheedling away with Ferd and Porter and the rest on the beach. You even caught me: who went to the meeting? Who didn't? Why is that fucking meeting so fucking important? Why is it so important whether Riaan was there or not? Are you from the CIA or something?"

Vanessa van Rensburg used a corner of her sarong to wipe a slight dampness from her eyes. She took a deep breath.

"I want to tell you something to change your mind. So that you stop asking all your questions and leave us alone. Perhaps when you have heard what I have to say you will understand how dangerous all this is. The only reason I am telling you this is to try to head off a huge mess that none of us will recover from. Do you want to hear it?"

"Yes."

"Off the record?"

"I can't guarantee that. But I will try. You have my word."

"You have heard of Spencer Guillaume?"

I had indeed. Spencer Guillaume had been the security police's secret weapon, a top-drawer operative with tentacles that spread through an empire of informers and double agents, turncoat guerrillas and naïve patsies. Guillaume's cover had been to portray himself as an enemy of the system, a friend of The Struggle. Once he had won trust, he used it to burrow into networks of anti-apartheid campaigners, tunnelling away under their foundations until the edifice collapsed

"Riaan knew Guillaume?"

"He didn't know who he was or what he did. He thought Guillaume was his friend. They drank together. He told him things. Not big things, just stupid things. Who was with whom. What people thought about this and that. Small things. No state secrets. Just gossip. But he never realised who he was talking to."

"Why are you telling me this?"

"Because Riaan thinks you know already and will unmask him."

"How could I unmask him?"

"It's not general knowledge."

"Meaning?"

"He thinks Zoë doesn't know."

"And that's important?"

"I sometimes think that is all that is important to my husband."

"Well. Let me ask you something. Do you think this acquaintanceship with Guillaume played any part at all in his decision not to meet with Nyati that night?"

"Tom, that's a question I have often asked myself. I don't know. I wish I did. But if you find an answer, you understand, don't you, how destructive that could be? After all these years. Very few of us, from Old Deep, have left the circle or introduced new members into it. All we have is each other. We go on vacation together, like now. We have parties. We phone. We e-mail. We marry. Our children know each other. Old Deep is our point of departure. It's our guarantee that we can trust one another. Like a cabal. A secret society. A lodge. We measure ourselves against what we were then and we are proud of what we have become. We have our alpha males and our not-so-alpha males, our den mothers, our courtesans. We make allowances for each other, those of us who made it this far. Some died. Some survived. And the survivors have built their lives on those same friendships they formed in The Struggle. On each other. But, right down at the bottom of it, we have our rules, our beliefs, our faith, if you like, that we all in one way or another held the line. To discover now that one of us …"

One day earlier, her disclosure would have seemed like a clincher. Riaan van Rensburg had been one of the principle suspects. His wife's confession would have confirmed his position at the top of the list.

But as I hurried to my suite, up the curving sweep of the staircase two steps at a bound, along the long corridor covered in a chic, rough weave of sand-coloured seagrass carpeting, I was thinking only of the scribbled address Jessica de Vere had given me.

Kobus Theron. Fifth Street. Nature's Valley.

Nature's Valley was another, far less glitzy vacation resort no more than a 20-minute drive along the coast, a hideaway amid indigenous forests favoured by Afrikaner vacationers reliving their pioneering days in darkly shaded log cabins. Kobus Theron, the self-confessed murderer of Solomon Nyati, was the architect of the entire conspiracy at Crystal Sands, and with him lay the answers to Lily Nyati's questions.

I entered the suite and hurried to retrieve the black concertina file from the antique dresser. At first glance it looked undisturbed, exactly as I had left it. But as I spread its folders open to again go over Theron's testimony at the Truth and Reconciliation Commission,

I saw quite clearly that one compartment was empty. A page had shifted from one folder to another. Part of the transcript was in the wrong numerical order. The missing pages included those concerning Nyati's meetings with me and Jess.

Something else was missing too, but I could not quite place what it was. For the first time since I had taken the suite, the phone rang. I did not initially recognise the unfamiliar buzzing. I imagined that the caller might be Vanessa van Rensburg, and was prepared to be curt with her. But instead, I hear the voice of Zoë Joubert.

"Disturbing you?"

"Not at all. Never!"

She laughed gently.

"I wondered if you would be free later on. Maybe after dinner? For a night cap?"

"Of course. I would love to. But don't you have commitments?"

"Mills has a sleepover with her friends and everyone else from the house has other plans. We would have the place to ourselves." I heard the rush of wind over the phone and guessed she was calling from a cell phone.

"Where are you?"

"The Robberg. We're all waiting for Riaan, of course. He's been held up somewhere. No, wait. Here he is. So will you come? Later on? Please."

"Of course."

"Riaan wants a word."

There was a pause as the phone changed hands, covered to muffle some indistinct exchange. Then he spoke.

"Hello, Mr Ambassador, Mr Spook," Riaan van Rensburg said. His voice sounded as if he had cupped a hand around the phone so as not to be overheard.

"Before you plan any socials, I thought I'd let you know that I'm planning a little meeting tonight with all the ODAC set. Extraordinary General Meeting, so to speak. You might want to be there, Kinzer. Or should I say TJ?"

Part Three

Nyati wriggled his legs through his manacled hands in the back of the car and started unexpectedly to fight back. Theron fired a single 7.65mm round over his shoulder. The resistance came to an abrupt halt. Theron retrieved the brass cartridge case but not the bullet. Later, De Kock suggested he throw his damned Skorpion into the sea. But Theron could not quite bring himself to part with such a treasured, trusted companion.

Part Three

Twenty-One

TURNING EAST ALONG THE N2 highway, I drove out of Plettenberg Bay, barely taking note of the irrigated fairways at Goose Valley and the moored legions of motor boats on the Keurbooms River. There had been a time when the country's disparities would have produced righteous indignation: sprinklers for the golfing elite while the caddy-class lived without running water; floating gin palaces for some while others could not even aspire to a bicycle.

But liberal umbrage was no match for the concerns that were beginning to dawn on me at the prospect of finally tracking down the one person who knew the full story, a person whose genius for lethal violence was a matter of public record. On the emotional register, egalitarian pique falls a long way behind the stirrings of fear.

The road on the outskirts of town was clogged with family saloons and SUVs towing trailers full of beach gear and boogie boards, but as I progressed further, the traffic eased. Long-distance buses and heavy tanker trucks monopolised the inside lane, heading on for the long haul on the toll road towards Port Elizabeth and beyond, cutting through the luscious foliage of the Garden Route, soaring over ravines where signboards told motorists not to feed the baboons.

In my rear-view mirror, some way back, I espied the familiar outline of a white pickup, but such cars were common. I thought little of it, concentrating more on finding my way.

All I had was a street name and no inkling of how Theron would receive me. In a matter of days the statute of limitations would liberate him from the likelihood of any further inquiry into his past. More pressing, Riaan van Rensburg seemed to be hoping that by discrediting me he would save the tatters of his own reputation – in the eyes of Zoë Joubert above all. I had a sinking feeling that, somehow or other, he had learned far more about my inquiries than was healthy for either of us.

As an offering for Theron I had brought a carton of locally produced cigarettes and a bottle of imported Famous Grouse Scotch. No single malts for assassins! As a precaution – in case of a formal interview – I had packed a tape recorder and legal pad. I was not sure why but I had stashed my sharp-bladed Swiss Army knife in my pocket – an improbably optimistic weapon against a battle-hardened operative of the dreaded Koevoet.

A large, green signpost pointed the way to Nature's Valley and I turned right onto a narrow, two-lane black-top across a flat plain. Smaller roads splintered off at right angles leading to distant homesteads and farms clinging to a narrow shelf of land between the sea and the ridges of the Tsitsikamma range.

Soon the road began a steep descent, twisting and turning along the side of a ravine where rock-falls had left football-sized chunks of debris. The light weakened, filtered through creepers and thick-trunked, ancient trees. Then, the road released me onto the flatlands of the coast.

It seemed an improbable bolt hole for the leader of an apartheid-era death squad.

The tide surged through a narrow, rocky inlet, then slowed and fanned out in spangled shoals and flat beaches. Children frolicked in the sand or floated on airbeds in the slowing current, staring into the mysteries of water – shells shifting, whorls of light refracting tiny rainbow prisms, crabs scuttling on secret missions, far more impenetrable than mine.

I tried to clear my mind, the way I had been trained; to make a mental list of priorities. Zoë Joubert and the future of our relationship figured prominently in my calculations. Every amorous instinct was telling me to abandon this fool's errand, to return and silence Riaan van Rensburg with whatever threat I could devise to defuse the time bomb of his disclosures. But I could not again break my pledge to the widows.

Van Rensburg had clearly plundered my trove of documents (had his wife helped him, like a conjuror's assistant whose sequined attire and leggy looks distracted the audience from the sleight-of-hand?) Vanessa van Rensburg had called me Hercule Poirot, but it was her husband who was planning the drawing-room crescendo, the finale of disclosure, the unmasking of the villain. Yet the cast of suspects was wider than he could conceive, certainly more fragile than I had imagined when I embarked on the mission assigned by Lily Nyati.

Guided by the scrap of paper from Jess Chase I drove through the grid streets of Nature's Valley. It struck me as a dark and forbidding place, the wood-frame houses set back in shaded foliage where you would not be surprised to find a venomous menagerie of snakes and spiders. The house numbers were marked on small wooden boards made indistinct by years of exposure to the heat and humidity of the coast. I drove slowly.

The address I had for Theron on Fifth Street matched a plot with a small, wooden home but no street number on display. I drove past and reversed into a leafy turn-off some 50 yards further on. All I could hear when I switched off the engine was the distant rumble of the surf.

A white pickup was parked in the driveway – not the fancy kind with four-wheel drive and fat tires, but an old working model with a battered flat-bed and chipped panels. The tail gate was crusted with ochre dirt from long journeys on unpaved roads. A stout one-piece fishing rod with a worn Penn surf-casting reel and heavy-gauge nylon line was clipped to the hood, stretching back over the cab in a taut curve.

Theron was a man who had spent his adult life at the cutting edge of security forces, feared and envied across Africa. As a field commander he had called up airstrikes, napalm runs, reinforcements, medical choppers for the wounded – daka-dakas, as the military argot had it. As a security policeman he represented the final executor in a chain that stretched directly to the highest echelons of power in Pretoria, hangman, judge and jury – usually in that order.

His actions had the imprimatur – if not the formal, written

authorisation – of those untouchable colonels and brigadiers who sent him on his missions with a nod or a wink: the paper trail of accountability stopped at his desk, his office, his Skorpion. If he announced himself as Theron of the security police, the introduction bore an unspoken threat of cells and beatings.

During the emergency years, people in his position had been formally indemnified against any appeal by their victims. Apartheid made them immune to justice.

I resisted the thought that his relationship to power was not so far removed from mine as Ambassador Extraordinary and Plenipotentiary. We both drew authority from office. We demanded access by right. We were the extension of remote and all-powerful authorities. In the end, we could both say that we were only following orders. But they said that at Nuremberg, too.

Now, like me, he was a man without a calling card, without the validation of a laminated ID denoting the embrace of great institutions. The collapse of white power left him naked. His formal title, Captain, was a rank from a lost army.

He was Kobus Theron. Just as I was Tom Kinzer. But I doubted whether such formalities meant that Theron had forgotten his many years of training and expertise in darker arts than I could imagine. He was still a seasoned killer – and I was still a former functionary versed only in the niceties of diplomacy.

The afternoon seemed to slow. There was no movement from the house and I began to think that maybe Theron was at the beach, or out shopping with his wife, or in bed with a mistress. I realised I knew nothing about him, or how he would react to being cornered in his lair by an upstart American.

What I wanted was one name from him. But I had no idea what price Theron would set on that information and I had no plan to prise it out of him.

"And you, I imagine, would be Thomas Kinzer. Ambassador. Or should I maybe say: Dr Kinzer, I presume."

I had not heard or sensed anyone approach. The passenger door of my rental car had opened and he had clambered in without invitation.

He smiled ruefully, as if we were old, familiar enemies, too weary for battle, ready for truce. He offered a hand to shake. I took it without thinking.

"Kobus Theron is my name," the man said. I must have recoiled for he tightened his grip. "Don't worry about my hand. There is no blood on it right now."

His appearance had not changed all that much from the images in Ray Gilliomee's book.

His close-cropped, gingery beard traced his jawline, while his top lip and neck were clean shaven. He wore faded blue rugby shorts, a lightly checked short-sleeve shirt and veldskoen suede ankle boots without socks. His legs, forearms and the V in the neck of his shirt were all tanned in a deep, nutty way that had nothing to do with vanity.

The face of his watch was hidden by a leather flap – a device to guard against the scratches of wait-a-bit thorn in the bush and to cloak glints of reflected light that might draw enemy fire. His narrow-brimmed hat was made of faded camouflage material. A jagged tear along one side suggested a narrow escape – a lucky charm, a talisman.

He sat easily, poised to run or relax, depending on the requirement of circumstances. I had half-expected a boozy, gone-to-seed blowhard – hence the supply of whisky and cigarettes I had brought with me – but there was no obvious hint of decline or vulnerability.

"So you came to see me. I had been expecting something, sometime. From the widows' side, maybe. From Miss Chase. I did not know what. "

The voice was deep, rough – a smoker's voice – strongly accented. He was not looking directly at me, but peering out of the car.

If you could imagine sitting on a park bench in Berlin in 1950, chatting casually with a camp Kommandant, the gruesome oddity of the situation would be the same.

This was a man responsible for a roll-call of martyrs – the Pebco Three, the Cradock Four, Biko, Goniwe, Nyati. At the TRC, Theron had been named in some of the most appalling testimony concerning the Vlakplaas farm in the Transvaal where they cremated their victims over barbecue pits and drank beer to while away a long night of incineration.

"You picked a pretty poor spot for a stake-out, Mr Ambassador, if I may say so. In one of my units you would not have lasted five minutes."

"I would not have wished to last one minute inside one of your units."

"As you wish," he said. "So what brings you here?"

"Did Jess – Mrs De Vere – tell you what I'm doing?"

"Not so much."

"But you did talk to her."

"She had my number. Yes."

"And you agreed to this meeting?"

"That is why I let you find me."

"So what did Mrs De Vere tell you?"

"She said you would help me square things with the widows," he said as he slid out of the car.

A group of women wearing the pale green uniform of domestic staff walked by and he said something to them in isiXhosa, the language of the Eastern Cape, eliciting what seemed to be genuine laughter.

Their voices receded in the hot, still air. There was no other sound, not even crickets.

I locked the car and joined Theron to walk to his house.

"I do different things now," he was saying. "Dangerous things, but better things."

"Like what?"

"Mines," he said. "Bloody mines."

It sounded like: mahns, bleddy mahns.

"Anti-personnel. Anti-tank. You name it. They plant them, whoever they are. I lift them. Plenty times, back in the old days, the Koevoet days in Ovamboland, my Casspir hit mines and up I went. Flying through the air. Ever been hit by a mine? I thought not. You spiral in slow motion. When you land, if you are still alive, you are deaf as a post. People run up to you and ask if you are alright and you can't hear a bleddy thing. So that's what I do, I go into minefields and I lift mines. Angola. Mozambique. Cambodia. Balkans. Humanitarian work, they call it. You see those piccanins with stumps for arms and legs and you know it was wrong to put those mines there in the first place. So in my own way, I put things right."

"What else?"

"Sometimes, I do close security, for the bigwigs when they don't trust the locals so they want a few of the old timers along for the ride. But mostly it's mines. Not so much the anti-tank kind, the big TM-57s that blew my Casspirs sky high. They need a lot to trigger. One twenty, one fifty kilos – a damn sight more than some African lightie in a village or even an old man on a bicycle. But it's the anti-personnel mines, the fragmentation mines, the PFM-1s and the OZM-4s that I hate, the kind that do not always kill, that maim and cripple, and move around so you cannot find them. These days they say you can use sonar and all that to look for them but in the end you have to be out there on the ground and you may never come back, not in one piece at least – like you in this country, hey, Mr Ambassador, walking into a minefield? You hit the mine and, bang, what is there? Red haze. Nothing else. But I am happy with my job. I lifted the mines along the power lines to Mozambique so they could open the new game park across the border from Kruger Park. Seven times I got shot at because there was still a war on and I must have made a juicy target. Once I made it out on foot with a wounded comrade – black guy, before you ask – because there was no med-evac like in the old days. And when they opened the game park, Mandela came and cut the ribbon. And he shook my hand. Mandela shook this hand. With a lot less fuss than what you did. So how about that? Look at it. Is it clean? Can you see blood?"

We had reached his front door and I hesitated to enter.

"You know, Ambassador. Kinzer. Thomas. Whatever. If I wanted to take you out, I could do it. If I had wanted to take you out years ago when you drove past my OP and into Nyati's house, I could have done it then. I could have done it when you parked your BMW in Nyati's garage and thought no one had seen you. In a silver BMW! I could have taken out the old Kombi they hid you in to take you around the township when they thought no one was on your tail. I could have taken you out in company in that motel on the PE road. Permanent Removal. If you weren't worth it then, why bother now?'

We sit opposite one another in his kitchen. There are odours of tobacco and sweat, mixed with fried breakfasts and disinfectant where the help has scrubbed the white tiled floor. The walls are panelled with varnished pine that matches the table and chairs and cupboards. Theron has laid out his cigarettes, pen and cell phone like soldiers in a neat row. He has removed his camouflaged hat and I am surprised to see that he still has a head of thick, gingery hair. He has brought a bottle of Klipdrift brandy, a bucket of ice and a litre of cola. As he pours, his hand is rock steady.

"When I used to do interrogation, when we captured the terrs, you could tell very quickly whether they would turn and join you against their comrades," he began. He spoke in a gentle, remember-when voice. "You had control of them. You could hurt them and they knew it. You could help them or not help them. You could eat with them and then they were indebted to you. You could show them the bodies of their comrades and tell them they were going the same way. You could threaten. You could intimidate, the way the removal of personal freedom intimidates most people. But, right now, here, I am not sure who is interrogating who and for why."

"Tell me again why you told Jess where I could find you."

He took a drink – no more than a cautious sip – and eyed me in a somewhat histrionic way, as if mimicking a poker player. He leaned back from the table and clasped his hands behind his head.

"That is simple. I had not heard from her for quite some time, some years, in fact, but I had met her and talked to her back in the Eastern Cape days. Not interrogated. Just talked. I told her things that were happening. I told her who was dangerous and who was not. Ach, you know, man, I talked to a lot of them reporters. Not just the on-sides bunch like Gilliomee. Tried to make them see sense. Sell them the line. But she was different. There was something she had that made everyone want to talk to her. And she listened so you felt you had something worthwhile to say. I even told her some private things that maybe I should not."

"But then we went different ways, after Nyati, because she knew things she could not prove and I knew things I could not tell. In the end, I left the security forces because it was going nowhere for me. I was getting older and they gave a good pension to get us out. We were an embarrassment, people like me. We had done the jobs, and now the mucky-mucks did not want to know us. They were too busy saving their own skins after Mandela was free. And there was plenty other work. The kind of jobs for people with some training and background in military things, weapons, logistics, deployments, et cetera. And one job was for the famous Mr De Vere – a few days in DRC Congo, scoping copper and cobalt prospects with his cronies. Private jet in and out. No immigration. No passports. No questions asked. So we fly out to Shaba, Katanga, whatever they call it these days, and keep an eye on him in the bush."

He wishes to amuse me, draw me in to a sympathetic hearing of his story. I nod encouragement, but cannot bring myself to smile.

"He meets up with some contact or other, Congolese chap who kept a big white launch, Bertram or some such, like you see in the fishing magazines, on one of those great rivers – the Lualaba, I think. So it's a sort of crazy assignment. There we are on the flying bridge, old hands from the bush, armed to the teeth with Kalashnikovs and RPGs, sweating like pigs, swatting the flies. And down below, in the air-con, there's these big mining guys with their contact offering all kinds of deals and concessions. Concession! What a word, hey? I give you my country's wealth and you pay me in Switzerland and it's a concession."

He laughed again with a degree of bitterness.

"Anyhow, while we are cruising on the river, some oke in the bush on the bank decides to take a pot shot at us with a bow and arrow. A bow and arrow, man! And the Congolese chappie shouts up to the flying bridge to open fire, but Mr De Vere, he's smart. He says: no way. We don't want to cause an international incident. So all he had brought us along for was show. But the Congolese guy, he pulls out his pistol and blasts away at the bush where the guy with the bow and arrow was, and kills him. And – plop – he falls out of the bush and into the river. And you know what? It's a kid. Some fool kid trying it on with a homemade bow and arrow. Dead as a post. Croc-bait. Africa! And they call *me* a cold-blooded killer!"

"And then?" I had begun to revise my opinion of De Vere. He

was not, it seemed, some rich guy frittering away the family silver. It took a degree of courage – and greed – to embark on a river cruise with the kind of warlord Theron seemed to be describing. It made it easier to see why Jess Chase had been drawn to him. I had a sudden memory of her avid consumption of early Wilbur Smith novels, the kind set in Africa, where men were men. Real men.

"So we skedaddle off that boat" – he gestures with the open palm of his left hand striking the clenched fist of right hand – "and we fly back and she is at the airport. I could not believe my eyes. Miss Chase. Now Mrs De Vere, what I did not know. And, man, was she angry! He hadn't taken her with! She was no one's little woman, she told him, right in front of all of us – execs, close protection, everyone – and she'd seen more shit in her time than he was likely to in his entire life … so don't even think that a few concessions in the Congo were anything for her. She could hack it. Then she saw me. She knew my whole record. I didn't want to lose the connection – it was good money with the mining guys, even better if you kept quiet about things like what we had just seen. So I asked her – you know, quietly, when she had calmed down – please not to tell her husband about the Eastern Cape. She had it in for me because of Nyati and all the others. Nyati most of all. She really liked him. But she did not want her husband to know that she knew me! Or him! What do they say? Wheels inside wheels! So she made a deal. She said she wouldn't rat on me to De Vere, and neither would I with her, but I must keep in touch and one day she would call and tell me how I could start doing some payback. Atonement, she called it."

"So who was the Judas?"

"Judas who? Iscariot?" He laughed his coarse, smoker's laugh again.

"Who told you where Nyati was that last night in PE?"

A note of protest entered his voice, as if to say I was pushing too abruptly.

"Tom. Thomas. Ambassador. What am I supposed to call you?"

I said nothing.

"Listen, man. My legal situation is precarious. If you have done your homework, you will know that they refused me amnesty. When

I had sung my little heart out to all their fancy Jo'burg lawyers in front of all the cameras and tape recorders and the reporters and Archbishop Tutu and everyone, and told them who did what, that's when they said: no amnesty for you, Kobus Theron. Then they said I would be on trial for murder and go to prison with all those guys who would love to get their hands on an old white security officer, if you know what I am saying. And now they are saying there will be the statute of limitations and there will be no trial and I will be free if I just wait a few days."

"Free? How can you ever be free of what you have done?"

Theron had rehearsed his words too frequently to be hurried or halted. He rose from the table to grab a white plastic bowl that he filled with potato chips. He refilled both our glasses, even though I had barely sipped at mine. Then he took a second bowl and decanted salted peanuts, as if he was settling in for the long haul. This was a moment he had been anticipating – a captive audience, an opportunity too precious to miss. Certainly he would not hurry to meet any deadline Riaan van Rensburg had set for me.

"This was war, man. Like in Israel. It was a war we would have to fight forever for our people. When I was a teenager I read all the books about the communists in Africa, the Congo, Uhuru, Mau Mau, all that. Blood and mayhem. You Americans, you outsiders, you all figured the terrorists were freedom fighters. But we, the security forces, were reacting to threat. We were fighting for our lives. Our freedom. The freedom of our people to be themselves, speak their language, run their affairs, go to their churches, feel safe in their homes. We did not see that it was them reacting to us. We did not care less about hearts and minds. We did not see that you could not win the way we were fighting because we weren't offering carrots – only stick. But we had no doubts that our actions were correct. We had a cause, too – our cause, the cause we had been brought up to in our schools and churches and homes. We ignored the reason why these people had become freedom fighters. If they were our victims, we were their victims. If we perpetrated acts against them, they perpetrated acts against us. If we tortured, they burned. They burned their enemies! They burned people who had done nothing to them. They would have burned the whole damn place if we let them – remember what Winnie Mandela said: 'With our matchboxes and our tires, we will liberate our country.' Man, she meant it."

"And at Vlakplaas. Who burned people there?"

"Listen," he said. "It was our duty to defend our country. There were bombings in shopping arcades and nightclubs. Terrorism. It was war and we fought on opposite sides but by the same rules. You see? It was only later that some of us realised we had to have a justifiable cause to win because you could never win on the battlefield alone. And, of course, it was different when it finished because the enemy got amnesty and we did not, and they got justice and we did not, and they got freedom and we did not but we had both been fighting in the trenches like the French and the Germans at the Somme or the Americans and the Viet Cong in Vietnam. We were all soldiers but some soldiers got victor's justice and the others did not."

"You Americans today are like we were then, in the old days. You want to be liked and to be admired because you are taking a stand. You are doing what you think is right. And when you are not liked or admired, you are surprised and hurt. But you must realise some time – as we had to in the end – that no one likes a bully, no one likes someone who lays down all the rules but doesn't play by them himself. No one likes someone who messes up your life and then tells you they did it for your own good."

"Come on, Theron. There may have been a war in Ovamboland fighting insurgents. But by the time Nyati died you were a cop and they were civilians. It was straight, calculated, cold-blooded murder. Assassination. There was no insurgency."

"Maybe not by your definition, but there was a revolution. You should know. You were there! I remember now seeing you through my binos, on that funeral day when they buried Nyati. There weren't too many whites in the crowd so you and those reporters and cameramen stood out and I remembered you had been secretly visiting Nyati with Miss Chase, because we had a big file on her and we had one on you through the diplomatic section, and I thought: yes, that's one more good reason to get rid of Nyati because he was becoming an international figure, like Mandela, and we didn't need two of those."

I heard crickets in the dense forest outside, and, more remotely, the sound of a cheery, indistinct conversation as two people pedalled by outside on bicycles.

"Say that again. Say what I think you are trying to say."

"We knew you, Thomas. Ambassador. Press attaché as was. So-called. Maybe something else, for all we knew. Agent provocateur. Enemy agent. "

He was speaking in a different tone now, more slowly, as if trying to make complicated ideas accessible to a witless child.

"There was a file on you. Haven't you read the testimony? Your name is in it, along with Chase and some of Nyati's other visitors from the outside. Ted Kennedy. Not done your homework? Before the order came for Nyati – permanent removal, extreme prejudice, whatever you would call it – we didn't just barge in. There were reports, committees, decisions, surveillance. Bureaucracy. Preparation. It was a big step because he was causing a lot of grief. We didn't just wake up one day and go and take him out. There were two plans. One was what I called the soft option: if we gave him his job back, promoted him, he would come back into the system. That was what the Department of Bantu Education wanted. Bring him back in, co-opt him, give him a good job and a fat paycheck and a new place with a big house and the unrest would cease. It would never have worked. The man was a revolutionary. Like Lenin. Or Castro. He was sending out the comrades to training so they would come back with AK-47s. He was making the place ungovernable, same as Goniwe in Cradock and Mkhuseli Jack in PE. And that was the big threat, when you think of it, because for all we had been told that blacks were not able to govern, there they were, running the show in their townships. Taking the initiative. Beyond our control."

He paused to sip his drink and I tried not to join him in this macabre toast, this companionable reminiscence. But I weakened and took a slug of brandy barely diluted with Coke. In the heat, the ice had all but melted, leaving just a slender frozen disk to float on the surface. I coughed and my eyes watered. He waited while I composed myself, offering a clean white handkerchief – still folded and ironed – from the pocket of his shorts.

"Then there was Plan B – permanent removal from society as the ministers and them called it. That was the security option from the police and army and special branch. So we put him under extra surveillance. We had a *tamatie* – a bug – right in his living room, in the plastic flowers on his coffee table. How could you not have suspected? We were amazed to hear you talking like there was no tomorrow."

I remembered the moment in every detail. I remembered listening to Nyati's story, then taking a deep breath before I overstepped the boundaries of the policy. How could I have been so stupid?

"You know, I have my files, too, my records, tapes, with my lawyer," Theron was saying. "All genuine stuff from the old office in PE. I have all the transcripts of you saying how the United States of America would do this and that if you could persuade your ambassador. You wanted to end constructive engagement, as I recall, you wanted to tell Reagan he was wrong to support gradual change, evolution. You wanted them to shift their policy so that they would back Nyati and his like and of course that was no good for us because constructive engagement was a lifeline to the outside world – our only lifeline – and once we lost that we were finished, though the politicians never told us we were finished anyhow. They let us go on with our permanent removals. Even while they were talking in secret to Mandela. But the moment that counted for Nyati was when our bosses looked at all the tapes and the transcripts and figured that we could handle a little local troublemaker, but we couldn't afford to have Uncle Sam in bed with him. So his fate was sealed."

"If you are trying to blackmail me, Theron, it's a bit late. I no longer have an official position. And if you're trying to sell me something, I'm not in that kind of market anymore."

"You can call it how you want. Blackmail. Selling. I am trying to help. I am trying to explain the facts to you, as I know them. More than what came out at the Commission. I am trying to help everyone put this behind us with the truth."

His eyes shone: hey presto, Mr American – who do you think killed Nyati now?

"So who was the informer?"

Twenty-Two

A CAR PULLED UP. ITS ENGINE RATTLED into silence. A door opened, then slammed shut. A woman of around Theron's age entered the kitchen. She carried a brightly coloured plastic bag from a supermarket chain. She was about to light a cigarette when she noticed me. I scrambled to rise in formal greeting, scraping my chair on the polished white tiles.

She was taut and angular, her tanned skin stretched over her shoulder and collar bones above the shallow divide of her sternum. Her hair – strands of grey mingled with auburn highlights – rose from her forehead in a rigid, bouffonned quiff held in place by a permanent wave. Tiny lines fringed bright red lips, as if from an enduring pout of disapproval or worry. She wore a strapped top in cream and a calf-length skirt with some kind of paisley pattern in russet and yellow. Jutting from rubber slip-slops, her toenails were painted in the same bright tones as her fingernails and lipstick. Accompanying her, a black and white Jack Russell terrier bounced as if on springs. Kobus Theron swatted it away and the dog yelped. The woman flinched but said nothing.

"Anna-Marie!" Theron exclaimed. "Mr Ambassador, this is Anna-Marie Theron. My wife."

She smiled awkwardly. Her pale brown eyes – almost amber – betrayed suspicion, whether of me or her husband, or both, I could not be sure.

"Ambassador Kinzer has come to talk about the old days."

"Ag, the old days, Kobie. The old days is past. I keep telling him it's past. Isn't it, Ambassador?"

Theron rose from the table and took the shopping bag from his wife. He squeezed her arm gently, as if to prevent her from bolting. Somewhere in Theron's life, I realised, there was a core of protection and warmth – an area of safety denied by this same man to Lily Nyati and the widows.

"Did you buy enough for three?"

"Are you staying for supper, Ambassador? You see, Kobie, he's not sure."

Finally, she lit her cigarette with her red plastic lighter.

No Cartier gold here; no bauble of the kind that had been in my hotel room when I left for lunch and was no longer there when I returned. Riaan van Rensburg would be preparing his presentation now, ready for the show, gathering the Old Deep set, Zoë Joubert among them, for the unmasking of the true Judas. He had already identified him: a man called TJ.

Anna-Marie Theron inhaled, glancing with some disapproval at the bottle of Klipdrift and the molten ice.

"Go start the braai, Kobie," she said. "Please."

As he left, Anna-Marie Theron took a photograph from the mantlepiece, returning to sit next to me at the kitchen table. I had a feeling that I had stumbled into a well-rehearsed scenario in which my own part had already been scripted. Ambushed would be another way of describing it. As Jessica de Vere must have known I would be.

"Kobie has told me who you are. I knew you would be coming here. I've always been waiting. He didn't want to tell me, but I made him. After that woman called – Chase, De Vere, whatever – he was upset by it all. He doesn't like to go back to the past, but he cannot get away from it. I have been thinking about it all. Over and over. In my head. You see this?"

She hands me the framed photograph. She and Kobus Theron are pictured by a swimming pool behind a high fence, cloaked in bougainvillea, topped with razor wire. Two boys have identical red hair and slender frames. Anna-Marie wears a modest, full-length swimsuit in turquoise. Kobus Theron is in skimpy Speedos. His torso is strikingly pale. The area behind the pool is littered with bicycles, cricket bats, a rugby ball. You can see a black, deep-bellied grill with its lid off, a hint of smoke rising into the harsh sunlight. On a lounger, a two-way radio shares space with a Jack Russell terrier and a machine pistol, a Skorpion.

"That was in the operational area, in South-West – Namibia they call it now. Our garden. These are our boys. Deon and Willem. Of course, they have grown up now. One is at Stellenbosch doing Law. The other is a doctor with Doctors without Frontiers. He's in Rwanda at the moment. Rwanda! Talk about getting from the fire into the pan! Kobie was with the security forces and we lived in this house in Ovamboland and he'd be away for days, weeks on end and we'd be mortared quite regularly. You see here, in the corner of the picture, those doors? That was our bomb shelter. We spent quite a lot of time in it, me and the boys. And I'd take them to school in a convoy and do the homework behind a security fence. I had a gun – a rifle – next to the bed and bars on the doors and a radio to call up help from the local Kommando. And then Kobie would come home and we would be a family again and he would never talk about what he saw and did. The boys would try to make him tell stories ... but he never would. He would be a dad, and make the braai and play rugby and cricket. Then he would go again and we would wait and wonder if he was coming back and that was how it was. And that was why I nagged and nagged him: get a transfer, Kobie, one of us is going to get killed – you or us – let's move to SA, Kobie.

I have my duty, he said. But you can do your duty without a uniform, I told him, without chasing terrorists, without leaving us here to be mortared in our compound. So one day, he came home early. The boys were at school. I was doing my clinic – I used to be a nurse so I would treat the locals, the blacks, for their little coughs and sneezes – and he walked in and said: how do you like PE by the sea? And that was it. That was how Captain Kobus Theron became a security policeman."

"You knew I was coming?"

"I knew you were coming, Kobie told me, and – forgive me – I know how you Americans think about us. I used to think you were our friends. But you think we are worse than your old plantation owners. You have forgotten what you did with your slaves because it was so long ago and you like to think we are like you with our blacks. But we are not. We grew up with these people, you see. We know them. We didn't buy and sell them. We didn't bring them from Africa in ships where they died and got diseased. They were here already! They came to our land from way up in the north, from the Congo. Of their own accord. We didn't make them. We may not have taken them to our hearts, but we could talk to each other. We taught them our language, our Bible. We didn't hate them. We do not. We went to church. We prayed to the same God, okay in different buildings. But we prayed the same for forgiveness for our trespasses." She took a long drag on her cigarette and peered up at the ceiling as if she were reminding herself of the lines she had been rehearsing before my arrival.

"We are all Africans in the end, whether we like it or not," she said. "My parents – my ancestors – left Europe more than 300 years ago, so what's Europe to me? I have never been there. I cannot even get a visa to visit the land they came from. So tell me: what is Europe? A holiday brochure the same as Thailand or Australia. Anyhow, that is not what I meant to say. When I heard you were coming, I decided it could not be a complete coincidence. There had to be a reason. I believe in fate, destiny. I believe it was a chance to get someone to help us because there are not many left who will help the people who once protected them from the *swart gevaar*, the *rooi gevaar*."

The words meant black menace, red peril. She smiled to see that I understood the terms

"So I thought: Just as it was fate to go to PE and Kobie being a security policeman, it was fate what brought you here today so I could say one thing, can you help him?"

"Help him? Mrs Theron, you know what he did. You might think we are bad because of slavery. But we have a different idea of right and wrong now."

"Right, wrong. When did you outsiders care about right or wrong when you came into Africa to play out your own dramas? What was it for you? A stage? A background for your films? And when you told men like Kobie that it was good to fight the communists and you would support them, what was that? Hmmm? Was it your game, like the British and the French and the Germans – the African scramble, you and the communists? But we live here. We live with the results. Collateral damage you call it. I'm not talking about good and evil. I'm talking about suffering. I'm talking about finding peace. I'm not talking about all this limitation and amnesty. Neither is he. He does not care for all this legal mumbo-jumbo. They told him years ago when they sent him on his missions that what he did was legal. Indemnity. Freedom from prosecution for acts committed in the pursuance of the Emergency Powers" – she drew imaginary quotation marks in the air, leaving a tendril of cigarette smoke – "but the law seems to change in our country depending on who sits in the Union Building in Pretoria. He won't have told you about his nightmares, his dreams. He does not tell anyone. But I know. He does not sleep a full night. He is haunted. Since he was at the Truth Commission and saw the women, the widows. They come back to him, their faces. He sees them and then it all changes in his dreams to the killings. It is all mixed up. The men, the women, the suffering ... and the killings and the war. For me too it was hard to come to terms with all that he did. I didn't know all the details until it came out in public. I knew he had a tough job but I did not know – I swear to God – that they made him kill people in cold blood. Can you imagine how we felt when we heard that? Everyone looked at the widows, Mrs Nyati and them. But no one thought: what about this other woman who has just been turned into an emotional widow, who has just found out her husband is being called an assassin who touched her body and soul with blood on his hands and death in his heart? Who will heal her? Who will she forgive to make it all better, knowing where her man had been when he came through the door at six in the morning and showered hot and cold for hours on end?"

She paused and lit another cigarette.

"And have you thought about our sons? What about them trying to make their way in the new Rainbow South Africa?" She offered the title with just a hint of scorn. "They go for a job and the black man asks them: so what did your father do in the old days? Have you thought of that? What are they supposed to say? He killed your comrades, your brothers, but he has hung up his pistol now – is that what they are supposed to say? When can they say: he was a policeman and that is all, it is over now, forgiven?"

"He used to pretend he was on radio duty or guarding. How could he say: I am going to kill people for my government? He didn't want me or the boys to know what he did. How he earned his salary. How he put the *wors* and *pap* on the table. But it was a war. We knew that in Ovamboland and it was the same war in PE. There were two sides. Two sides to the story. Do the others have nightmares? I don't know. How can I know? All I know is that he played by the rules. He always played by the rules. The government's rules. Even at the TRC. He could have run away. He was in Bosnia, Cambodia doing his mines. He didn't have to come back. But he did. He came back because he believed in reconciliation, he believed in justice at the end of the day when the war was over and everyone was as free as everyone else."

She began to busy herself with the evening meal, setting a warped aluminium pot on the stove, mixing a kind of cornmeal from a bag marked Iwisa No. 1 with water.

"So he was just obeying orders."

"You don't have to sneer. He was loyal to what he believed in, even when everything changed and you cannot say that of the politicians, or diplomats, can you, Mr Ambassador? To listen now you would think no one knew about apartheid and it was always someone else's fault."

"Are you frightened of him, Mrs Theron? Did he tell you to say all this?"

"Do you know what it is like to live with someone else's – what is the word – demons? Yes, demons. Men like him have demons but that does not mean they are bad after everything they have seen and done."

"But what on earth do you think I could do? And why should I do anything? Nyati was my friend. I liked and respected him. I thought he was the future."

"You know, Kobie once said to me, later on, when it was near the end: if I was a black in this society, I would be a terrorist, too. Like Nyati and them. He understood. Yes, he obeyed orders, but he had started to understand that the people who gave the orders were wrong

– liars, cheats who did not have to live with what they ordered the way Kobie does. Do you see the cabinet ministers, the generals confessing like Kobie? The old state president, PW Botha, who ordered all this, lives like a nice old *oupa* by the sea. Do you see him or his henchmen at the Truth Committee? No ways. And the ANC, what about them? They are in government for all the massacres and tortures they did in their camps in Angola. They are just the new version of the old ones, slicing up the pie. They have peace. But not my Kobie."

"But I still don't see where you want me to come into this."

The pot of corn porridge began to bubble on the stove and she stirred it as it thickened. Then she returned to the table, but did not sit, leaning against the back of a chair, flexing her surprisingly muscular arms so that she was peering down at me.

"You know them, the women, the widows. He said you knew them. He said you visited them while Nyati was still alive. You were at the funeral. You know where they live. You must take him to them, face to face, so that he can apologise and you can explain and they can forgive him. I am a woman, too. I lost my husband to all those nightmares and the murder charges so I know what a woman would say to someone who came to say they were sorry. Because if they see him they'll know he is truly sorry, that he suffers for what he did. That he was misled, like they all were, the soldiers, the troopies, the police, fighting for something they thought was forever when the Bothas and De Klerks were selling them out to you Americans and the British and the blacks. Without that war he would not have done this. He is a kind man. A loving father."

"Like Nyati would have been?"

"That is not fair. Kobie is a good man. A good husband. He didn't drink or fight or chase other women. He brought his kids up to be good members of the church and society. He fought in a war like a good soldier and now he wants to say he's sorry. I know Kobie. He has said to me: Anna-Marie, if I could take back all the hurt, if I could bring back all the bodies, I would do that in a moment, but I cannot change the past. I can only say I'm sorry."

"And to you? Does he ever say sorry to you? Does he apologise for hiding the truth from you all those years? Or maybe he did not hide it. Maybe you did not need to be told what was happening. Maybe you understood without needing the words."

"That is disgusting. And it is not me we are talking about. We are talking about those women. And anyhow it was a war. There were others plenty worse than him."

"So why does he not just go and say sorry to them? He does not need me for that."

"Because whatever else has happened this is still South Africa and he does not know how to."

Theron had returned from the yard. He was holding a can of fire-lighting liquid and the flames from his barbecue cast a flickering light around the doorway like some kind of halo. His wife gathered up the Jack Russell, hugging it to her body, and looked at me with pale, dry eyes.

"If these *kaffirs* can have their victory," she said, "Why can my husband not have his peace too?"

Part Four

When the remaining bodies had been doused in petrol, Theron radioed the incineration order. Four slender columns of smoke curled above the dunes, all a little way off from each other, joined by a fifth rising from Nyati's car. Later, Theron would regret leaving behind the phony licence plate on the burned vehicle – damaging evidence. But everyone makes mistakes; there were other tasks at hand. Dawn was rising on a new day – a battle over, but not the war.

Part Four

Twenty-Three

By the time I abandoned Theron and his wife to their evening meal, Africa's quick dusk had fallen. I could not shake off a stubborn feeling that, simply by touching the hand that pulled the trigger, I had entered into some kind of dreadful complicity with Nyati's killer. He had committed the crime, of course, but I was part of the motive.

Without my self-serving visit to Cooktown with Jess Chase all those years back, Nyati might still be alive.

What could I offer his widow now – or the Old Deep set – other than my own head on a platter, my mea culpa? I had embarked on this mission as judge and jury. Now I was the accused. And the only witness I could call was weighing his options over a plate of grilled sausage and mielie pap.

The car's headlights picked out fantastic shapes of creepers and misshapen branches that might have illustrated a compendium of tales by the Brothers Grimm.

During my diplomatic days in South Africa people had made much of the idea that the revolution confronted everyone with unavoidable, life-defining choices, no matter where you stood in the racial spectrum. It was a time when, quite literally, you nailed your banner to the mast and left it there.

The only question was: were you with the new order or not, ready to advance with the battalions of change or not? Zoë Joubert and Riaan van Rensburg and Rod Harris had made their choices long ago, gambling that they had guaranteed their place in a future as bright as the past was dark. But, this night, with Riaan van Rensburg as an unlikely inquisitor, they would be drawn back, forced to re-examine the flaws, the legends constructed on shallow foundations of deceit.

When we are young, in our innermost thoughts, in the moments of revelatory self-scrutiny never exposed to others, most of us know our own secrets. But, as time erodes our private honesty, we visit that bright core of truth ever less frequently. We come to prefer our fiction. Our untruths set into permanency, hardened by the glaze of invention. Our obfuscations solidify and become accepted truth. That was as true for the Old Deep set as for anyone else, myself included, as Theron had reminded me.

I pulled over and stopped the car, ignoring the road signs that warned of rock falls in the cluttered ravine heading back to the main N2 highway. I reached for the package of booze and cigarettes I had brought for Theron and tore it open. I swigged at the whisky. I lit a Chesterfield filter. I coughed and spluttered and felt no better.

Theron was playing mind games. He was lying.

The assassins had not operated with the outside world in mind. They had pursued their own agenda. Think of Mxenge, Goniwe, the whole procession of ghostly heroes lining the path to Mandela's freedom – they had not died because of rash promises by junior diplomats. They had died because they had been in the authorities' face. They had risen to oppose apartheid's great ramshackle juggernaut and must therefore be crushed by it.

Their deaths were foretold in bleak interrogation rooms and cheery police canteens with polished linoleum floors; in spattered, stinking cells and bland committee rooms painted bureaucratic beige.

How could that have anything to do with me?

Yet Theron had known things that were not in the transcripts. He had described the layout of Nyati's living room, the plastic flower pot where they hid the bug, the easy promises I had offered to a suspected revolutionary in defiance of the God of policy. And I could not deny that I had made them. I could recall my words as clearly as when I spoke them: you have my promise, Mr Nyati, that I will work for a change in American attitudes; I will work for the legalisation of your organisations and the freedom of Nelson Mandela. How could I have foreseen what these words would lead to? And how on earth could I ever have assumed that anything I said in Nyati's living room would simply remain there?

Theron had known where we hid the rental car on the day of my first visit. He knew how we had been ferried around Cooktown under grubby sacking on the muddy floor of a Kombi. Throughout our conversation he had been telling me how much he knew, not just about me but about the embassy, about Jess, about the relationship I had with her and the motel room where it began.

I switched on the car radio. A disc jockey was mid-way through a retrospective selection of '80s music – Dire Straits, 10 cc, the kind of stuff that Jess had played on cassette tapes when we travelled together: "I'm not in love", "Money for nothing", "Brothers in arms".

Theron had been saying: we were brothers in arms, you and I. We are tainted. We share guilt.

But he was wrong, wrong, wrong.

I would visit Lily Nyati and tell her he was wrong. I would take him with me and force him to confess his lies. I almost swung the car round there and then to return and grab Theron by the scruff of his neck and shove him into my car in manacles – better still onto the flatbed of his pickup – and drive him cruelly cross-country like they drove Biko, and take him to Cooktown all the way along the coast in the Eastern Cape and deliver him to the widows and say: here he is, here is your man, your culprit, prime evil, the source of your grief, your path to redemption – no Judas, no tricks, no mysteries, just one straight killer, one single state assassin; do with him as you will.

There was, of course, another option.

I could simply resolve – here and now – never to see any of these people again. I could turn right on the N2, to Port Elizabeth, past the turn-off to Humansdorp where Molly Blackburn had died, past all the phantoms of Nyati's death. I could drive to the airport, book a ticket on the first flight out. Abandon the entire project. Cut and run. Have my chattels sent on to me. Port Elizabeth–Johannesburg–London–Washington. The cost of freedom – if not release – was a few thousand dollars, less than my fee at the conference.

Or, I could turn left, grab my bags, fuel the car for a fast late-night run to Cape Town, reversing the whole sorry route that had brought me here – a feeble Marlow, scuttling down-river as the awful message from Kurtz became too onerous to bear.

The horror, the horror! Mistah Kurtz, he very much alive!

I wished Theron had miscalculated on some far-flung minefield, dissolved in his "red haze" to spare me his droning disclosures, his psycho-games, his faked truth.

I reached the junction with the N2. Either way the road looked dark, uninviting, as if everyone else knew something I did not and had resolved to stay home.

Then I thought of Riaan van Rensburg, plump, sweating, holding forth like some kind of ludicrous Torquemada in beach shorts.

As I turned, the headlights of a vehicle approached from Nature's Valley, hanging briefly in the rear-view mirror like twin moons.

With one hand on the steering wheel, I took another pull at the whisky bottle, then lit another cigarette. The speedometer crept up above the limit of 120 kilometres per hour – 75 miles per hour according to my mental calculation – but there was little traffic on the road. And besides, I was a foreigner, an outsider. If the traffic police pulled me over, what could they do? Deport me, an ex-ambassador still on the State Department database? Send me home? How convenient would that be for those who defined the purpose of my stay as "conference purposes only".

The speedometer nudged towards 150 kilometres per hour – 90 miles per hour – but apart from a single vehicle a long way back there was no one else going my way. In the opposite direction an Intercape overnight bus rumbled by, pursuing a heavy tanker truck, duelling for dominion of the night. The sky was remarkably clear, the stars etched brightly on the darkness. I rolled down my window to allow a chill draft to ventilate the car.

The flashing light appeared suddenly close in the rear-view mirror.

The speedometer indicated that I was travelling at 130 kilometres per hour – 80 miles per hour – and I took my foot from the gas pedal.

Instinctively, I brought the rental car to a halt at the roadside, scrambling to push the whisky bottle onto the floor as the tires skidded on the gravel. In the wing mirror I saw a flashlight approaching while the blue light blinked directly behind me.

"It's an old trick, the flashing light," Kobus Theron said as he kneeled by the window of my hire car. "But effective."

Apart from the flashlight, he was carrying a worn machine pistol.

"Here is the deal, Mr Ambassador," he said. "I will tell what I know. You will take me to the widows."

"And the gun?"

"Insurance. Take it or leave it."

Twenty-Four

WITH HIMSELF AT CENTRE STAGE, on the same deck as had been the venue for Zoë Joubert's party, Riaan van Rensburg had arranged loungers and deck chairs in a semi-circle.

At Theron's urging, I chose not to declare my presence, but to remain hidden in the shadows off-stage, like an understudy in the wings awaiting the call.

Van Rensburg had positioned hurricane lamps on the balustrade and at various points among his audience so that, from a distance, the gathering might have been mistaken for some kind of formal assembly. A coven perhaps, or a Greek tragedy, or the appropriately macabre setting for the denouement of a particularly grisly murder story. (Which, of course, is what it was intended to be.)

He wore black cargo trousers and a loose, dark shirt, his black hair slicked back. As the members of the Old Deep set took their designated places – ordered to this lounger or that chair by a gesture from the satanic Poirot himself – he paced back and forth on his webbing sandals, deep in thought, sipping from a heavy tumbler.

If he was pleased with the turnout, he gave no indication of it. Around him, looking variously anxious and curious, mystified and querulous, the players in his orchestra awaited the tap of his baton – Jessica de Vere at the centre-rear, as if a timpanist (Chris de Vere was not in evidence), Zoë Joubert and Rod Harris as the wind section, Ferd and Cobra off to the right like ponderous, quarrelsome double-basses, Vanessa van Rensburg close to the maestro himself, doubtful and troubled, taut as the strings of a fiddle. Theron held me back in the darkness, the natural milieu of our erstwhile trades.

"I have been doing some homework," Riaan van Rensburg began. "Something that affects us all, where we come from, where we're going."

A snuffle of suppressed laughter from the double-bass section brought him to a halt in mid-sentence and he paused, raising a hand.

"Guys, this is no joke."

From a pocket of his cargo pants, Van Rensburg pulled a folded sheet of yellow A4 legal paper. Wrapped in it was a letter in a grubby envelope with gaudy stamps showing fish and birds.

"Exhibit A, m'lud," one of the lawyers said scornfully, drawing ripples of laughter from the others on the deck.

"I'm obliged," another chimed in.

With the moon high behind him, Riaan van Rensburg scanned his closest friends. Among them, he knew, he had been mocked for his serial failures, a forlorn cuckold, yearning always for the successes that lay just beyond his grasp. Now, they had no choice but to listen to him.

His latest wife was sitting to his right. No sign of her companion. Her eyes pleaded with him not to proceed, but he ignored her.

At centre stage, he caught another questioning look from Zoë Joubert. How haughty and superb she looked; how she would admire his handiwork once she understood its purpose – purging the group of its rottenness; not simply expelling the outsider, Kinzer, who had proved so disruptive – so threatening – but cleansing the Old Deep set itself of the hypocrisy on which it had been founded. A Judas, a traitor would be exposed; a new era would begin with a clean slate. As the inquisitor, he would finally be worthy. And if he won her, it would not matter that he lost all else – wives or children, lovers or friends.

The ocean stretched to the horizon, black and silver, below a clear, southern sky embroidered with the familiar markers that brought comfort to navigators in treacherous waters – Orion's Belt, the Southern Cross.

"There are two things I have to say. One relates to our visitor, the American Kinzer. The other relates to us."

At the mention of my name, the group became still, steadying itself after the initial ribaldry. Zoë Joubert looked up sharply and caught Van Rensburg's eye. He smiled to reassure her but, in the up-light of the hurricane lamps, his face seemed to crumble into a clownish grimace.

"This," he said, waving the documents he had taken from the pocket of his cargo pants, "is evidence, exhibits A to Z. What it shows is that Kinzer is not some passing conference delegate, some ambassador. Remember all those questions? Who was there with Nyati? Who attended, who did not? Who was with whom? Who knows who his real masters are? The CIA? Our own NIA? Maybe some private outfit, out to get the dirt on all or one of us for who knows what purpose."

He was looking directly at Jessica de Vere. "But there is no doubt, no doubt whatsoever, that his intention was to discover something about us, all of us, that would divide us, discredit us. Read this letter and you will see how cleverly he had arranged his cover so that he looked like an emissary of Nyati's widow, so that he had the ultimate credibility of support from a genuine heroine of The Struggle."

He handed the letter around. Still no smoking gun.

"But this," Van Rensburg went on, brandishing the single sheet of yellow A4 legal-pad paper with scribblings in my own handwriting, "this is the real clincher. This is the poison he was trying to spread."

He glanced to Zoë Joubert for approval but she was shaking her head, staring directly at him, her eyes fixed on him. Vanessa van Rensburg glowered – in rage or pity it was hard to tell.

Rod Harris reached out to take the hand of Ricky Rajbansi. But his acolyte withdrew and seemed to melt away. Harris tilted back his head, peering up at the stars. Then he looked across at Zoë Joubert, shrugging his shoulders, smiling a wan smile, as if to say that no secret lasts forever. Porter, the academic, stared out at the ocean, unconcerned, shielded by revolutionary purity.

The sheet of yellow paper passed quickly around the gathering.

"This is inadmissible. This is nothing," Cobra said with his courtroom sneer, less familiar now that he had joined his former comrades in The Struggle in the scramble for a niche in the rainbow's spectrum.

"Absolutely." Rugby-boy spoke now. "We know nothing of its provenance. It is just a sheet of paper. It has no status in law. And this is not a court."

"Unless it's a kangaroo court," Cobra added, not so sotto voce.

"This is not just a piece of paper," Riaan van Rensburg said, his voice rising. "This piece of paper is in Kinzer's handwriting. It was in Kinzer's hotel room. It is his list of suspects. Most of our names are on it, but only one has been ticked. You can all see whose name that it is. Rod Harris!"

The poet made to rise in defence, but Vanessa van Rensburg jumped up before he could speak.

"Ticked? Lists? What is this, Riaan? McCarthy?" she said. "Some kind of old Russian-type show trial? Sure there are lists. So what? There were always lists – lists of good guys, lists of bad guys, lists in police files, lists of lovers, lists in our heads, for God's sake. But you don't presume guilt because of a tick on a piece of paper. Who ticked it? You? Kinzer? The room maid? Maybe the tick means good guy and the rest are all bad guys. And wouldn't that be closer to the truth? Can we all say we were so virtuous? Were none of us ever called in? Did none of us get the offer: how about a little cooperation, a little *koöperasie*? Isn't that part of who we are now? Just survivors who managed to scrape through The Struggle intact – not saints, but no sinners either".

A voice from the crowd said, "Speak for yourself, Vannie, baby."

"And you, of all people, Riaan," she continued. "How can you stand there as if you were so holy?"

"We all know about Riaan." Zoë Joubert had risen to speak now. "He wasn't the only one."

The deck fell silent.

Riaan van Rensburg stared at his friends, looked from one to the other with hangdog, questioning eyes. Each of them nodded assent. Finally, he looked for confirmation from his wife and she nodded, too. They had known! And the one who chose to slide home the stiletto with such effortless, sweet-faced ease was Zoë Joubert, who was speaking again with a new urgency.

"We've all seen this piece of paper now. What can I say? Blame me. I brought this American into our midst. I thought I knew him. I was conned as much as Riaan was conned, as much as Rod Harris was pressured."

Until this point, she had been looking directly at Riaan van Rensburg but then she turned and scanned the assembled membership of the Old Deep set. Her eyes came to rest on Jessica de Vere, staring back at her, biting her lower lip.

"I happen to know why Rod's name has a tick next to it," Zoë Joubert was saying. "Rod is who he is, how he is. That has not been exactly a secret for a long time. But it has nothing to do with this list. The people involved – and they are not all here – know the reason. They know how wrong it is to depict Rod Harris as a traitor when he was a greater hero than any of us for the sake of the one person who could really be hurt by all of this. I will not say more. But please let us not squabble. We have survived. We have been each other's best friends, neighbours, sometimes more than that, sometimes less. We don't have to ask how many sugars we take in our coffee, or what we have for breakfast, or which newspaper we read, or where we were when Nyati died or when Madiba was freed. We know. We are family. We take each other on trust. We assume that if people were less than noble, they acted for a purpose, that there was no malice aforethought and any damage was limited. We know things, collectively and singly, about each other. We don't always say them. The Old Deep set is more complicated than it looks. It always has been. It exists on our sins as much as our virtues, whatever they may be. But we cannot do anything but destroy it if we go on like this. And ask yourselves, look around. Take all these people out of your lives and what's left? Who would we call on in bad times? Who would we share a concert ticket with? Who would you rely on to listen to your story without taking advantage? And who would you expect to tell their story to you?"

Now, finally, Rod Harris rose to speak. He removed his odd, Alice-in-Wonderland hat and held it clasped between his hands.

"Condemned by a tick on a piece of paper. Poetic justice? Poet's justice? Justice for the poet? Well, if you all want to condemn me, fine. I don't plan to dignify these proceedings with any kind of defence. There are much more important things at stake. People. Tender souls. And I will not be the one to break trust. But I ask all of you this: if you seriously believe I betrayed Solomon Nyati, then consider also the person who is bringing the allegation. The same person we have protected and sheltered all these years, even though we all knew his secret."

"Terrific," Riaan van Rensburg said. His voice had thickened. "Condemn Van Rensburg as a collaborator, the scapegoat more like. No judge or jury, mark you. Shoot the messenger. And everyone else is fine and cosy with their little secrets. But I think the secrets and the subterfuge have gone on long enough. Take this lot out of your lives and so what? At least there'd be some honesty. Everything we have built is built on lies. Who did what to whom when. To listen to La Joubert and her ex-husband it sounds as if it was all okay to play footsy a little with the regime. But the whole point was that we were in The Struggle. We were better than that. I have gone through hell because I once mistakenly said things I should not have said to someone I should never have talked to. I told him Rod Harris was gay. I told him the marriage to Zoë was a sham. And I spent years paying for that. Suffering, drinking, losing wives and partners. And now you all turn around and say: oh, we all know Riaan was a turncoat. We all knew he was on the security police books. Don't you understand that's why I didn't go to the meeting with Nyati? So that I wouldn't have anything to tell them! So I wouldn't know where it was or who was there. All I did was drive the fucking Kombi while you were all playing sticky fingers in the back. And you all knew, did you? Did you know the times I got this close to ending it, with pills, with a razor blade, in the gas oven? Did you know how often I woke up knowing one more woman had taken a look at my sorry, drunken mess of a life and decided not to bother, thank you very much and walked away or climbed into bed with someone else? So, now we all know about me, what about the rest of you? Shall we do a roll call? Shall we say who was there that night, one after the other? Shall we say who we told about it later? Because for all your forgiveness, Zoë, someone told the Special Branch about that meeting. Someone betrayed Nyati. Someone was responsible for his death. So let's see who else was not there? Let's ask where they were, hey Jess, Miss Reporter. You weren't there so where were you, then? And Porter and Mr Poet? What were you up to because I'm damned sure that whatever else I might have done I did not betray Solomon Nyati."

"None of you did."

Twenty-Five

NOT EVEN RIAAN VAN RENSBURG could have been hoping for this *deus ex machina*. The faces in the lamplight turned towards us. The expressions: bewilderment, incomprehension, surprise, fear. Theron, remember, was carrying the machine pistol with which he had killed Nyati.

"What the ...," I heard someone say. Riper expletives rippled around the audience. Then silence as Theron moved into centre stage. Riaan van Rensburg shrank away.

"If you do not know who I am from the TRC, I am Captain – ex-Captain – Kobus Theron, formerly of Koevoet in Namibia. If you are looking for the person who killed Solomon Nyati, then look at me. I did it. With this gun in my hand. I have told it already. And my reasons."

He raised the machine pistol aloft. The assembly seemed to close in on itself.

"There was no informer. That was just a line what I told the TRC. It was just mischief to hide the truth. The reason we knew his whereabouts was that his car was bugged. We had the technology from our overseas friends. We didn't need informers. We knew where he was every hour of the day. We took him out when it suited us and it suited as that night on that road at that hour. *Klip 'n klar*! There was no Judas."

"How do we know you are telling the truth?" Cobra rose, drawing himself up as if confronting a witness under oath.

"Ach, the lawyer," Theron said. "The lawyer who drew up all those contracts for the sanctions busters while all the time he was telling us how bad we were. Shall I go on?"

Cobra sat in abrupt silence.

"I thought not," Theron went. "I could go on like this. I could say how many of you met my colleague, Mr Guillaume. In Geneva. In New York. On your trips. But I choose not to. I could tell you who went to whose bed and who stayed at home and waited. I can tell you who was turned and who was not. I can bring you the tapes, transcripts. The photographs, even. But I do not choose to."

"But if you think any of your good selves played any part in this particular sorry mess, all of you is wrong. Would you like to know why? The answer is simple: we did not need you. What were you? A few names on a few files. Fifth columnists. But you did not change events. Solomon Nyati would have died on that night anyhow, whoever he had met in PE. Because I had chosen that night, because it suited me. It was business. Business in a war. There had been matters like it before and later. None of you was important. Sure you were an irritant. Some of you I admired. "

"Some of you had real courage" – he glanced towards Rod Harris – "Some of you didn't. Some chickened out" – this time his judgement fell on Porter, the tough-guy revolutionary, who could not meet his eye and scrambled to leave the gathering, Cobra in close pursuit.

"But there were only two real players in this war," Theron said, "people like me and people like Nyati. We were the combatants. The rest was window dressing, white liberals talking to foreign reporters like Miss Chase here – good evening, Mrs De Vere – then going home to the white areas we kept safe for them to write it up for the overseas papers and TV."

Jess fumbled in her handbag for a cigarette, then searched in vain for her gold cigarette lighter. When she did not find it, she glared at me.

"Sure we liked to have lots of names to play with, match up, blackmail and so forth. There was plenty of idle chitchat. But when it came to the real war, there had to be a winner or a loser and all you were doing was picking your bets," Theron went on. His rumbly, smoky voice seemed to enter your head and reverberate from within.

"And you won your bets! You cashed in the chips with big houses and nice cars while we who had protected you went before the TRC to confess our sins and worse. Because we fought the war and you did not fight the war. You were spectators. Now, Nyati and his people, they were fighters, warriors, soldiers. And they knew that people die in wars. He knew he would die. He even knew who would kill him. We met once and I tried to turn him. Did you know that? I had him in a cell in PE and I knew it would do no good to beat him any longer, so I threatened him – with his family, his friends, his reputation. Nothing fazed him. So I told him: "You go now but one day, soon, I will come for you and you will die if you don't change your ways, Mr Nyati."

"And he said: 'you can do what you want to me but I will not change and the only thing that will change will be this. When you kill me, you will sign your own death warrant. When you kill me you will make me one more martyr and sooner or later there will be too many martyrs for the world to take.'"

"So we both knew where we stood. He signed his death warrant. I signed mine. Call it our covenant. He died. My life was ruined. So tell me now who killed who. If you want to blame anybody, blame your American friend here for poking his nose in where it was not wanted. Blame Ambassador Kinzer for trying to make Nyati into a Mandela. And me, of course. Blame me. I took the rap when no one else would."

The deck began to empty, a rapid tide ebbing without farewells. Perhaps it was the sight of the ugly, worn machine pistol, or simply the appearance of Kobus Theron, this monstrous throw-back – the enemy, forgotten in all the bonhomie of the new era, the darkness that fell across the nation's dream.

The silence filled with the sound of engines starting, cars driven away in reckless haste.

Riaan van Rensburg remained, Poirot to the end.

"So that's it, hey?" he said. "The American walks in with his stooge, his assassin, and the show's over. We need to know nothing else. Uncle Sam's puppet has told us the truth so we can all go home. Doesn't that tell us everything? I mean, if you had asked whose side they were on, back then, they would have said they were the good guys, like they always want to be. But who is it now? So whatever Theron said, that's not the truth, Kinzer, not the whole truth and nothing but the truth. Why should we believe Theron? Why should we believe an apartheid killer, especially one with a gun?"

Theron rolled his eyes and placed the machine pistol on the wooden deck, squatting beside it. He raised both hands in the air in mock surrender. Van Rensburg's audience was dwindling. But Zoë Joubert had not left. Her eyes, fixed on mine, smarted with betrayal: how could you bring this into our midst? How could you bring this killer to denounce us all? How could you promise love when all you wanted was some warped testimony?

When I glanced towards Jessica de Vere, she looked away in disgust, as if my appearance with Theron represented the most appalling breach of faith, or at least etiquette. I had committed the very stupidity she had warned me to avoid.

Rod Harris moved his deck chair closer to Zoë Joubert. Vanessa van Rensburg moved across to her husband and took his hand. The ranks had thinned but the line-up was obvious: Theron was my only ally against them.

Van Rensburg was not done with his questions.

"So what is the truth, then, Ambassador? Your henchman, the killer, says none of us was to blame. But why believe him? He's already lied to the TRC. He's lied because the truth is a stranger to him, just something to be manipulated. You were even mentioned at the TRC visiting Nyati. What were you doing? A bit of advance work for Theron? With Jessica here?"

He brandished the missing pages of transcript from my hotel room.

"Stop it, now, Riaan," Zoë Joubert said, but, to my surprise, Vanessa van Rensburg came to his defence.

"Why should we stop it, Zoë? Don't we always stop it before it reaches the point of no return? When you decide? I know where I was. I know who I finished up with. I have my alibi for the night Nyati died. Shall I tell you who it was? Does it matter, except to embarrass some wife or girlfriend or boyfriend? Of course not. But what about everybody else. Where did you go after the meeting with Nyati, Zoë? What about you, Jess, where were you? You set it up, but you never pitched. So what's your story?"

Riaan van Rensburg reached into a pocket of his cargo pants and pulled out a golden cigarette lighter. He held it aloft, turning it so that the light of hurricane lamps was reflected in its cross-hatchings.

"Does this help remind you?" he said. "I found it in Kinzer's hotel room. Does your husband know this?"

"Of course not. It was all before Chris decided what he wanted, who he wanted. But he will know everything now, tonight."

"And this lighter got where it was because? You left it at Nyati's all those years ago? I don't think so. With love from Chris," he read from the inscription. "How sweet!"

He tossed the gold lighter across the deck to Jess Chase. Her hand reached for it in mid-air but it fell onto the wooden decking. She knelt to retrieve it. When she rose, she looked straight at me.

"Maybe you should ask the ambassador."

Before I could say anything, Zoë interrupted.

"Jess was not the only one waiting for Chris," she said gently. "I know that all too well. So before any of you go throwing accusations around, please remember that. It ended then, so let's leave it that way."

"But did it end, Zoë, the double-crossing?" Jess Chase had stepped across the deck and stood facing Zoë Joubert. "I know, for me, it ended when Chris snapped his fingers. But not everyone was quite so single-minded in their relationships, were they? Did it end with you and Chris when I broke with Tom? Did it? Can you answer that? Honestly? Or was it always that little joke – Boys' night out. Wasn't that the excuse? Like the other day? Once in a while. In Plett or Davos or somewhere. Boy's night out for old time's sake. Girl's night out. Or even day out when I was not around. Well, for your information, I played it straight. Even when I left this lighter behind on *my* girl's night out, I played it straight down the middle. But you can't say that, can you, Zoë?"

She did not wait for a reply.

The moon was high over the water, turning the surf line silver. The chairs Van Rensburg had laid out were abandoned. One or two had been knocked over in the rush to leave and no one had bothered to right them or collect glasses of half-finished drinks littering the wooden planking. Vanessa van Rensburg took her husband's hand and led him to their battered Jeep. Theron took a cold beer from the fridge.

Briefly, Zoë and I were finally alone together. She leaned against the balustrade. It wobbled, dangerously, as if some vital carpentry had begun to unravel. A section of the rail fell away and landed below in the garden. I took her arm but she recovered quickly.

"So, confession time," she said. "Don't interrupt. You wanted to know how it all happened, why it was so important not to go digging up the past. I will tell you and you can make your own mind up whether it has been the right price to pay for Lily's peace of mind. I was at Old Deep. Chris was at his mansion. Sometimes I crossed the line, going back to my own roots, really, away from all the tin roofs and the noisy crèches and the endless political debate. In theory I was married to Rod, but he was struggling more and more with pretending to be straight. A marriage of convenience, if you like. Cover for him, protection for me. So it suited Rod if I disappeared for a day or two and he could disappear for a day or two as well. And then with Chris it got a lot more serious. I thought we would become the couple people had always expected us to be. If there's someone else, you sense it. But I didn't know who it was and, frankly, I would have been amazed if I'd learned who was sharing Chris's bed while I was back at Old Deep and you – poor Tom – were attending diplomatic cocktails. It's obvious now though I didn't realise it until just tonight. You were the backup in case none of this worked out. In case I won."

"When? When did De Vere decide?"

"I suppose actually it was all just after the Nyati meeting. It made me quite famous actually. Now that I think of it, Jess made me quite famous with her articles about white liberals meeting the doomed black nationalist – that kind of thing. So perhaps she knew her stories would have repercussions. I think my name all over the papers put Chris off, a bit. Too prominent. Too publicly rebellious. So it all happened quite quickly. I went to tell Chris I was pregnant. He beat me to it by telling me it was all over between us because there was someone else. So I kept my news to myself."

"He didn't know? About the child? Mills?"

"Not for quite a time. Rod stuck by me during the pregnancy and the birth. He was fantastic. He did all the coo-cooing and the 3 am diaper changes and the cups of tea for tired, breast-feeding mama. Of course, he needed his space for his poetry and his own thing. And after a while, the way men do, Chris started having second thoughts – Jess turned out to be higher maintenance than he expected. So we would meet up occasionally. Boys' night out? He was the father of my child! We had known each other since the year dot. We could talk and laugh. We read the same books, liked the same opera. We belonged together, really. And as Mills grew up, he started asking questions about her, about the timing of her birth, about Rod. And I told him he had a daughter. He and Jess had Charlie by then – she was no slouch in getting the son and heir into play pretty quickly to keep Chris in line. And, I suppose, like some old English king, I rather think Chris enjoyed having his public son and his daughter on the side. But Mills never knew. And Rod never let her down. He never forgot a birthday or a prize-giving – and believe me there were plenty of prizes. He was Father Christmas and the Easter Bunny. And he loves her and she loves him."

"Of course."

"So, poor Tom. You sank our little ship and didn't realise you'd sink with it yourself. And the funniest thing of all is that when I saw Chris last night, I told him there'd be no more boy's nights out because I had found someone I thought would last – you – and I think he was quite relieved."

"I tried to bring you the truth."

"The truth was always there. We just didn't need it thrown in our faces."

"The truth. That word," Theron said as we left. "Maybe one day she will tell you the whole truth and nothing but the truth."

"Meaning?"

"Meaning what I said."

Part Five

In the first instance, they would deploy knives and bludgeons. Then they would pinion the body and pour petrol. Justice would be done. The people's justice.

Twenty-Six

I PACKED AND CHECKED OUT. I WOULD not be coming back this way again. Depending on how the visit to Cooktown unfolded, we might never be coming back at all.

The main highway from Plettenberg Bay traced a familiar route across great bridges spanning rivers that rose in the Kougaberg and Baviaanskloof and the Grootwinterhoekberge. At one point, as the highway rose over the flanks of the mountains, a sudden dense mist reminded me of why the foliage was so verdant from frequent drenching by damp weather sweeping in from the ocean. The little traffic there was on the road slowed right down. Spectral headlights suddenly appeared from the gloaming. Along the coast, the signposts pointed a way to pleasant-sounding places – Oyster Bay, Paradise Beach. We skirted Port Elizabeth, past the turn-off to the airport, alongside the auto plants and tire factories, and back down towards the coast. The road signs brought up old memories: New Brighton, Kwazakele, Uitenhage – places where I had watched the revolution unfold and Theron had struggled to thwart it.

The highway would pass the turn-off to Crystal Sands – I was not relishing that.

Theron snoozed in the passenger seat. We had retrieved his white pickup from the roadside and, at his behest, pulled in at Nature's Valley in the early hours of the morning so that he could pick up freshly laundered clothes and sculpt his beardline. He had chosen a dove-grey two-piece suit and a white shirt with a regimental-looking tie, loose around his neck as we drove on. He had packed a tote bag and slung it heavily onto the rear seat of the rental car. It was not that clear where he thought we were going or for how long. Our journey overlapped the route Nyati drove on his last night on earth. We would pass the ambush point itself.

Against Theron's advice, I called ahead to Lily Nyati to tell her I would be arriving with a visitor who wished urgently to speak with her about her husband's last moments on earth.

"You have taken away our surprise," Theron complained as I clicked off the phone. "You may regret that later. And who else is listening to your phone?"

"We are not fighting wars anymore," I told him.

He sighed loudly and lit a cigarette.

After a while, I mentioned to him the incidents with the pickup truck at Elim, the punctured tires of my rental car.

"Did you do any of this?"

"Not guilty, your honour."

"People kept telling me that 'They' are still out there and I assumed that meant people like you."

"People like me, but not me. The ones people call 'They' are the ones that got away – the generals, the handlers, the bombers, the cabinet ministers. They are out there, and they don't want to be disturbed, or reminded. They don't want the boat to rock."

"And Faku. Do you know a police officer called Faku? Nieuwoudt? Who is Nieuwoudt?"

"Where does those names come from?"

"The transcripts. The TRC. And they were at the airport when I arrived. They picked me up."

To my surprise, he smiled as if he saw some irony, some bitter joke that eluded me.

"So I trained them good, right? They were in my team and I trained them to keep out an eye for unusual things, names, inconsistencies, people who had been places where they should not have been. And they would have remembered your name alright, Mr Ambassador, after all the fuss you made with your Miss Chase and your BMW. So they would have just done a couple of checks when they were looking over the manifests. Did they find some papers on you? I always told them to follow the paper trail."

"A letter from the widows."

"So that is what is behind all this?"

"At the start."

"Then you are perhaps less of a smart-ass than what I thought."

"In the transcripts Nieuwoudt was a lieutenant and Faku a sergeant. But at the airport, Nieuwoudt called Faku captain."

"Mind games," Theron said. "They always liked mind games. I was their professor. Welcome to the new South Africa."

"So why are they still policemen and you are refused amnesty, Theron?"

"Because they was following orders. And I was giving them. So I am the fall guy." He was silent for a while. Then he turned on me with a quick flip of temper that alarmed me.

"Man, I wish you had told me sooner. If Faku and Nieuwoudt have got wind of where we are going, they will arrange a hot reception for us. For sure. It was me that taught them how to play that game, planting ideas, supplying the tires and the petrol. Black-on-black violence, we used to call it, but it was often enough with white supervision. And money. A few bucks for the ringleaders and you would get anyone to necklace anybody you wanted. And we know what *meneers* Faku and Nieuwoudt were up to the night Nyati died, don't we, Ambassador? They might not like to be reminded of that. They might think that is all going to come out in the new South Africa. They have grudges from those days. They do not appreciate my sacrifice for the team."

"But if that's what's going on, why are you doing this? You don't have to. Why not just wait for the statute of limitations?"

"Because no statute will chase away the nightmares. Because I cannot think of anything else. Because I am at my wit's end. Because my wife believes this is all fate. Because she thinks I must. Because she is a woman and believes other women will think like her. Because my sons say I must or they cannot stay in this country. Because, because. Why always because? Sometimes, in the bush, you did things and you did not always know why but then you'd find out there had been an ambush or a mine and you had driven around it without knowing a bloody reason."

Bleddy. Mahn.

"All my training, my instincts are saying: don't do this, because you are driving straight into an ambush and there'll be mines all over the place."

"You think we'll be ambushed. By widows?"

"Not by widows. Not even by the old comrades you knew back then. You have not been keeping up, Ambassador. We are talking about generation X, the kids that never learned to do anything except throw rocks and burn tires. Burn people. Middle name violence with a capital V for Victor. If she has these guys around her, like Winnie Mandela with her football team, they won't be making fancy arguments about the TRC and all that. Poverty and corruption makes people just as angry as apartheid did. And these days there are no police like us to hold the line."

He was speaking to me as if we were allies, bonded by pigmentation and shared threat. And I was listening to him as if he were right to do so.

"What makes you think we are on the same side?"

"No need to lose it, Ambassador. I'm only giving you my advice as a professional."

"Professional killer?"

"Whatever you like to say. But I know these people ..."

"I grew up with them bare-assed in the Macabuzi River. Isn't that what you were going to say?"

"Something of that kind." He sounded as if I had given offense.

"Well I didn't grow up with them calling them piccannins and *kaffirs*. I met them as people. Not slaves. Not *blecks*. And that's how I will treat them."

"You want to go alone?" He let the idea sink in. I said nothing. "No, I thought not. I am not surprised you do not want to go alone. Because you people always seemed like having my continent as your playground. But you leave us to do the fighting."

I fumbled a cigarette out of my pack of locally made Chesterfields. In the studies that emerged after the TRC, of which much had been made at the conference in Cape Town, there was a theory that, in the cautious duet of victim and perpetrator, it was often as not the victim who made the first move towards reconciliation. But in return they demanded the truth about their loved one's last moments on earth – total confession; total remorse.

"You must tell your story, Theron. They must hear it from you. You must be their witness. You must tell the truth."

"And watch your back, Ambassador. You want me to watch your back, don't you, Ambassador? Like a professional."

We pulled over for petrol. Theron stocked up on biltong and pies – *padkos*. We drank chilled Coke from plastic bottles. We smoked incessantly with the windows rolled down. I was following Nyati's route to his death in the presence of his murderer. Some tribute! Some wake! A station called Radio Algoa was playing country music and slightly outdated rock. I had driven these road before with Jess Chase, years before, tingling with hope that, on this or that clandestine voyage, unhooked from my diplomatic credentials, we would become lovers and I would be initiated into a new world. Her world. However briefly, the dream had come true.

I was invincible, shielded from all harm by the intensity of love and righteousness. I would see Nyati and grasp the lesson we often forgot in America in our haste for material betterment – freedom is the prize above all, and life without it is no life at all. I would outwit the authorities – the Therons and the Fakus and Nieuwoudts. To hell with policy and protocol. To hell with the risk of exposure for behaviour "in a manner incompatible" with my diplomatic status, as the cold war parlance used to put it. These same back roads had been my passage to enlightenment.

But how often had Theron driven here, too, with his underlings and superiors – Snyman and De Kock, Taylor, Nieuwoudt, Faku? What had they discussed among themselves – tradecraft, rugby scores, children's grades, chances of promotion, the perfidy of colleagues, coding systems, favoured weapons, victory, defeat? In their unmarked cars with the phony plates, had they discussed who they would next visit at 3 am? Did they talk about the enemy as worthy adversaries or as *"dom kaffirs"*? Had they cackled over the tapes from their phone intercepts, their bugging devices? Had they laughed at people like me who thought they had outflanked the system, outwitted them? Or had they been silent, macho, checking their radios and the magazines of their weapons, knowing what had to be done without needing to go into the detail of precisely who would break down a door here and who would stand guard there, who would roust a sleeping man from his bed and pistol-whip a protesting wife before the cuffs bit home on the captive's wrists?

"You know this road?"

"Like the hand on my back." Theron laughed and looked across at me. "Did you never do that? Did you never mock the Afrikaners, the police, for the way we messed up your language? Did you never say it was duck's water off my back? That you made me out of a monkey. So, I know this road like the hand on my back."

"So did Nyati."

"Oh, yes. Nyati knew it very well. He travelled it often and if you tailed him he would slip away and meet his recruits and tell them how to get to Lesotho and Botswana on the way to training to pick up their landmines and Kalashnikovs. That is why we needed the radio bug your CIA gave. He was too slippery and he knew all the roads like a hand on his back."

"But in the end it was you who put a hand on his back."

"A bullet," Theron corrected me. "I put a bullet through his skull. I do not joke about that."

We approached a rise in the road where the combination of a steep gradient and a sharp curve to the left forced travellers to slow down. Off to the right, a narrow cul-de-sac on a dirt road offered cover for anyone lying in wait. As we passed the place, Theron looked back over his shoulder, a final, retrospective evaluation of its suitability. Neither of us spoke. The circle was closing.

The Cooktown turn-off came sooner than I wished or expected. Theron fastened his shirt collar and adjusted his tie. He reached onto the back seat and pulled on the jacket of his suit. He took his tote bag and placed it neatly across his lap. He switched off the car radio and cleared his throat. He packed the detritus of the *padkos* in plastic bags and knotted them carefully. He lit a cigarette, then stubbed it out.

In his heyday as a counterinsurgency commander, he would not have displayed such nervousness at a moment like this. Any doubts or hesitation would be hidden by the orders to charge weapons, lock and load; any sense of vulnerability would fade in the knowledge that, out on the flank, Casspirs full of armed men were in position, a radio-call away from deployment.

But not now. There was no back-up here, no *daka-daka*.

A signpost from the black-top pointed to a dirt road leading across a scrubby field, past an abandoned slaughterhouse with a peeling, faded signboard in Afrikaans. *Slagpale*. The place seemed bigger, tawdrier, the burned police houses rebuilt, the cemetery swollen with AIDS victims outnumbering by far those who fell in The Struggle.

The rear-view mirror showed an empty road. No children rolling barrel-hoops; no vendors selling wire sculptures of windmills and motorcycles. Only hawk-eyed young men in small groups on strategic corners. Theron scanned the township, checking for familiar landmarks, escape routes, lines of attack.

He had been here often enough in the dead of night, cruising between the tiny homes, armed and dangerous. He had been here to arrest young men in raids before dawn – young men, who, if they survived the ministrations of the security police, had probably fathered this newer generation. White control, really, had been no more than a painful chimera, a bloodstained interlude.

"Better pay respects," Theron said, directing me to the burial ground on the outskirts of the township that looked out across a river-bed to the bald, dry hills of the Eastern Cape

From his bag, he drew a tired bunch of flowers in cellophane bearing the name of a supermarket chain.

The martyrs' graves – no more than piles of dirt on the day of the funeral – had been covered with a newer adornment, in grey granite, like a small Greek temple, a budget Parthenon. An inscription read: "Their blood shall bear the fruit of freedom."

A notice credited the South African Heritage Resources Agency with the construction of the monument.

Above small white urns there was another motto. "Long live the fighting spirit of our leaders."

Theron looked at it, then looked at me. He removed the wrapping from the flowers and laid them at the grave.

"Ancestors," he said, without explanation.

We climbed back into the car.

"Shit, man, this is wrong. We should get the hell out of here," he said.

I checked the rear-view mirror again. The knots of young men had coalesced into human barricades blocking the exits. In the distance, a slender column of black smoke rose from a burning tire.

"Too late," I said.

She was waiting outside the house that I remembered from my first visit. She was wearing a dark beret and a white apron over a woollen jacket and long skirt. The building was slightly bigger than most in the township, befitting the home of the school principal, perched on a rise so that it seemed to dominate the broken, dusty streets like a command post.

She gestured for me to drive into the garage – the same garage as Nyati himself had made available on my first visit with Jess. (She had been driving at that time, and seemed familiar with this subterfuge to keep the car hidden, not from young black men but from men from like Theron.)

Theron insisted that we reverse into the garage, poised for escape. Lily bolted the doors closed. The engine fell silent. A chicken pecked around the car, squawked when I opened the door. Speckles of dust floated in a shaft of lemon light spilling through a crack in the roof. The garage walls were lined with an array of rusting hoes and rakes and scraps of metal on hooks and frames.

The remains of an entire bicycle, its wheels and frame bent out of shape, hung from a length of cord in the ceiling – maybe the same one Nyati had been riding in his narrative so long ago. In an art gallery in New York or Berlin, it would have qualified as an installation.

Lily Nyati led the way through an inner door, past the kitchen where I remembered her making huge vats of soup for the funeral (the room was still and cold now, its odours antiseptic, neutral, as if she no longer lived here permanently, a temporary sojourner at her husband's modest mausoleum).

We embraced awkwardly and I introduced her to Kobus Theron.

She started back, holding the white apron to her mouth to cover her shock. When she spoke, it was to reproach me with such bitterness that I thought all my calculations had been stupendously flawed.

"I know who this is, but I never thought he would have the nerve to come to this house. I never thought you would have the nerve to bring him here."

"There is a reason, Lily. I promise," I said.

"I hope. Or I will never forgive you."

In the living room the three other widows sat in a sad row on a single sofa, huddling together for comfort at the sight of Kobus Theron and his tote bag. They whispered to one another and to Lily Nyati in their own isiXhosa language. To my surprise I heard Theron speaking it, too.

Lily Nyati translated his words. "He says he is sorry if we are surprised. He says he is nervous, too. He says he is grateful if we will listen to him."

"And will you listen, Lily?"

"It is not what I expected."

From the kitchen, Celiwe Nyati entered the room. She shook my hand with stiff formality. When Theron went to greet her, she turned away. This time she wore black jeans with matching sneakers and a T-shirt in green, yellow and black – the colours of The Struggle. At the front, across her chest, her father's portrait and, at the back, a slogan with the promise: "One Settler, One Bullet."

Through the lace curtains and security netting on the window, I noticed that the young men had formed into a phalanx, either guarding the house or keeping us prisoner in it. With the car hidden in the garage, there was no sign of our presence for any subsequent investigator to note as evidence that we had even been there.

Celiwe Nyati crossed quickly to a small window with four polished panes and gestured to her comrades, but I could not interpret the signal. Theron shook his head from side to side.

On a coffee table – the same one as had been there in Nyati's day when its mock floral arrangement hid a security police listening device – his widow had laid out a teapot, cups, saucers, milk, sugar and cookies under veils of thin gauze weighted with bright beads to keep away flies. Theron's gaze fixed on the plastic flowers in the centre of the coffee table; he did not raise the question of whether the bug had ever been found, silenced or removed.

It was tempting to imagine its forlorn signal beeping faintly in the silence of some forgotten control room long abandoned by the listeners, drums of recording tape hanging from storage racks. Lily Nyati poured tea with the requisite additions of cream and sugar. In theory I had come to report to her and so should begin the meeting. The heavy stillness of the sitting room became unbearable.

"We have been here before," I gestured inclusively to myself and the widows. Nothing much had changed in the room since I first saw it – the same brown suite of sofas and armchairs, the same glass-fronted display case with its framed photographs, school diplomas, and, from more recent times, a letter signed by Mandela himself praising the fallen warrior.

"I recall Celiwe being here, too, as a very young child," I went on. "Captain Theron has also been here."

Celiwe Nyati gasped. "This is not a family visit. You are not my uncle. This is not Christmas. You have brought a killer into our home. Our home! You have brought my father's killer into his own house! Again!"

Lily Nyati sighed and peered upwards at some imagined point on the plaster-board ceiling.

The silence closed again and I continued with the speech I had been contemplating on the drive. My words seemed stilted, inappropriate.

"I do not want to give offense, but some things do need to be said. We all know where we came from; we all know the roles we played. Captain Theron has confessed some of what he knew at the TRC."

Lily Nyati looked at me sharply when I used the word: some.

"And I was here as a junior diplomat, a representative of my country, my government, when I made a promise I have not kept. None of that is disputed. None of that is new. What is new is what has happened since you all sent me a letter reminding me of my promise and asking me to investigate more recent events. I have now done both and, in the course of that, have met up with Captain Theron."

"Ex-captain, former captain. I am no longer a police officer."

"A police officer? A murderer!" Celiwe Nyati's voice had risen, carrying to the young men outside. Tears brimmed in her eyes. Theron ran a finger around his unfamiliar tight collar, as if seeking to loosen a noose.

"Mrs Nyati. Ladies. You asked me to find out who betrayed your husbands. I have discovered that no single person did that. Of the young white liberals he met the night he died, several have confessed to being informers of one kind or another, wittingly or unwittingly. But there was no single traitor of the kind Mr Theron described at the Truth Commission. When he said that, he was lying."

The widows on the sofa shook their heads, and clicked their tongues, but were not really surprised. Theron was a serial assassin, the killer of husbands, the author of pain and loss. Who would expect honesty? Only Celiwe displayed anger.

"He should be dead, dead like my father, like the Cooktown Four and all the others. He deserves no sympathy. No forgiveness. Do you know what he did before he came here? He went to the grave, the monument, and put down flowers and in his heart he was probably pissing on it."

I turned to Lily Nyati.

"Do you want me to continue? Shall we leave?"

Her daughter answered for her.

"You are not permitted to leave. Do you hear? You have no permit!"

She laughed at her own joke: permits to enter segregated townships had been an instrument of control in the apartheid era. And now, it seemed, they were again. I had a sudden recall of the days before I met Jess, of following the rules and reporting to the police in some settlement or other to fulfil the bureaucratic protocols of control. The officer who copied out my details in painstaking script kept a framed photograph on his desk. I thought it might be of his wife, his family, but it turned out to be of his pet bulldog. In a corner of his office, a *sjambok* was propped against the wall.

"Continue," Lily was saying.

"The reality is this. Theron planned to kill your husbands for a variety of reasons. One of the reasons was that Solomon Nyati was too important to The Struggle. Another, so he tells me, is that he was becoming too well-known outside the country because of people like me and Miss Chase."

The widows seemed older than I had anticipated, their faces filigreed with wrinkles. Each sleepless night, each restless moment, each cry of pain had been etched forever so that, if you studied the fine lines, you would see the agony had been unending, a curse that would not be lifted.

Zinto. Ngalo. Mboniswa. Nyati's comrades, murdered by Theron and his men. Four widows, sitting where they had tarried so often with only memories for comfort..

"So there was no single traitor?" Lily Nyati asked me.

"As far as I know, there was not."

"But there was a reason?"

"There was a reason."

"And you are part of that reason?"

"It seems."

"Seems? Yes or no?" Celiwe Nyati demanded to know.

"Yes."

"Then it is you, too, Ambassador or whatever you are, who should be seeking forgiveness," the daughter said in more restrained tones. "Not just this monster you have brought with you."

Her arms were stiff against her sides, her hands curled into fists.

"I have committed two errors. Firstly, I made a promise to your mother and the other widows that I could not keep and in my heart of heart knew I would not be able to keep. And, secondly, I came back here believing that the truth would make up for my failure. I believed that the truth would help you heal."

"It is more than truth, can you not see that?" Lily Nyati took up the cross-examination, gesturing to her three friends.

"What do they need?" Lily Nyati was saying. "Truth? Redemption? Money? Do they need only the reason why they have raised their children alone, slept alone, lived cold and empty lives tending martyr's graves? And you thought you would walk in and resolve this."

"You invited me in, Lily."

"And now you need me – us – to invite you out."

"I was not the killer!"

"And I suppose you will say you were only obeying orders."

"I was never obeying orders. I did what I believed an American should do. Then and now."

"And him?"

"He must speak for himself."

Twenty-Seven

Theron lowered his tote bag.

"Mama Nyati," he began. "Ladies. Miss Nyati. Ms. I am sorry." He looked from one to the other, but only Celiwe Nyati held his gaze. His voice had lost the confidence of his delivery to the Old Deep set on the deck back in Plettenberg Bay.

"As I have told the TRC, I killed Mr Nyati directly and I ordered and organised the murders of Mr Zinto, Mr Ngalo and Mr Mboniswa. If I had known then what I know now, I would not have carried out my mission. I would have refused. I would never have done this if I had known that our leaders knew, even then, that we would lose the war, that we had lost the war."

"This murder was war?" Lily Nyati said.

"I felt it so to be. I had been in war in South West. Namibia. And this was the same war, like your husbands were in. We were combatants. I saw Nyati – Mr Nyati – as a soldier. An enemy of the state. When I killed him, I could not see him as a human being, only a soldier."

"Not as a father? Like yourself?" Celiwe Nyati barely whispered. "A father with children. Like me."

"But you had weapons," Lily Nyati said.

"And they had weapons, sometimes of a different kind. They had a just cause. You had a just cause. So did we. But we did not tell it properly. We were fighting for our survival, or so we thought. We thought we could not survive if we did not rule. We had more guns, it is true. They – you – had numbers. You had the strength to say no to us and when you said that in such large numbers, we realised we could no longer make you say yes."

"Yes, baas, you mean." The women joined in brief, sour laughter.

Theron hunched forward, his hands reaching out, showing the pinks of his palms.

"It was wrong," Theron said.

"But it does not bring them back," Celiwe Nyati interjected.

"Nothing can do that."

"Our hearts are empty," her mother said.

"I cannot change that. If I could I would. If I could bring them back and take all your pain and their pain on my own shoulders, I would do that."

One of the widows, Gertrude Zinto, leaned forward and touched his arm, just for a second, then drew back as if jolted by a physical shock.

"But you can explain," Lily Nyati said.

"I could say I was carrying out orders and I was. There were orders that Nyati should be permanently removed from society. That meant only one thing. Our bosses had decided, the police and the military, that he was causing too much trouble, too much *onrus*."

"But why did it have to be you? What entitled you to take his life?" Celiwe's voice had sharpened again, taking on a harsh edge. "He was fighting for justice, for peace. He wanted us all to live together in peace. As humans. And you shot him like a dog."

Theron paused and reached into his tote bag. From it, he withdrew the machine pistol with which he had killed Solomon Nyati.

"With this I shot him," he said.

The widows shrank back among themselves and one, Lucy Mboniswa, bolted for the door. I followed her and placed a hand on her arm. But I was not quick enough to prevent Celiwe Nyati running to the gathering crowd outside, shouting in isiXhosa.

"She is telling them who I am," Theron said after listening to her for a moment. "She is telling them I am armed and they should be armed. Is that not true, Mama Nyati?"

"It is true," Lily Nyati said.

Theron placed the machine pistol on the coffee table, turning the snub, worn barrel towards himself and the wooden pistol grip towards Lily Nyati. Notches had been carved in it, too many to count at a glance.

"With this gun, I killed your husband. He was a brave man. He died fighting me. He was unarmed and I shot him. I have brought it here if you want revenge. With this gun, I killed people in Zimbabwe, Namibia and South Africa. I give it up to you. It came to me when I captured its owner, a freedom fighter. Now it is time to give it back. The killing is over and I want peace in my country and in my heart. Only you can tell me that your husband would now forgive me, because he would know that I was a soldier and I lost and the victor can afford to be generous."

"You talk clever talk," Lily Nyati said. "But let us see where the truth lies." She stroked the machine pistol, allowing her fingers to run over the trigger guard. She swivelled it so that the barrel pointed exactly between Theron's legs.

"This took my husband's life, this thing made of wood and metal?"

Her voice rose to an interrogative crescendo.

"You show me the murder weapon and expect what? You think I can punish a gun, make it weep, make it show it is sorry and has remorse. Make it feel my pain. But that is a trick because it was not the gun. It was not really the gun at all. It was a man, a killer, who pulled the trigger. You are the man. It was you. You killed him. Did you kill him or did the gun kill him?"

"I killed him."

She raised the weapon now and levelled it at Theron's head.

"You shot him where?"

"In the head."

"How many times?"

"Once. It was a struggle in my car. A fight. He was trying to escape."

"With his hands tied?"

"Handcuffed."

"And he would have died anyway? Even if he had not struggled."

"Yes."

"And you are sorry?"

"Mama Nyati, I am sorry. If you wish me to go on my bended knees I will say I am sorry. I am sorry to you and all the widows. I am sorry from the bottom of my heart."

"And when you had killed him you disguised it, like all the others, to make it look like another kind of killing."

"Yes. Black-on-black. A black-on-black killing."

"Black-on-black. That is a quaint expression. And what is this now. Black-on-white? If I pull this trigger it will be black-on-white? Is it less killing if it is black-on-black? Are black people less dead? Do white people live more, count for more?"

For the first time I noticed stains of perspiration on Theron's shirt spreading from his armpits. Beads of sweat stood out on his forehead. He spoke carefully, weighing each word. The gun barrel swung a little crazily, but never left its target completely, sometimes locked onto his chest, sometimes his groin, sometime lined up for a straight head-shot. The weapon was capable of firing a stream of bullets, emptying its 20-round clip in a matter of seconds. In its day it had been popular with Special Forces operatives who prized its compactness – it was not much bigger than a conventional handgun – and its impressive rate of fire. For much the same reasons, it had also been favoured by mobsters and urban terror organisations. At this close range, Theron would stand no chance at all. She held the barrel with one hand while the other strayed over its mysterious workings – the trigger and trigger guard, the lightly oiled slide, the safety catch which she flicked between its settings in the safe, semi-automatic fire and full automatic fire. If she pulled the trigger, no one would ever report her action. Theron's death – maybe mine, too – would be cloaked in Omertà.

Step by step, Lily Nyati led Theron through the sequence of events that formed his testimony: the choice of ambush location (why there, at the pass? because the cars would be slowing? easy to catch?); the way the police cars were hidden; the flashing blue light and the separation of the four men into two vehicles once the snatch had been made.

She prompted him when he stumbled as if she were his confessor – or inquisitor – prizing out the reluctant detail: who killed who, and when and where? She had gone through his story so often from the transcripts that she knew it better than he did.

Celiwe Nyati had returned to the room, following the recital as if to ensure that Theron left out no detail as he described the moment of the ambush and the silence in the cars as they drove towards

Crystal Sands. Then the rising protest as the captives realised they were not being taken off to some police camp for the routine beating and interrogation, but something far worse. Then the separation for disposal by bludgeon, knife and fire. Permanent Removal.

Celiwe paced back and forth, sometimes checking from the window on the crowd outside. When the young men caught sight of her, they roared. "*Amandla!*"

Finally, Lily Nyati homed in on the detail of her husband's last drive with Theron, the words they had exchanged, the silences, the manner in which he had attempted to strangle Theron and his failure to do so.

Had he begged for his life?

No.

Had he tried to plead for the lives of the others: let them go and take me in exchange?

Yes.

And why had you not granted that wish? Because it was too late. Because we had planned it this way, not that way.

Then the shot, the final single shot to the head.

"So how did you feel during this struggle in your car?"

"I felt nervous. It was an operation. There is adrenaline. You do not think. You act as you are trained to. You do not think until later."

"And later, for you, you went home to your wife and family and had breakfast?"

"Yes ma'am."

"And told them?"

"Some lies about late duty."

"Some lies? My husband's death was just some lies? These killings of four men – Nyati, Zinto, Ngalo, Mboniswa – were just some lies? Did you go straight home?"

"First I must report to my superior."

"What did you say?"

"I said it was done. That was all. They knew what was happening."

"So then you went to your family?"

"Yes ma'am."

"But Solomon did not."

"He was dead, Mama Nyati. How could he?"

"How could he, indeed?"

"Do you know how old I was?" Celiwe broke in. "Do you know how I was an infant on my mother's back, wrapped up in a blanket. Do you know that I never knew him? How could I? Did you know how long I would ask my mother when my father was going to come home and she did not know what to say?"

Lily Nyati rose and strode back and forth in the small sitting room, still carrying the gun, then turned on Theron as if imitating the prosecutor in a television courtroom drama.

"Are you being honest with me?"

"Yes, I am being honest."

"So I will ask you once again: how did you feel?"

"I was doing my part in the war. To protect my people. To prevent a communist takeover. It was an operation. A necessary, military operation."

She knelt beside him and rammed the machine pistol into the side of his head.

"You do not seem to understand," Lily Nyati said. "I asked you to tell me how you felt about it. Before and after and during. What did it mean to you?"

The noise level was rising outside the house, among the growing crowd of young men. I could hear slogans from the past, the thumping rhythm of a toyi-toyi dance. In my earlier days in South Africa, the sound had filled me with exhilaration. Now it elicited a terrible fear. The rage had risen. I was its target just as much as Theron.

"Go and talk to them," Lily Nyati told her daughter. "Tell them to be patient. Tell them it is not yet time."

She sat back in an armchair with a beguiling look on her face. The machine pistol was steadier now.

Celiwe Nyati was leading the singing among the crowd – the old, haunting melodies, the chilling lyrics, composed in an era she knew only by hearsay – her father's era.

"*Senzeni Na*?" What have we done?

It was a question I was asking of myself.

In the distance, part-hidden behind a row of shanties, I could see a late-model Toyota, parked and immobile. Maybe it was a trick of light but I thought I saw two white faces alongside that of a black man.

Theron licked his lips. He looked at the floor, then back up at the ceiling, then straight at Lily Nyati.

"In one way I felt nothing."

"It left you cold?"

"It left me cold."

"And the other way. What was the other way? You are talking as if we are all the same. Are we?"

"We are Africans. All of us." Theron's eyes flickered towards the other three widows as he said this, then returned to his questioner.

"Ha! You think so? You think African and Afrikaner is the same thing? Master and Slave. Victim and perpetrator. Overlord and underdog. Are they all the same?"

"No. They are not. But I belong in Africa because of hundreds of years of my ancestors. I do not belong anywhere else. Not Holland or France or Germany where my people came from. I was raised to be believe we had a duty to rule Africa. But now I cannot belong anymore in Africa unless you give me my space in Africa. You were here first."

"Yes, we were here first. But you took it, plundered it, stole it. Like you have stolen my husband from me. So if you want to be here in my Africa you must be honest. Can you be honest?"

"Yes, Mama Nyati. I am an honest man. A father of two wonderful boys. A husband. Blessed with a wife who says she loves me despite everything. I work for peace, against violence. I lift mines so that they can no longer hurt people. I risk my life to pay for the lives I have taken."

"And when you took them, those lives, was it in cold blood? Or was there something else? Were you thinking: one less of these blacks to deal with? Did you hate us? Did you hate my husband?"

"No Mama. I did not. He was a soldier. It was not personal."

"Not personal! You killed him! Is that personal or not?"

"It was war."

"And now it is not war and you are sorry."

"Yes, I am sorry."

"So did you hate him?"

"No."

"But he was black and you were a white policeman."

"Yes."

"And what did you call blacks? *Kaffirs*?"

"No. Yes."

"Say it. Say what you felt."

"*Kaffirs*. You want me to say I hated *kaffirs*?" A spot of wild red colour had spread across his cheekbones. Perspiration smeared dark stains across his shirt.

"But I did not. I did not want to live in your house or you in mine. But I did not hate."

"But you mocked us. With your police friends. You laughed at us. You made jokes."

"Sometimes."

"Because of the way we talked?"

"Yes."

"And our voices in the servant's quarters? The way the maid stole your sugar and the gardener believed in the spirits? Because we had tribes? Because we wanted to take back everything you had taken from us? Because our voices sounded strange to you?"

"*Ja*. All of that. *Ja*." Theron sounded as if he were short of breath. His words came in a staccato burst.

"And our smell?"

"Yes."

"And our stupidity?"

"Yes. Yes. Yes. All those things. Because you hated me, you wanted what was mine. Your men wanted my women, my car, my house. I hated that you were sly. I hated that you had slaughtered my people and bombed our houses. I hated that you did not do what you were told. But I did not hate you in person, not anyone. We made a covenant with God to survive in this damned continent. So how could that be turned into hatred?"

"But some of your own officers were black, weren't they? Were they *kaffirs*, too? "

"But I did not hate them."

"And are you being honest now?"

"Yes I am being honest. I could not be more honest because I have said things I would not say to my own wife, my own children. I want them to grow up decently. In Africa. With other Africans. Like you and your children. His children. Nyati's children."

"Do you think he would want his children to play with the sons of his murderer?"

"But we must all do that in our country. We cannot visit the crimes of fathers on sons."

"Do you think my husband, my late husband would forgive you?"

"Or my father? Would my father forgive his murderer?" Celiwe Nyati had returned to the house. "Would the comrades outside this house forgive the killer of their hero?"

"They would have no reason to. But you could explain to them, Miss Nyati. Ms. They will listen to you. Your father wanted only the best for his people and what I see outside the window is not the best for his people. The violence must end sometime, if not today then tomorrow or the next day, and when it does there will be consciences to settle, questions to answer, prices to pay. I know that. God knows I do."

"Do not mention God. How can a killer mention God?"

"Please, I beg you, for it is you and your generation who can do this: break the cycle of violence. Turn the other cheek like we all learned in all our churches. Do not make my mistakes. Do not believe that violence can solve problems without creating many, many more. You are young. You have a life. Maybe you did not know your father. That is my fault – 100 per cent – and if I could change that in any way, I would. But I did know your father, in my way. And I know how much he loved his children and his country and how he fought against people like me to provide you with a future. Like Gandhi. He was a Gandhi and I called him a terrorist. But he sacrificed so you could have that future. You have won. He would not want that victory to be stained with more blood."

His words flowed so flawlessly – almost oratory – that I wondered how often Theron had rehearsed this pitch for mercy. Or was it just one more excerpt from a well-thumbed playbook, the high-stakes endgame?

Celiwe Nyati would not meet his gaze but I saw that she was

weeping. When I looked at him, there were tears on his cheeks too.

"What must he do to prove he means what he says?" I asked her.

"I would do anything. I would lay down my life," Theron said.

I did not think that the comrades outside would necessarily distinguish between his life and mine if his gambit failed.

"Would my husband kill you? If he had had this gun, would he have killed you when he could have?" Lily Nyati's fingers roamed over the weapon. She clicked the safety catch on and off, a murderous metronome. Hypnotic. And left it off.

"I doubt he would think I was worth the effort."

"And now what do you think of us? Do you think we are human now? Do you see what pain you have created? If I had killed your wife, would you forgive me? Would you receive me in your home?"

"No, I could not have. My heart is not big enough for that. You are better people than I am," Theron said, his shoulders slumped.

"Go," Lily Nyati said, as if suddenly tired. She clicked the safety back on.

"Celiwe, tell those people outside to go away. The show is over." She laughed bitterly.

"I have asked them," her daughter said. "But they refuse. They want vengeance."

"Tell them. From me. From all of us. The widows. Tell them we want it to be over."

Celiwe stepped outside again, grabbing the bullhorn she had used so skilfully in Cape Town. Dust rose from the war dance – young men firing up their passions as earlier generations had done in exactly this same place. Light flashed on a large blade. Columns of smoke rose from burning tires. Two tires seemed to be held in reserve, along with bottles of petrol. When I looked again, the distant Toyota had disappeared. Someone had grabbed Celiwe Nyati's bullhorn and hurled it to the ground, crushed under the feet of the toyi-toyi dancers.

"We cannot leave," I said. "Not everything has been said. He has told the truth, Lily. You must respond. You must say if his truth was enough."

"The truth does not exist in a vacuum," she said. "It does not heal all wounds. It opens them. Does his confession ease my pain, our pain? I see what you want. It is what you Americans call closure. All the loose ends tied up. He confesses. I forgive. He is free. I am free. But it is not like that. Life is not like that. Truth is not like that. Perhaps in your country where your lawyers make people pay for their sins in dollars and cents you can pay for the loose ends, too. But not here. There are too many loose ends, not enough dollars or even cents. We have loose ends from the slavers and from the Christians with their missionaries. We have loose ends from the traders and colonialists and the gold mines. And all that was even before apartheid, the mother of all loose ends! We have history and you arrive as if you can wipe the slate clean. Listen to them outside. Is there closure for them? The only closure they know is the toyi-toyi. An eye for an eye. It is their judgment that counts now. Not mine. Or ours."

"You do not believe he was telling the truth?"

"If he was telling the truth, then he will be forgiven."

"And me?" I said. "Have I done what you asked of me?"

"You have done more. You have done too much. You did the opposite of what I asked."

I had come to the end of my arguments. Theron rose and Lily Nyati stared straight ahead as he walked towards her.

"Can I shake your hand, Mama Nyati?"

"Never," she replied. "How can I forgive you?"

"Miss Nyati. Tell me what I must do."

"You said you would lay down your life. Then prove it."

Theron picked up his machine pistol and made a more to walk outside.

"Leave the gun," Solomon Nyati's daughter said.

A window smashed. Rocks rained onto the roof, a satanic hail.

"We must call the police," I said.

"There will be no police today, not of the kind you imagine," Theron said.

Lily Nyati picked up the telephone but the line was dead. She tried her cell phone and looked at it, baffled. "There is no signal."

Twenty-Eight

THERON WAS DOWN. HE HAD LEFT the building with his hands held above his head in surrender. I do not to this day know why but I followed him. A Molotov cocktail landed at his feet, exploding in a bloom of oily orange smoke, but he walked on. You could smell the sweat, the burning fuel, the rage. The rocks came, hitting him in the chest and on the shoulders and in the groin. But he kept on walking.

In the crowd, the blades were drawn – long agricultural machetes, pangas freshly honed. A boulder the size of a soccer ball somehow flew at him. He faltered, stumbled, fell. He twisted around to look at me. I saw no fear, only the bewilderment of a prize-fighter who cannot grasp that all is lost. A hail of smaller rocks hammered at his ribcage. Somehow he rose again, first to his knees, then upright.

"Go back," he mouthed to me. Blood sputtered from his lips and gums. The crowd closed behind us, locking us into their trap.

Theron's tormentors grew bolder. They pushed, shoved, spat. With nowhere else to turn, he came to a halt. Someone produced a sharpened bicycle spoke, already dipped in blood, and punctured his arm. The fabric of the dove-grey suit, scuffed and dusty, darkened in a crimson ring around the entry wound. Theron closed his eyes briefly, then stared back at his executioners, the toyi-toyi dancers. A weighted club – a *knobkerrie* they called it – thudded down on his shoulder so hard that you heard the bone splinter and crack. He grunted, staggered. His knees buckled but he pulled himself upright, one arm aloft to shield his head, the other suddenly useless, hanging by his side.

He turned to me again and I saw the beginnings of panic. Perhaps he had imagined that his redemption would be quick, clean, one way or the other. But vengeance demanded a death as painful as any he had enforced on his victims. Above the crowd, passed from hand to hand, an unburned tire was moving towards him. A machete slashed at his lofted arm so that it, too, fell to his side and the tire coiled around his neck.

"Ah dear Christ," I heard him say. "The necklace ..."

Theron finally sank to the ground. His face was level now with a clear bottle held by one of his assailants. It was filled with petrol. Someone grabbed him by the hair and wrenched his bleeding head backward as the fuel was poured over him, as if in some macabre baptismal rite.

"Murderer!"

"Killer of Comrade Nyati!"

"Pig!"

The cries multiplied.

"One settler, one bullet."

Then silence.

The leader of the group held aloft a cigarette lighter and made an attempt to strike it, ridiculously without result. You could smell petrol, sweat, urine, faeces. I knew where this was all leading but the great luxury of translating will into action had deserted me. I knew I had to escape but could not move. The crowd was too dense, my resolve too feeble.

I knew the petrol would soon blossom in a hideous flash and ignite the tire around his neck and his skin, burning it to the bone, like napalm, and the crowd would dance in jubilation and watch him turn to cinder. When I tried to push back, young men behind me pushed me forward, towards their fiery guillotine, the next in line.

It was not me, I wanted to say, I did not kill Nyati. Theron and I are not the same. Take him. Spare me. But sentence had already been passed.

Theron was praying.

"*Onse Vader wat in die hemel is, laat U naam geheilig word.*" Our Father, who is in heaven ... The words came to me. I had not uttered them for a long time, but I did now. No one heard.

"*Gee ons vandag ons daaglikse brood.*" Give us this day our daily bread.

"Where is your God? Your God cannot save you. Boers have no gods."

"*En vergeef ons ons skulde, soos ons ook ons skuldenaars vergewe.*"

"You have trespassed too much." Laughter rippled through his executioners.

"Your prayers will not help you."

"You will go to hell."

"*Lei ons nie in die versoeking nie.*" Lead us not into temptation.

They took up the chant now.

"Go to hell. Go to hell."

"*Maar verlos ons van die bose.*" But deliver us from evil.

"Stop," the girl said.

The crowd fell back.

Celiwe Nyati was carrying Theron's treasured and trusted companion, his Skorpion machine pistol with which so many murders had been committed. She carried it at port with both hands before her.

She advanced towards him where he knelt. His shirt dripped blood from fresh wounds. A gash had opened the skin of his forehead. Dust and mud covered him, transferred from the boots and bare feet that had kicked him. Petrol formed runnels through the grime that coated his face.

She lowered the gun, taking its weight in her left hand, her finger extended along the trigger guard. No one spoke. No one danced. No one shouted slogans.

The young men hung back now, silenced.

Celiwe Nyati brought the gun barrel level with Theron's head.

His voice was barely a whisper. "Do it now. Shoot. Please. For God's sake."

Then she extended her right hand.

"Take it," she said. "Take my hand. For my father's sake. Not for mine. Not for yours. Not for your God."

Part Six

They had covered the bases. They had the electronic surveillance in place on the vehicle. All they needed was the signal, and that would come willy-nilly from the woman who thought she had escaped their attentions. Who thought she had been so damn clever.

Part Six

Twenty-Nine

THE LETTER ARRIVED BY PERSONAL courier – FedEx or DHL – two months after my ignominious retreat. I was still licking my wounds, counting my blessings and secretly wondering if, against all the odds, I could salvage something from the whole debacle.

The episode outside the Nyati home had left me badly shaken. You can theorise all you like about the purifying fire of revolutionary violence, but when you encounter it, eyeball to eyeball, it leaves deep scars. I was moody, anti-social, reluctant to pick up the phone. I slept badly. The nightmares invariably transported me back to Cooktown as the object of the crowd's rage in place of Theron.

Some of my Washington friends had gone so far as to suggest that I seek counselling for post-traumatic stress disorder. But how preposterous would that have been? My travails paled to insignificance compared to the havoc my visit had called down upon the others. In any event, I have never been easy baring my soul to strangers, certainly not on the basis of a cash transaction and a ticking clock.

The letter's arrival made me jittery. My personal address was on very few circulation lists. Yet an anonymous man in uniform was at the door asking for my signature to hand over the package. I signed for it with some alarm. This time, there were no coloured birds or fishes.

I had not, in the end, decided to embark on a Cape-to-Cairo odyssey; or a visit to the Pemba Channel Fishing Club in Kenya to hunt for marlin; or a safari in Serengeti or the Masai Mara; or even a quick foray to the Victoria Falls and the tiger-fishing of the Zambezi. The options belonged to a previous existence when a certain stranger called Thomas J Kinzer had the luxury of time to be filled, before events and experiences burst in upon him, demanding that he somehow come to terms with them.

I fled Cooktown after the ambulance came for Theron. I dropped the rental car at the airport in George and took the first available flight north to seek a long-haul connection to Europe. Anywhere out of Africa – the final cop-out.

There was no effort to salvage any vestige of respect or friendship from that awful night on the deck of Zoë Joubert's vacation retreat. Too much had been broken. So many lives had been turned upside down by the events I had so foolishly triggered, just as I had been one catalyst among many of even grislier events many years earlier when Nyati died.

So I ran.

I ran, stashing the beginnings of this volume in my carry-on.

I ran from Zoë Joubert and Faku and Nieuwoudt and Anna-Marie Theron and Vanessa van Rensburg – the whole lot of them. I ran from Jessica de Vere, née Chase. There was nothing we could say to one another that would revive what he had once had, or undo what I had precipitated.

Pandora's Box. Genie's bottle. Can of worms. Choose your cliché.

Even at the last moment, at OR Tambo Airport in Johannesburg, I thought they would stop me. I was a day over the limit on the visa and a lifetime away from its restriction to "Conference Purposes Only". At the long gauntlet of exit booths, an immigration officer disappeared with my passport and I figured that maybe I would not escape without answering a whole raft of questions about incidents in Cooktown that had somehow made the local prints. But she returned quickly, rubber-stamping me out of the country with a speculative glance, comparing my clean-shaven photograph to the dishevelled fugitive standing in front of her. I looked around me, half-expecting to see Faku and Nieuwoudt in some dark corner, waiting to see me off the premises. Or worse. But there was no one.

On the flight I made no pretence of restraint. I was drunk and snoring before they brought dinner.

And now the letter.

It was handwritten in a graceful, almost calligraphic hand, suggesting a golden nib and expensive ink. The paper was hand-laid vellum, harking back to earlier times when serious amounts of thought preceded the commitment to words that could not simply be retracted at the tap of a cursor.

Either it had been drafted and re-drafted or written with great confidence and deliberation because there was no indication of corrections or deletions or revisions.

"Tom,

I'm not really sure how to start this and maybe I shouldn't start at all. I'm still here in Plett. Everyone else packed up and went home pretty much when you did, so it's a lonely old town. Mills was anyhow due a visit with Rod so there has been very little to distract me from my thoughts. I went for a long walk along the Robberg Beach today, past Chris and Jess's place (I could see it was all shuttered and there are rumours that it's on the market) and past our picnic spot, where, of course, there is no trace of all our fun and games: the ocean is a pretty good housecleaner. There have been massive storms, too, with huge rains that brought a spate of floodwater down the Keurbooms River, completely changing the landscape. After the flood-waters punched a way through, part of the old Lookout Beach was completely washed away and the bar near your old hotel overlooks a new mouth into the lagoon rather than that lovely, long beach. Some of the speedboats at the boat club were wrecked. There are whole new obstacles on the river where trees and logs have been carried along by the floods and dumped, like those dams that beavers apparently make. What do they call it – the pathetic fallacy? – when we project our feelings onto inanimate objects, although there was nothing inanimate about the storms. Still, they made me think of your visit among us.

I was always taught that you shouldn't rush your feelings into words and, if you do, to leave them fallow for a while in a bottom drawer and look at them in the cold light of dawn. (Excuse the metaphors!) But I can't do that this time. I tried to keep quiet, but I can't. And I promised myself that once I had written there would be no censorship or edits or re-casting or excisions. That's why it's pen and ink. No revisions! The minute I finish this I will send it to you by courier so that there is no prospect of it getting lost. When – if – you finish reading you will understand why. I hope you will reply in kind without any one of your old diplomatic obfuscation. It will, incidentally, be the only copy so its destiny is in your hands.

Here goes.

When I last saw you, I was terribly angry. You had taken my world and deconstructed it without even trying to reassemble it. You had broken my trust and, I feared, my heart. You had betrayed me and everything I thought, or hoped, that you wanted for us. The relationships on which I had built my adult life – all my friends and, yes, lovers – were fixed in our little galaxy. We all knew our place, our orbits. We tolerated our myths and fibs and foibles. What had been was a past we all shared, a bond, held together by our common acceptance of one another's flaws. It was, if you like, our treasure, our emotional patrimony. We didn't need it thrown in our faces like kitchen dregs in some kind of cheap soap opera.

When I read the newspaper reports of the trouble you had caused for Lily Nyati, I was even more enraged. How could you bring the murderer to her home, the killer to her hearth? What on earth did you think you were doing? What trauma were you causing her poor daughter? I was not surprised to see articles saying you had provoked riots. You had inspired emotional violence here and then went on to Cooktown to stir up physical unrest. I confess that my feelings were self-serving. Of course I knew you as an individual – an individual who had tried to sweep me off my feet and had come pretty close to succeeding, who had reawakened so many feelings and hopes that I had submerged in the name of my work – although, as I think you guessed, the real motives lay in my protectiveness towards my beloved daughter. But, after the reports from Cooktown, I couldn't help but cast you as the archetypal blundering American that the rest of the world sees in your nation, walking into situations you don't understand, believing that whatever standards you would like to think obtain in your own country should apply universally. Well, I happen to believe that those great ideals of transparency and democracy of which you are so proud are very rarely followed in the USA itself. And your attempt to use my country as a test-bed for them was pretty brutish. Of course, in the spirit of honesty to which I have dedicated this letter – maybe confession is a better word – I should say that I was secretly relieved. Your inquiries had barely scratched the surface of what really happened, at least in my case.

Then I called Lily and, I have to admit, I got pretty confused. Her account of that awful day with you and Theron was completely different from the newspaper reports. I had not realised, in fact, how much she desperately wanted to hear her husband's killer make his confession and his apology to her and the other widows. I had not understood the extent to which she seemed to think that you had redeemed yourself in her eyes not only with this apparently cathartic moment, but also in coaxing Celiwe into a frame of mind that her father would, I think, have welcomed. But most of all, none of the newspaper reports told the story that Lily told me. The press accounts all seemed to have been following the original "scoop" by that dreadful Gilliomee, an apartheid stooge if ever there was one. Maybe "script" would be a better word than "scoop," because there was nothing fortuitous about it as far I can see. He had written it as if he had been there as an eyewitness with the police. But how could that have been?

Lily seemed to think you were quite the hero, making sure that her daughter did not change her mind and risking the awful fate that awaited both you and Theron. Stepping out with Theron into the crowd must have needed a lot of courage. I am not sure you realise just how volatile these moments are; how it just takes one slogan, one chant, one denunciation to trigger a necklace killing. Perhaps you did.

I still don't understand your motives but when Lily told me that you had actually been stoned and pushed around yourself, then I must say I began to look at things in a different light. It is quite possible that, if you had not done what you did, Celiwe would have allowed Theron's execution to go ahead. And who knows what would have happened to our rainbow nation after that? Who knows what monsters from the old days would have emerged to embark on reprisals? We were probably on the brink of a paroxysm of mutual retaliation that would have strained, if not destroyed, the social fabric.

Maybe that was what some of them wanted. And certainly the inflammatory tone of Gilliomee's articles seemed designed to achieve in print what could not be achieved on the ground. But there was another aspect of your intervention that struck me. When you arrived in South Africa, when we had those cosy dinners in Cape Town, when you came to my party on the deck for inspection by my friends (you did not pass universal muster, I can assure you!) you were aloof, cold, different, fenced off. When you stepped out into that crowd, it seemed to me, you were finally acting as if you understood where we all figure in this new order; how we stand ready to take the lumps and hope for the best and pray for tolerance.

Every day we risk retribution, and every day that it does not come – in a carjacking or a burglary or some such – is a bonus. Maybe we are living on borrowed time, but we are drawing down the debt and every day hope a little more fervently that our country will become a normal one, if that is possible. South Africans, I think you know, don't regard themselves as just one more humdrum lot. We punch above our weight. We've won more than our share of Nobel prizes. We punished and revered Nelson Mandela. We engineered a transition from tyranny and the brink of all-out war to freedom and democracy. But we know that, ultimately, the onus – the burden of guilt, if you like – is on us, the whites, the former rulers.

Now we have to make one more supreme effort to make it work. And if that involves stepping out into the crowd, figuratively in most cases and literally on that day of yours in Cooktown, then so be it. One thing I realised from your intervention is that we cannot simply stay in our cocoon, hiding from the society whose birth we once tried to hasten. Yes, you upset us. But you also made us look at ourselves more honestly, to see where the complacencies had grown over our memories and our ideals. No one liked the mirror you held up to us. But we all had to look into it.

So that, in a way, brings me to the point where I have to take my own advice and fill in the final piece of the jigsaw about events in Port Elizabeth and Cooktown that night, and in the broader emotional tangle. Maybe Kobus Theron has already told you this, since he would almost certainly have known. Maybe he wanted to keep one or two secrets up his sleeve for later. Maybe he even wanted to spare you the unhappiness of too much knowledge.

But the fact is that the encounter with Solomon Nyati in Port Elizabeth that night was not my first with him. Far from it. I told you once that the scar tissue on my shoulder was a war wound. In a modest sort of way, that was the truth. When the Truth and Reconciliation Commission hearings were in progress, I spent every day wondering whether my secret would come out. Whether I would be subpoenaed, whether I would, in fact, need to apply for amnesty. But nothing came and I had to assume that the people who knew the truth had decided to remain silent. That is the way people like Theron work, squirreling away their little bits of knowledge for future reference. It is their stake money, their pile of chips. They play their hands like your Mississippi gamblers. And, of course, once you try to keep something secret, you merely increase the value of their capital. They have the drop on you. As the years go by, it becomes ever more difficult to own up, to tell the truth. So, after all the forced confessions and allegations that night on the deck, it is time for me to come clean. In a way, it is easier now that many of the friendships that we sustained with our myths and fairy tales about one another have fallen away and the ones that remain are the true ones. I supposed I have you to thank for that very ambiguous restructuring of my social network.

If I am honest, another reason for keeping quiet was my embarrassment at my own foolishness. I had acted in such a gullible way over the years in my desire to be close to The Struggle that I came very close to undermining it – not terminally, but enough. When I have told you what actually happened, you may decide that the breach in our relationship should be permanent. I hope that is not the case. But there is no way of resuming our friendship – if that is what it was – without honesty. I think that you have been forced now to consider your own role in our struggle, however much of a bit part it might have been – ouch, did you say? – so I will finally tell my story, too."

I imagined her breaking off, at this point, setting down her fancy fountain pen, perhaps making tea, or walking out onto the deck to survey that so-familiar vista of ocean and mountains. I imagined her in bright sunlight, lightly clad in the warm, summery weather of the southern hemisphere as I contemplated the murk of a northern winter, following her story in a pool of light cast from a reading lamp positioned next to my favourite, winged, red, leather armchair. I had no reason, of course, to see her that way. For all I knew she may have been writing to the tattoo of hailstones and thunder as lightning crackled over the storm-tormented sea. After what came next, that might have been the more appropriate metaphor.

"So, yes. I had met Nyati before. It seems in another lifetime now, shortly before I went abroad for my studies where my parents thought I would be inoculated against all the pressures of The Struggle. I was supposed to be packing up to head for England and America. But I slipped away and went down to Port Elizabeth one last time to see friends in the Black Sash because I knew they had the contacts in the townships, which I did not. And so I met Solomon. He set the rendezvous. It was at Crystal Sands, the same place as he died. I asked him why and he told me that he had to find places the system could not follow him to. Every word at home was monitored, he said, and he only conducted conversations there that he either didn't mind the police monitoring or wanted them to hear."

Now it was my turn to pause, make tea, survey the view. I walked across my study to close the drapes. The words came back to me – "or wanted them to hear." Instead of tea, I poured a stiff jolt of single malt, with a splash of branch water. No ice.

If Nyati's tradecraft was unchanged by the time I met him, then clearly my conversation with him fell into the category of exchanges that were either insignificant or designed to be shared with his enemies. If what I was reading was true, Nyati had pretended to be talking to me that day in his bugged home in Cooktown. But, in fact, he was talking to Kobus Theron, sitting somewhere nearby with the headphones clamped to his ears to catch every intonation. And when

I said the things I did, Nyati knew full well that, despite my lowly rank, my words would be amplified by being reported back to the highest level. At his meeting with the Old Deep set in Port Elizabeth, hours before he was kidnapped and killed, Nyati joked that, one day, they might attend his funeral. At least he understood the risks he was taking, even if Jess and I didn't.

"Anyhow, we went for a walk in the dunes. When I heard where he had been killed all those years later, I knew then that we had not been as alone as he thought. They were there. And when they chose where to kill him, I assumed they were sending a message. In any event, Crystal Sands was as good an isolated spot as any for a brutal murder to be committed without witnesses. Two birds with one stone. They were nothing if not pragmatic. As we walked, I told him that, ever since the Soweto riots of '76, I wanted to be part of The Struggle, really part of it, the whole thing, the operations, the spying, whatever was needed. I wanted to join the guerrillas, Umkhonto we Sizwe, the Spear of the Nation. If young black kids could hack it, so could I. I would be his little drummer girl. He laughed – that annoyed me because I thought he was laughing at me. But he wasn't. It was just his way to cover his thoughts while he computed all the odds. Looking back it all seems strange – white college girl, black revolutionary, a walk in the sand. But people forget that it was never all so monochrome, monotone – what is the word I am looking for? Simple?

There is so much shorthand used to describe events that cry out for a much finer script. I supposed that is the nature of propaganda: boil complexity down to a single emotive slogan that reinforces one side of the argument and hides the other. My country was depicted in terms of black or white while, for some of us, the reality was etched in half-tones, greys, off-whites. And, of course, for all the heroism of the comrades and Madiba, so much of The Struggle was riddled with betrayal. The regime had spies everywhere, single agents, doubles, trebles. If a young white woman arrived on a black man's doorstep offering help with the revolution, what on earth would he have thought? A plant? A honeytrap?

But then, after we walked on a bit, Solomon said: 'Okay. One day you will get the call.' Or something like that. Maybe it was: 'we will call on you'. Other people we both knew had vouched for me and I know they had made inquiries to check me out, so I guess he was prepared to take a gamble. I remember, as if it were yesterday, the moment when he reached his decision. He stopped and turned to look me straight in the eye. His voice changed. We weren't chatting any more. He was the commander. The call will come, or you will think it has come, he said, but before you go any further with any operation – I repeat any operation or mission – you must check with me. He explained the passwords I was supposed to use and the response he would give if a mission was to go ahead. None of that is important now, except that I waited a long time for the call. All the time I was abroad, I guess I was what they would call a sleeper. I got on with my studies. I was diligent, industrious. Then I came home."

Thirty

I felt a sudden aversion to reading on. What on earth would I learn now? How many more layers had been hidden from me on this madcap venture? Above all – how could I have been so foolish, so solipsistic? When you embark on some personal odyssey – a.k.a. ego trip – to reformat your own history, how much consideration do you give to the impact it will have on other people? And how much do you calculate the distortions of their perspectives? Stories, versions have their orthodoxy: A did this and B did that and C just did nothing. But when you start playing around with the equation you get a different result. A+B might equal C but A times C produces a different B. The factors acquire new values. People emerge in different lights. So do you as the instigator. If you have a secret, you behave in a different way than you do when it is exposed. Your confidences are the adhesives holding together your relationships with the people who don't know what you know. Remove them and the relationships change. There's no glue anymore. Things fall apart. The centre, like the poet said, cannot hold. I had stripped away the secrets of an entire cohort. But not all of them, as Zoë Joubert now seemed determined to demonstrate.

"In the years I had been away things had changed. I had left a country of simmering rage. Now it was boiling. The townships were becoming ungovernable. The young people, the comrades, could not be restrained. I think there was a feeling that so much was happening inside the country that the guerrilla war from outside had been overtaken. The revolution was building even without the freedom fighters to give it a push with their AK-47s or their bombs. So maybe my mission – my first mission – was just a tactical move to show the new comrades in the townships that the old guard comrades were still out there in Lusaka or Harare or Maputo fighting for them, sending insurgents into the country to sabotage the system. My orders were simple enough if you know South Africa. Or, at least, I thought they were. I was to drive a bakkie – a pickup – to a border area and wait. Two men wearing farm labourers' coveralls would emerge at the rendezvous point and get onto the back. They would have a bag that I was to hide under the front seat. I would drive them towards the big oil-from-coal plant at Secunda. Then I was supposed to drop them off and drive as fast as I could to a rendezvous near Soweto to hand over the bakkie, but without drawing attention to myself by speeding. (We had pretty strict speed limits in those days.) It should have been flawless cover. There is no more common sight in the farming areas than a white person driving labourers around on the flatbed of their pickups. I'd travel up there overnight, pick them up just before dawn and drive them to Secunda in broad daylight. It was a bold idea, turning the prejudice to the freedom fighters' advantage. We'd have no problems with the road blocks, because I was white. My orders were to tie up my hair, put on a baseball cap and try not to look like a student. If I was stopped, I was to speak Afrikaans, which, given my roots, was no problem. I went through all the codes and procedures I had been given to verify the mission with Solomon. I was given a cut-out, an intermediary I trusted from way back, a black reporter. (His name isn't important. And I still feel bound by some vestigial sense of honour to keep it to myself. But I suspect you would have met him without realising how active he was. He was a pretty good reporter, too.) I knew that he was close to Solomon and that I could trust him. We arranged the pickup point and the handover of the keys. At that time, cell phones weren't all that common but you could get a pager service and I gave him my pager contacts. The way the system worked, you had to call a number and give the message verbally to an operator who would then forward it to the designated recipient. It would appear on the pager's tiny black and white screen. Of course, the messages were monitored, so we devised an innocuous code. If we were good to go, the message would say: 'Call me now or never'. If the operation was cancelled, the pager would say: 'Happy Birthday, Doll!' We had quite a laugh about that, the reporter and I, probably because there was a lot of tension in the air at the time. Solomon was not happy about the mission because he did not know the men who would be crossing the border. There had been a lot of penetration of the ranks by the regime. Betrayals. Torture. The Armed Struggle diluted, weakened. Umkhonto we Sizwe had been trying to repeat its success blowing up a Sasol plant, so Solomon believed it was worth a go. Looking back now, I wonder how secure his own precautions could have been in the climate of the times.

In any event, I drove up the road towards Botswana. I can't say I felt 100 per cent enthusiastic. Yes, I was opposed to apartheid and I was prepared to prove it by embarking on the mission. But this was what the state – and my parents – would call it terrorism. At the time, Umkhonto we Sizwe had a policy of avoiding civilian casualties at all costs. So there was a moral fig leaf. But, frankly, I knew my father and mother would not see it that way if I was caught. Neither would a lot of my closest friends, not least of them Chris de Vere. While I was abroad he had dropped by to visit me on his business trips so our old relationship never really broke off. Most whites would excoriate me, among them a lot of my anti-apartheid friends who simply did not believe in violence of any kind. Frankly, I was scared, too. I might get shot or killed. I might get arrested. I had no training for this kind of thing. I doubted I would be able to withstand the pain of torture and I knew, deep down, that I would betray Solomon even before they switched on the electrodes, or whatever they chose to do. The more I drove that night, the more I asked myself what I had got myself into. In principle it all seemed so heroic – like Orwell in the Spanish Civil War, an act of valour in real conflict with real guns and real risks. Finally, I was joining The Struggle. But I was out of my depth. I had offered a commitment that was too much for me. I did not have the courage of the young kids I'd be picking up. I began to blame Solomon, too. If he was not too happy about it, why had he exposed me to this danger? Was it some kind of test? There was no way I could call him back at that hour to ask. But what if I just turned around and headed back? Then what? What would happen to the freedom fighters at the roadside? What would happen to The Struggle? And, of course, what would happen to me when the comrades in Lusaka or Maputo discovered that I had been the weak link in the chain? I was trapped. I would have to go through with it, whatever the consequences. I had been a protester. Now I was to become a terrorist.

I was about 10 minutes from the pickup point when my pager went off. It was still dark but I could see the message quite clearly in the little LCD screen: Happy Birthday, Doll!

The message looked even more ridiculous a few miles from the Botswana border than it had when we devised it. But I did not need a second asking. I barely slowed down. I did a 180-degree turn with the handbrake, and nearly rolled the bakkie right over. And then I was heading back down the road. I never knew who it was but someone shot at me and the bullet grazed my shoulder. I ditched the bakkie and the baseball cap as soon as I could at the first town I came to and did what I could to stop the bleeding."

My glass was empty. I had not noticed the storm brewing outside my windows in Washington but now it had built to a fury, tossing and tormenting the trees out front as the rain swirled in the street lights. The refill was more modest than the first jolt. I was reading closely and did not want to be distracted. The most perilous part of an aborted mission is always the getaway. If the alarms have gone up and the enemy listeners are alerted to any unusual chatter, then the simplest phone call can be a betrayal. You have to have absolute faith in your contact. You have to have a bolt hole. If there is a question of a wound, you need medical treatment. In other words you need a network. A secure network. Inadvertently, apartheid had built a network – the blacks-only townships where a fugitive could go to ground. But, of course those places were honeycombed with police informers, bugged homes, agents of the system. And wounded whites with bleeding shoulders were hardly the most inconspicuous of visitors.

"They had made me memorise one single phone number in Soweto. I found a pay phone and called it. An answering machine. I spoke my location and hung up. The wound was not all that deep but it was aching. A second after I put down the phone my pager beeped. I was somewhat baffled. The little message screen said: 'Now or never'. If anyone was monitoring the pager service, a coded message would look pretty suspicious. I had no idea what it could mean now that the mission had failed. I felt terribly vulnerable. If the police were looking for me, I had nowhere to hide. I stood out. Whites have homes to go to. They don't loiter outside phone boxes. They have cars, trucks, 4x4s. My behaviour marked me as an outsider in a small country town. But then things began to move. A little boy came up to me – a black urchin maybe 9 or 10 years old, with dusty bare feet and the look of a glue-sniffer in his eyes.

'You must come – now or never,' he said, tugging at my jacket. I followed."

The boy led her in a suburban street to where a scratched and dented mini-bus was waiting. She clambered into the back and was pushed to the floor. A blanket covered her. The vehicle moved off and a voice told her to be silent until the order came to step out quickly into a bare yard strung with wire. She recalled a line of laundry drying in a desultory wind, the scratch and peck of scrawny chickens, a maize patch. She took two steps from the mini-bus and into the kitchen of one of those matchbox houses that spread like rashes in the poor quarters outside Africa's major cities – homes that, in comparison to mine in Washington, were tawdry cramped places. In the townships, where squatters lived in tin shacks, they were – relatively speaking – palaces. A black man in a white, doctorly coat raised a finger to his lips to indicate that she should be silent. He wrote on a notepad: "Please say nothing. You will be moved out tonight. But do not speak." Then he paused and added: "Or scream. No anaesthetic."

The man doused her wound in a mercurochrome antiseptic wash. He teased out bits of fabric and used an ear-bud to complete the cleansing. She bit her tongue and kept it bit as he took a sharp needle to stitch the whole mess closed. He finished with a pad doused in iodine and taped a dressing tight over it. Then he pulled off his white medical coat to reveal matching olive green pants and shirt displaying the logo of a local veterinary service. He handed her a pack of aspirin and left.

"A woman I had not noticed in the shadows of the kitchen took over now. She, too, gestured for me to remain silent. She took me into the main room of the small house and sat me at a table covered in oil-cloth with a faded pattern of pink and blue flowers. She brought me bread, butter, jam and tea. Her manner suggested she was used to waiting on tables for white people. I smiled but she turned away and I suddenly realised what risks she was running in taking in a fugitive from justice, for that is what she would be accused of if the authorities found me. Aiding and abetting terrorism. A very serious charge indeed. That day lasted forever. I was tired and I dozed a lot but my mind kept on computing the possibilities. Clearly the mission had been betrayed. But at what stage? And how much had been known at each step along the route that was supposed to have led from free Africa to the target in Secunda? Did the police know they were looking for a white woman, or not? Did they have a name? Did they know it was me? No one spoke to me. It was obvious that I was an embarrassment, a risk, a danger. If the police came for me, then my reluctant hosts would be taken in and might never return – a way of living that was familiar enough to black people at that time, but not to most whites, of course. My shoulder was throbbing. I worried about infection. I wanted antibiotics and medical attention. But I think I realised even then that I would never be able to ask a doctor at home to look at my wound; it would need too much explanation. I had crossed a line. I was on the run. The thought brought a frisson of excitement but it did not last for long. To be a terrorist in my country was to be hunted, condemned to a life of backward glances and perpetual fear of the 3 am raid and the door splintering open. Sorry. I will pause for now."

The mini-bus returned for her after dark. It took her part of the way towards Johannesburg where her journalist contact awaited her in a less obvious vehicle, a late model Nissan. He was dressed as a gardener and asked her to drive while he sat in the back seat like an employee so as not to draw attention at the roadblocks. The mission, he told her, had been blown somewhere in Botswana right at the last minute. The local police had gotten wind of the whole plan and became determined it should be stopped. And stopped it was before it could go any further. Word had filtered back across the border. The South Africans had laid an ambush at the handover point but had not had time to put blocking forces in place to prevent her from fleeing. Their only chance of finding out who was supposed to pick up the freedom fighters was to capture the white pickup. If she had not thrown the 180-degree turn when she did, she would have driven straight into the trap. When her contact told her that, she pulled the Nissan over onto the roadside and vomited.

"Of course it was a dreadful secret. I could tell none of the Old Deep people what had happened. Did I trust them all? Not completely. Did I want to avoid putting them in an impossible situation? Certainly. If they knew what I had done, they would be complicit. If I was identified as the driver of the pickup, then anyone who shared that knowledge would go down with me. And not just at Old Deep. The trail led straight back to Solomon Nyati. If I was identified, then the whole non-violent campaign would be discredited. He would be unmasked as part of the armed struggle. White liberals would look gullible and exploited. I had to live with the secret. I could tell no one. And, of course, when I confirmed my pregnancy, there was one more identity to be protected – an unborn child. Daughter of The Struggle, fathered by a billionaire. Imagine how the Ray Gilliomees of this world would have had a field day with the little yarn. I was more surprised than you can imagine just a few weeks later when Solomon Nyati got in touch again, though the same intermediary, to say the time had come to forge a stronger bond between the townships and the white suburbs, or, at least, the kind of liberals who lived at Old Deep. I was worried. I tried to tell Solomon in any way I could that I was damaged goods, tainted; that they might be on to me. But the message came back: 'Comrade Solomon knows what he is doing; trust him!'

Between us, we put on quite a charade.

I had to pretend that the initiative came from Jess Chase. Silly, really. I had a far better understanding of what was happening than she did, but still I had to pretend I had no direct line to Solomon. Cut-outs, they called it, like the M-plan – cells isolated from one another, unaware of what the other was doing. The theory was that, even under the most extreme duress, you could not betray what you did not know. So I used Jess as my double bluff, to protect my own ties to The Struggle, to protect the Old Deep set, to maintain the fiction that I – their leader – was nothing more than a peaceful activist. Certainly not a closet terrorist wondering when she would be arrested. Think of the stories Jess would be able to write about that! Of course I had my doubts. I knew that people like Kobus Theron were cunning. They could well have identified me and decided simply to let me run to see where I led them. It was a double life. All I could do was to pretend. I spent a life acting out the part of the self-confident leader Zoë Joubert until that night on the deck. When Kobus Theron said they had located Solomon and the others through a surveillance device in the car, I was relieved that it was not I who had inadvertently tipped off the police to his whereabouts. Although I guess that may have been just one more lie. So there we are. You are the only one who knows all of it, at least as far as I can tell. Forgive me for placing that burden on you, but I believe you have more than earned the right to hear the story. The truth, the whole truth – if there is such a thing. In the spirit of this mea culpa, Tom, I wanted to add one thing. If there is any place left in your feelings for me (and there is no reason why should there be after the way I misled you) and if you would like to try to reset whatever it was we had, I just want you to know that I would never deceive you again."

At some stage, I had transferred the whisky bottle from its place on an antique dresser to the small table next to my armchair. It was well down by the time I finished reading. The final paragraph of her letter brought back uncomfortable memories of Theron's words as he and I left the deck of her holiday home.

"Maybe one day she will tell you the whole truth and nothing but the truth."

Maybe Lily Nyati's questions had finally been answered. To the extent that they ever could be.

Epilogue

Not long after Zoë Joubert's letter arrived, another package of documents, transcripts, covert tapes and surveillance photographs found its way to me from a lawyer dealing with Kobus Theron's estate. A covering note from Anna-Marie Theron explained that, after the doctors patched him together following the violence in Cooktown, her late husband had insisted on returning to work but he seemed to have lost his skills or his concentration. There had been a terrible accident. He had not survived. Death would have been instant. A red haze.

Her note enjoined me to read his files carefully. She concluded with the words: "So now you will know his burden. And perhaps now he has found peace."

I have perused Theron's trove, but I shall let my narrative stand where it does. There is no need to undertake a major revision on the basis of unsubstantiated evidence, plausible though much of it seems. In this chronicle, I have disclosed what I learned and know to be reliable and true.

The same adjectives cannot be used to describe Theron's versions, although, looking back, I believe he did try to steer me away from my worst misconceptions. By now, we have all indulged our need for catharsis, and there are probably some secrets that need to stay that way, some imputations of guilt that would simply be impossible to bear.

But I did call Zoë Joubert.

I told her that I had been asked to teach a post-graduate course in Justice and Truth at one of our universities.

I told her that I would begin my lectures with a question relating to two white men driving into a South African township where they were not welcome. They were saved from an enraged crowd by an act of enormous courage on behalf of a victim. So whose justice had been served, if justice had been served at all?

I asked her if she would perhaps be interested in coming over to address my students. A professional assignment. Fees and expenses paid. No strings. But it would be so nice if we could meet again. Her letter notwithstanding. And, of course, I could offer accommodation if she would prefer that to some soulless hotel.

She arrived on a circuitous connection via Abu Dhabi, London and New York. She thought the navy blue Jaguar XKR a trifle ostentatious. She seemed amused by my affectation of denim jeans and leather pilot's jacket. It did not really need to be said, but her offer of a reset had been gratefully accepted: our mutual deceptions cancelled each other out. We were quits.

She told me that Jessica and Chris de Vere had sold their home in Plettenberg Bay and relocated to a stuccoed terrace in London's Belgravia with a vacation retreat in the Caribbean, far from Africa. Rod Harris was still the man Camilla embraced as her father, though Jessica de Vere had insisted on clandestine DNA testing of the girl and of her own husband. She kept the results in a private deposit box at her bank in Geneva, along with other land registry deeds, bearer bonds and equity certificates provided by Christian de Vere.

Riaan and Vanessa van Rensburg somehow bumbled along, the eternal unhappy couple.

Lily had launched a campaign calling for the repeal of the statute of limitations, but it had run into a wall of denial and refusal from the politicians. There would be no criminal proceedings against the killers who were denied amnesty, on either side.

Zoë Joubert brought with her a small file of newspaper clippings, some in Afrikaans, which she translated as we perused them. One – "Exclusive Eyewitness Report" – described in uncanny detail how a former American ambassador and suspected CIA operative, acting in direct contravention of visa restrictions, had provoked a riot that almost led to the necklace killing of a former South African police agent acting as his bodyguard. The officer was just days away from being freed from the burden of his past by a statute of limitations.

The headline proclaimed: "An American's Shame in the New South Africa." It was signed: "by Raymond Gilliomee". Its description of the events that final day in Cooktown recalled a Toyota saloon that had disappeared from view before the mayhem stopped just short of murder.

We exchanged some of this information over dinner and some, the more intimate details, in the whispering hours before summer's first light. I did not mention the Theron files in my wall safe. Perhaps, one day far into the future, I shall unseal them when they can no longer hurt her as much as they would right now.